THE
BILLIONAIRE
AND HIS
FOREVER

paige press

THE
BILLIONAIRE
AND HIS
FOREVER

SADIE BLACK

Paige Press
Leander, TX 78641

Ebook:
ISBN: 978-1-953520-96-8

Print:
ISBN: 978-1-957647-28-9

Also by Sadie Black

HIS NANNY TRILOGY

The Billionaire and His Nanny

The Billionaire and His Scandal

The Billionaire and His Forever

About This Book

We were always going to be an impossible fantasy.
There was never a future for us between the secrets and
the scandals, the temptations and the lies, and above all--a
child who never deserved this life.

But even when we hurt each other the most, when the
entire world is rooting against us, when we've been
betrayed and wrecked and somehow survived it all... how
could we ever let go of this imperfect forever?

**Sadie Black's all new world of cruel billion-
aires, naughty nannies, and angsty secrets
concludes in book three of His Nanny trilogy.**

Chapter One

Abbie

Everything was so perfect last night. Graham finally confessed his love to me, Jude was just starting to settle into being back at home in the country, we were a perfect little family with so much potential, and then *bam*. The sky fell. The colors contorted. I found myself falling through empty space without any clue how to get back on the ground.

All I could do was sit there frozen in shock as the police pulled Graham out of bed this morning and arrested him for the attempted murder of his ex-wife. What the hell happened? How would that have even been possible? He was with me the night she OD'd. He couldn't have done it...he *wouldn't* have done it.

I feel like I'm losing my mind. This whole situation is completely surreal. A living nightmare.

My summer wasn't supposed to go like this. It should have been the summer of my life. In the good way, not in the way you'd write a tell-all memoir about. But everything has been fucked. From being sent to the Ratliff estate in the idyllic Hudson Valley on a secret mission to steal Graham's heart to completely falling for him (and his kid) in the process, from all the sordid tabloid rumors about our alleged affair to being forced to endure relentless abuse at the hands of Graham's ex-wife when she moved back in to save his reputation. Nothing has gone as planned. And I have no idea how to fix any of it.

I've basically been hiding out under the covers since Graham was hauled off by the cops, but it's getting late and I can't hide forever. Especially not when Jude's going to be up any minute, and she's going to wonder where her dad is. So I slink back to my own room and get dressed, haunted by images of the man of my dreams getting dragged away in handcuffs, begging me to protect Jude.

I'm brushing my teeth when a soft knock comes on my door, shaking me out of my stupor. Glancing at the time on my phone, I curse—it has to be Jude. I do a quick rinse-and-spit and then rush to fling the door open, pasting on my biggest smile, no matter how much it hurts to fake it. Jude stands there in her nightgown, brows drawn together.

"Where's my dad?" she asks. "He's not reading his paper in the dining room, and he's not in his room, and even Esmeralda said she hasn't seen him but that's a lie. She always knows where he is. Do you think he went to visit Mommy at the hospital without me?"

My lip feels raw from all the biting I've already done on it this morning. How long can I lie about Graham's absence? Can I at all? I swallow the lump in my throat and opt for something semi-close to the truth, because it's the best I can do right now...and there's no way I'm dumping the whole murder accusation thing on this poor eight-year-old. She's got enough to worry about with her mother in a coma.

"No, of course not. He wouldn't do that. Your dad... he had a really important meeting." I try to sound bright and cheery, but Jude immediately pales.

"He said he'd be home with me."

"It was super last minute and kind of an emergency. You know how his work stuff goes sometimes."

She sighs, nodding. Graham has proven himself nothing if not a workaholic, so the lie is by no means a stretch for her to buy. I drape my arm across her shoulder and coax her downstairs so we can see about getting some breakfast. My own trauma needs to take a back seat right now.

"When will he be back, though?" Jude asks as we make our way down the hall.

"I don't know," I admit. All I know is that Graham has a very expensive, very fancy lawyer. Hopefully that works in his favor. "I'm sure he'll be home as soon as he can."

Jude looks up at me, worry etched on her face. "Did something bad happen?"

"It's just a meeting," I reassure her. Then I switch tactics, hoping to distract her. "Do you want to go to the kitchen and see if Mary wants some help?"

She shrugs. "Okay, I guess."

"That's my girl," I say cheerily, hating myself every second for lying.

Jude nods dutifully, giving me a brave smile that only makes me feel worse.

We find Mary in the kitchen, looking pensive as she sips a cup of coffee.

"Good morning," I say.

"Morning!" Mary immediately hops out of her chair and gives Jude a grin. "I didn't start breakfast since everyone seemed to be sleeping in. What should I make? Sky's the limit."

"Anything you want," I add, giving Jude an encouraging squeeze.

"Waffles?" she says hesitantly. "With strawberries and bananas?"

"Sounds perfect," Mary responds, whipping open the refrigerator. "What about on the side? Sausage or bacon?"

"Veggie sausage," Jude says.

"Can we help?" I add. "Jude's a little...anxious this morning. Might be good for her."

Mary puts us to work measuring out ingredients for the batter while she goes to the pantry to look for the waffle iron. Esmeralda shows up and joins us too, and soon the room is full of happy voices and the sweet smell of waffles. Jude can't stop laughing when Mary recounts the story about how she accidentally set a restaurant kitchen ablaze at her first professional chef job and the fire department had to come put it out.

Once the food is ready, Jude and I eat at the little table in the kitchen with Mary and Esmeralda. The cook and the housekeeper already had their own breakfasts, but they keep up the banter while they sip coffee. I know they're putting on a show for Jude, purposely steering the conversation away from any mention of Graham, trying to act like nothing happened. Which I appreciate. But under the bluster, I still have a heavy ball of nerves sitting in my gut.

I feel like screaming. While we're sitting here playing house, Graham is rotting in a jail cell in New York. I should be at the police station right now, meeting with Graham's lawyer, helping figure out a plan to get Graham out of this mess. But I can't. I have to stay with Jude. I made a promise, and I intend to keep it.

Not only that, but Graham's lawyer might not even want me there, getting in the way and potentially creating even more fodder for the rumor mills and the media. I just wish I knew Graham was okay. It's taking everything I have not to give in to the panic that's been threatening to overtake me ever since those cops busted into Graham's bedroom this morning.

My phone vibrates in my pocket, and I sneak a look under the table. It's my dad calling. Again. I've already missed six calls from him while we were helping with the waffles. I don't know what he wants, but I'm not picking up. I send his call to voicemail. Again.

"Is that my dad?" Jude asks, watching me.

"Nope, it's *my* dad. I'll have to call him back," I say, trying to sound breezy. "But since you're all done, why don't you go get dressed for riding and we'll head out to the stables?"

"Okay."

As soon as she's out of the kitchen, I lower my voice and look at Mary and Esmeralda.

"Have either of you heard anything from him?" I ask.

They both shake their heads, looking grave.

"I told Mary everything that happened with the police this morning," Esmeralda says quietly. "But Mr. Ratliff would never do what they said he did. No matter how much he fought with Mrs. Ratliff, no matter how difficult she could be..."

Mary nods along.

"I know," I say. "I don't know what to do. This all feels so unbelievable."

"There's nothing you can do," Mary says gently. "Just take care of Jude, keep her busy, and try to stay positive. I'm sure we'll hear something soon."

"Right," I agree.

It turns out Jude's busy schedule is finally good for something. She talks a mile a minute about her next riding exhibition as we make our way across the property toward the stables.

Cassie is ready and waiting for us, a look of worry on her face, but just like with Mary and Esmeralda, she paints on a smile as soon as she sees Jude. Desi sticks her head over the gate of her stall and whinnies, which has Jude laughing.

"She's so excited to see me!" she squeals, taking off down the center aisle.

"How can she not be? You're her favorite person," Cassie says.

We watch Desi nuzzle Jude's hand, and it's almost as if the horse knows something awful happened and it's her job to protect the tiniest Ratliff.

"Heard anything from Graham since they took him?" Cassie asks me quietly.

I shake my head. "This is all so fucked."

"I know," she says. "I'll do my best with Jude. She seems okay enough."

"That's because she knows nothing," I tell her guiltily. "We've all just been pretending he's at a meeting in the city. Can you just...keep it that way? I'm losing it."

"Of course," Cassie says, giving me a quick side hug before attending to Jude.

I go outside and sit on the bench next to the riding ring so I can watch Jude's lesson without getting in the way. Minutes later, my phone buzzes again. Crap. If I don't talk to my dad soon, he's liable to just show up here and cause problems. On the other hand, what if he can help? He went to law school in California before he got his MBA here on the East Coast...and besides that, my dad is the kind of person who always has a plan. Maybe he'll know what to do.

Graham is his best friend, after all. Or was.

"Hi, Dad."

"Wow. You actually picked up this time."

I can't help rolling my eyes. "I have a job to do. I've been trying to distract Jude all morning so she doesn't find out what happened. Which I'm guessing you did."

"It'd be hard not to. It's all over the news." He doesn't sound very compassionate, which shouldn't surprise me, but it still stings. "You know what I can't stop thinking? Is that if you'd just gotten married to him before this, you'd have the perfect excuse to file for divorce now and walk away with all his money. We'd be sitting pretty. But you didn't listen to me, did you? You wanted the fairy tale. You fucked up the plan. Again."

I clench my jaw, ice in my veins. "Fuck you too,

Dad."

With that, I hang up.

Staring down at the phone, I fight back the tears that I've been battling all morning. How can my father blame me for this? How can any of this be my fault? Graham was with me the night Natasha overdosed. We were together the *entire night*. He never even went near Natasha. But he also refused to tell the police where he was, because he wanted to protect me—so he has no alibi. I don't know how he's going to convince everyone of his innocence.

My hands are shaking so hard, it takes me three tries to hit Amanda's name in my contacts list. Closing my eyes, I press the phone to my ear and listen to the ringing on the line, desperate for her to pick up. None of the staff know about Graham and me, but Amanda does. She'll know what a big deal this is. She'll comfort me. Help me figure out what to do.

"Where are you? How are you? What can I do?" Amanda asks instead of saying hello. "I've seen all the coverage."

"They took him away in handcuffs. It was horrible." My voice trembles as I sniff back tears. "I'm at the estate with Jude but I'm fucking falling apart—"

"I cannot believe you've been banging a murderer. This is so freaky."

"What?" I blink back the hurt that's bubbling to the top. "*Amanda.* He didn't do it. He was with me that night, remember?"

"The whole time? No breaks?" Amanda asks skeptically. "You were literally awake the whole night?"

"I mean, we slept a little, but he couldn't have—"

"Honey." Amanda's voice is kind, but very firm. "Have you asked yourself who stands to benefit from this? It's you. And it's *him*. And you definitely didn't do it, right?"

"No. Neither of us did it!"

"Can you prove it, though?"

I swallow hard and close my eyes again, but I'm still swimming through the gray. I whisper, "Amanda, please. I just need your support."

"You have it. But I'm just saying. You need to prepare yourself for the worst."

"The worst has already happened!" I all but yell into the phone. I glance up at Jude, but she's trotting around the ring on Desi and she doesn't look my way. Dropping my voice back down to a whisper, I say, "Look, I just need to figure out my next steps. I need a plan."

"I think you already know your next steps, Abbie. You need to get the hell out of there."

"I'm not leaving Jude," I hiss. "And he didn't do it. Why is that so hard to believe?"

"I believe that you believe it," she says.

Jesus Christ. Even my best friend has turned against me. "I have to go."

"Abbie. I get why you're in denial. I know you love him. And I'm not saying he doesn't love you, too, in his way. But you can't stay there anymore. You have to face the facts—"

"I said I have to go."

I hang up and let the tears fall, feeling more alone than I ever have.

Chapter Two

Abbie

Sitting around brooding and panicking isn't going to get Graham out of jail. I need to do something. Anything.

I weigh my options as I walk Jude to her Spanish lessons in the library, and once she's settled in with her tutor, I go up to my room and lock the door.

It's time to call the police. I'm not naïve enough to think they'll agree to release Graham at my request or anything like that, but maybe I can at least find out when he'll be able to leave the station. I've seen enough crime news on TV to know that people who get arrested—even in high-profile cases—are usually released on bond. And since Graham has more money than a small island, I'm sure he'll be able to make bail.

Unfortunately, the cops aren't much help. I'm not sure which precinct has him, so I have to call several. By the time I find the right one, I'm already agitated and they are decidedly unhelpful.

"Are you Mr. Ratliff's attorney?" a bored-sounding detective asks in a Bronx accent.

"No, I'm his...employee," I finish lamely. "I need to know when he'll be home to take care of his daughter."

"Is this a CPS situation?" the detective asks, suddenly brusque and demanding.

"Wait, what? No!" I stutter, suddenly terrified for Jude. "She's got someone to care for her. Many people, in fact. We don't need Child Protective Services."

"If you aren't his attorney, ma'am, we can't talk to you."

"You can't even tell me when he'll post bail?" I'm proud of myself for remembering the verbiage. "So we can come down there to pick him up?"

The response is a dry, "No attorney, no information. We all done here? We're very busy, ma'am."

"I'm sure you are. Thanks for your time," I say coldly, and then hang up.

My first dead end. I don't know what I expected, but if anything, I feel worse. Still, I'm not giving up so easily. Maybe I can do some investigating here on my own.

I go back downstairs and sneak a peek at Jude and her tutor, who are studiously covering verb conjugation. Then I slip further down the hall to Graham's office. I have no idea what I'm looking for, but maybe I can find some kind of proof that he would never raise a hand against Natasha. Or proof that she was the one trying to hurt him.

I comb through his desk and filing cabinet and find absolutely nothing but piles of legal documents and the kind of paperwork that shows just how much money a banking empire makes. It's staggering to think about. The business has client accounts and huge investments all over the globe, each raking in more zeroes than I thought possible.

As I pick up another bank statement, something else occurs to me. If something happened to Graham, wouldn't Natasha get all his money? Is he already paying her alimony now? Or did they sign a prenup? And what about Jude? If Graham was in jail or otherwise out of the picture, Natasha would get full custody by default, wouldn't she?

I have more questions than answers, and it's only making me more anxious. I rake through every file in his office, hoping to see Natasha's name pop up somewhere. Nothing. His laptop is password protected, of course, so after attempting to log in with a few variations on Jude's name and birthday, I give up. After almost an hour of searching, I've gotten nowhere.

I straighten everything up and make my way back to the library to collect Jude. It's time for her tennis lesson.

"Did my dad call?" Jude asks as we walk out to the tennis courts. "When's he coming home?"

"I'm not sure, sweetie. I haven't heard anything yet," I say, giving her hand a squeeze. "I know he'll call as soon as he's able to, okay?"

"Okay." Jude looks glum but bounces onto the court anyway, racket swinging.

I wish, for just a moment, that we could trade places. That I could be blissfully unaware of the utter shitstorm going on with Graham and let someone else handle it. But there is no one else. Just me, the nineteen-year-old nanny, desperately trying to save the man I love. At least the rest of the staff believe he's innocent. That has to mean something, right?

Now that I think about it...maybe they can help. After all, they've witnessed Graham and Natasha's relationship up close and personal over the years. They know way more than I do. I should interview them. There has to be useful intel to be had. Natasha Ratliff wasn't exactly an angel, so I doubt anyone would lie to protect her. Surely she's left a trail somewhere.

At lunch time, I set Jude up in the living room so she can watch cartoons while she eats—a special treat—and then ask Mary and Esmeralda to meet me in the kitchen.

"How's Jude holding up?" Mary asks, making a few more sandwiches for us.

I sigh. "She wants answers. I hate lying to her, but I'm going to have to come up with a cover story. It seems unlikely Graham will be back tonight. He could be gone for days."

"We'll tell her he's on a business trip," Esmeralda says. When Mary and I stare at her, she gets defensive. "Do you have a better idea? We can't very well say her dad's in *prison*. I hope to God she doesn't see anything on the news."

"You're right. Business trip it is. She's not going to be a happy camper when she hears it, though." I shake my head. Then I switch tactics, lowering my voice to a conspiratorial whisper. "I know neither of you believe Graham is guilty, but...do you remember anything he might have said or done to Natasha in the past that might have hinted that he's capable? That he had a plan?"

I try to make myself sound uncertain, like I'm on the

fence about Graham's innocence, but the truth is, I'm playing devil's advocate here—in the hopes that they'll load me up with evidence to the contrary.

"What? Mr. Ratliff hurt *her*?" Mary clucks her tongue. "Never. He's all bark and no bite. I'm not saying they didn't fight, or that he hasn't smashed up his office in a fit of rage. But when it comes down to it, that man wouldn't lay a hand on that woman. Or *any* woman, for that matter. Mrs. Ratliff, on the other hand...well. I've seen her get violent. I was standing right there the time she poured a cup of hot coffee in his lap. What'd he do? He got up and walked out."

"Mmm. She thrives on discord." Esmeralda nods. "Always loved to stir the pot when she lived here. She'd have temper tantrums, throw her fists at Mr. Ratliff, rip priceless art off the walls just to destroy it. She crashed one of his cars once, and I know it wasn't an accident."

"She crashed a car on purpose?" I gape. "Just because she was mad?"

"She's got some serious mental health issues. I remember how she'd leave all her medications laying around the house. I was always picking them up, deathly afraid Jude would get ahold of them and think they were candy," Esmeralda says quietly.

"My God." I knew Natasha wasn't liked by the staff, and that she seemed to get off on treating her "inferiors" like dirt, but I didn't realize how truly awful she'd been when she lived here. She was a liability. Dangerous. Poor Jude. I can't quite wrap my mind around it.

"She puts on a good face for the public, but you have to remember that she's an actress. We've seen who she really is." Esmeralda shakes her head and leans back in her chair.

I have never in my life been so grateful that the head of housekeeping is such a gossip. Only a few weeks ago, I was worried she told the tabloids about Graham and me, but here she is, hopefully helping me build a case to save him.

"She wanted to keep Mr. Ratliff on a leash, too," Mary interjects, setting a heavenly lobster roll in front of me. "He wasn't allowed to do anything or go anywhere unless she was involved. But we all know how much she liked to galivant around on her own."

"I don't understand why the press seems to like her so much," I say. "Just a few months ago, it was all about her affairs, but now they're weeping over her being in the hospital."

"They're just trying to sell papers and keep people tuning in on TV. They don't really care about anybody. But Mrs. Ratliff does know how to work them," Esmeralda sniffs. She takes a huge bite of her sandwich, shaking her head as she chews.

"I used to worry she was hurting Jude," Mary adds. "Sometimes I'd help with baths when she was younger and they were in between nannies. I remember seeing finger-shaped bruises on Jude's arms. I was suspicious, but she'd swear it was from riding lessons or playing rough."

Esmeralda puts her food down, her face grave. "It wasn't just you. I found red marks on her neck once. When I mentioned it to Mr. Ratliff, I thought he would lose his head. They fought so loudly that night. Mrs.

Ratliff tried to blame it on me. Thank God he knew better."

"Why didn't he kick her out then?" I'm almost afraid to ask.

"I don't know. Maybe he thought she'd get better. She did seem to have this pattern of...ups and downs," Mary muses. "After she moved out for good, the bruising stopped."

I take another bite of my sandwich to stifle the growing rage in my belly. How dare she hurt her child like this. I always knew Natasha was awful, but *this*?

"I still can't believe Graham didn't report her," I say. "Jude is everything to him."

"It would have been his word against hers—she could even have turned around and blamed it all on him, and then where would that have left Jude?" Mary points out.

My heart sinks. "I hadn't thought of that."

"There are many reasons we hated Mrs. Ratliff," Esmeralda says, patting my hand gently. "That little girl is precious to all of us."

Just then, Jude pokes her head into the kitchen. "Can I have a dessert, please?"

"Of course, sweet thing." Mary leaps up and bustles away to help Jude.

Esmeralda shoots me a look. "I know what you're trying to do. You need to be careful."

"What do you mean?"

She makes sure Jude is gone again before saying, "I saw you in Mr. Ratliff's office. We're all worried about him, but be careful where you step. There are snakes in these grasses."

"The biggest snake of all is in a coma," I remind her. "I can't sit back and do nothing. Jude needs her father."

———————

LATER THAT NIGHT, I try calling the police station again, hoping I'll be able to speak with someone a little kinder this time around. No dice. It's seriously driving me crazy, not knowing anything. And Jude cried her little eyes out when I told her that Graham was going to be away on business for the rest of the week. I hope to God they don't keep him in police custody longer than that.

My next call is to Graham's lawyer, Elise Bowen. Having handled Graham's divorce, surely she'd know about the abuses that both Graham and Jude suffered at Natasha's hand. Maybe she can use that somehow to get Graham out of jail. I don't have her personal number, unfortunately, but her law firm is a pretty big deal, so I do a Google search and call the office.

"Bowen and Ellis," a curt voice answers the phone.

"Hi," I say, feeling awkward all over again. I swallow it down and press on, because Graham needs me to. "This is Abbie Montgomery, I work for Graham Ratliff. Would it be possible to speak with Miss Bowen?"

"Oh." The way the receptionist says the word makes my stomach turn. "The nanny."

"Um, yes?"

"Hold on," she sighs, as if I'm inconveniencing her. "Let me see who's available."

I end up speaking with a junior attorney, who refuses to give me Bowen's cell number.

17

"Can you call her for me, then?" I beg. "Mr. Ratliff needs to get out of jail as soon as possible. He's *innocent*. Mrs. Ratliff is behind this whole thing, we just need to find a way to prove it. How can they even be keeping him locked up when they have no solid evidence—"

"Look, Miss...Montgomery. Frankly, you playing Nancy Drew is not going to help his case. If anything, it only bolsters the adultery narrative that the prosecution will no doubt be running with as a motive. So stop calling. Stop digging. Let the grown-ups do their jobs, okay?"

Then he hangs up. I stare at the phone, cheeks on fire as if I just got slapped. Fuck.

At my wit's end, and with nowhere else to turn, I call my dad.

"I don't know what to do," I sob as soon as he answers the phone. "I can't help him, and no one will tell me what's happening, and I'm sitting here trying take care of his poor kid and..."

"Calm yourself down, Abbie. It hasn't even been a whole day," he interrupts impatiently. "I play golf with his lawyer from time to time, all right? So just give me a little time to work on this. There's nothing to worry about. I'll take care of everything."

Chapter Three

Graham

My FATHER's words ring in my ears: *Cock up, my boy*. Never have those words felt more appropriate than this moment, as I sit here fuming and fretting in a frigid interrogation room with handcuffs on, staring down a pair of hard-eyed detectives who think I tried to murder my ex-wife. The whole thing is so ridiculous it's almost goddamn laughable.

Natasha's overdose was a result of her own actions, and the round-the-clock care she received at the hospital afterward was thanks to an emergency call that *I* made in order to save her life, but here I am, having to fight for my innocence. It's preposterous. It's unfathomable.

Yet somehow, it's my reality.

We've been in here for what feels like hours, though without a clock on hand I have no idea how much time has really passed. I sit with my eyes trained on the wall behind the cops, unwilling to talk because I know better. I may have never been in this situation before, but I've seen enough films and TV shows to know that these detectives aren't here to play nice. If life were simpler, my alibi would suffice, but I cannot bring Abbie into this.

Our relationship has upended her life enough already. She doesn't need any more negative attention. She's completely innocent, and throwing her in with the piranhas all over again is absolutely out of the question. I knew coming to New York City was a bad idea, I just didn't know it would turn out this bad. I never should have caved in to Natasha's demands.

How the hell can anyone think I'm culpable when she *overdosed*? This shitshow is all Natasha's fault, and she's still found a way to put me square in the middle of it. So I cock up, putting on my best armor, and refuse the tepid, burnt-smelling coffee they try to offer me.

"This would go a lot easier for you if you'd just cooperate." This from the self-professed good cop.

They are quite the pair of stereotypes, the two of them. Good cop is played by Detective Krohl, older, grandfatherly, with pouches under his eyes and an air of world-weary exhaustion about him. He gives the impression that he just wants to help. That he'd love nothing more than to get this silly business over with so he can go home and put his slippers on and have a nice cup of tea with his wife, who probably looks like Mrs. Claus in a velour track suit. But all he's done this whole time is lean on me to confess, albeit gently, and by now I've lost all patience.

Because I have nothing to confess.

On his left sits Detective Hernandez, aka bad cop, who looks to be in her late thirties. She's lean and mean, with her curly hair scraped back into a tight bun, not a single strand out of place. The second she walked in, the sharp arch of her brows told me she's the take-no-prisoners type. She's done nothing but bark accusations at me, try to make me sweat, try to break me so I'll tell her something other than the truth—which she seems to have zero interest in because it doesn't fit the murderous, adulterous ex-husband narrative that she clearly already believes.

"I'd like to call my attorney, Elise Bowen," I tell them.

"Of course. We'll get there," Detective Krohl says.

"The fuck we will, scumbag," Detective Hernandez snarls, lunging toward me.

Krohl's hand shoots out to turn off the digital voice recorder on the table and then tug Hernandez back into her chair. "Calm down, Ananda," he soothes.

She breathes hard, glaring at me, as if she was this close to slugging me in the jaw if not for the intervention of her partner. This is how it's been. Round and round we go. Although, what more can I expect when they suspect me of attempted murder?

"You do know that you're legally required to stop interrogating me once I've asked for my attorney," I say.

"An innocent man wouldn't need a lawyer to tell his side of the story," Hernandez shoots back.

"Don't make this harder on yourself, Graham," Krohl says, his voice kind and patient, as if we're all just friends catching up. Then he turns the recorder back on. "Just give us your version of what happened that night."

"I already did. And you've already recorded it. I have nothing else to say," I tell him, nodding at the recorder. "My ex-wife is an addict, I am sorry to say, and she did this to herself. An unfortunate and frankly preventable accident."

Krohl sighs like he's disappointed in me and takes a sip of rancid coffee before reclining in his creaky chair and glancing down at his notes. "The thing is, we have multiple eyewitness accounts of the fight you had with your wife at Piatto. It doesn't look good."

"Ex-wife," I correct, though I'm sure it does nothing to help my case.

Hernandez smiles cruelly. "You *threatened* to *kill your wife* in front of an entire restaurant full of people, including your eight-year-old daughter. Tell us about the fight, Ratliff. What did Natasha do that lead to that statement? She cheat on you again? Or was it you doing the cheating this time, and she threatened to blackmail you with it?"

"Ex-wife," I monotone, my gaze drilling into the gray cinderblock wall.

But underneath the steely exterior, I'm a black hole of anger and regret. Dammit, I shouldn't have lost control like that in public. Usually I pride myself on my cool head, but Natasha always brings out the worst in me. She knows exactly how to push all my buttons —loves doing it, in fact. She makes me say terrible things I don't mean, and now it's come to bite me in the ass.

"Please, Graham," Krohl says. "Just give us something we can work with. I'd really like to hear your side of things."

"As I've told you, I'm done talking until my attorney is present," I remind them.

The detectives share a look and I clench my jaw. We're getting nowhere. This is hell.

"Don't want to talk? Fine, then. This is how I see it." Detective Hernandez reclines in her chair, matching her partner. "Everyone knows about your recent affair. That little PR stunt on Mrs. Ratliff's opening night aside, which by the way fooled exactly no one, I imagine things haven't exactly been pleasant between you two since the divorce anyhow. So. The nanny story hits all the news outlets, you look like a fucking pedophile, and she sees an opportunity. She threatens to take you to court. To take the kid away from you. That sound about right?"

Anger roils through me. How dare they bring Jude into this. And Abbie is an adult.

"Hit a nerve, have we?" Hernandez prods, eyebrow cocked.

I slide on the mask I use for all my board meetings and say nothing.

"Natasha Ratliff is a woman who gets what she wants," Krohl says, shaking his head, as if he's just now warming up to Hernandez's theory. "You know this. I know this. Shit, half the globe knows this. Maybe you were afraid...no, no. You weren't afraid. You *knew*. Knew she'd go after you for everything. Destroy your reputation, your business. Take your child, your home, your income. We know you've got quite the cushy nest egg."

He's really on a roll. I wonder if they practiced this skit in advance.

Hernandez leans forward again, piggybacking off her partner's momentum. "You were threatened with losing everything that matters to you, and you lost control.

Didn't you? You lost control in the restaurant, and she pushed you further. She pushed you so far you knew you had to get her out of the way. To save yourself, save the kid."

This is all bullshit. But there's nothing I can do, just sit here with these cuffs digging into my wrists while I'm forced to listen to false speculation.

"But how to get rid of her without ruining your life in the process...?" Hernandez continues thoughtfully. "A big, splashy murder just isn't your style. So you set it up to look like an accidental overdose. Something you could easily pass off as an accident. Something that keeps you in your home, with your child and your extensive wealth. Untouchable. But guess what? Your privilege can't keep you safe from the law, Ratliff. Not this time."

She almost looks triumphant, like this inane statement is her trump card. If it weren't for the handcuffs, I'd even be tempted to give her little performance the slow clap.

"I demand to speak with my attorney," I say through gritted teeth. "I've had enough of story time. This interview is over."

After an eternity of silence, Detective Krohl lets out a heavy sigh. Then he turns off the recorder and tucks it into his pocket with a weary shake of his head. "Okay. You'll get your call. But I'm telling you now, this won't make things better for you."

Moments later, I'm taken into a tiny office by another officer to make my call.

"Phone's on the desk. Make it quick. I'll be right outside," he tells me.

All I want in this moment is to hear Abbie's voice, but I need to talk to Bowen first. I wait until the door clicks shut behind the detective and then immediately dial Bow's cell. It goes straight to voicemail. My frustration rears its ugly head yet again. Where the fuck is she? There's no way she doesn't know what's going on. My arrest has been all over the news. I try again, to no avail. We're going to have words when she gets here. I pay her well to be available at all hours.

I dial her office number next, hoping to God that she's in.

"Bowen and Ellis," Destiny answers curtly, which instantly rubs me the wrong way.

"This is Graham Ratliff. I need to speak to Bow."

"Mr. Ratliff!" Her tone changes on a dime. "I'm so sorry, but Miss Bowen is currently out of pocket."

"Where the bloody hell is she?"

"I'm not at liberty to discuss it," is all she says. "Where are you right now?"

"I'm with the police. I've been in an interrogation room all day, and I need Bow to get down here as quickly as possible. Or Ellis, or whoever you've got."

"Ellis is unavailable. I can send one of our junior attorneys, Brooks Farris?"

I let out a laugh with no humor in it and pinch the bridge of my nose, trying to center myself. "Fine. Send whomever. Just make sure they get here immediately."

After I hang up, I sit and stare at the phone. A junior attorney? I don't like it one bit. It feels wrong. It feels like a bad omen looming over my head. I know nothing about this Farris, only that he's not who I pay for and not who I trust. But I don't have a choice.

Goddammit, Graham, if you'd only kept your shit together.

Behind me, the door opens. I brace myself for the detective to tell me my time is up and that he's taking me back to the interrogation room for more bullshit with Krohl and Hernandez.

"Well, well, well," a familiar voice tuts. When I look over my shoulder, I see Ford Montgomery standing there, hands in his pockets like it's a day at the damn beach. "Look who the cat dragged in."

Relief washes over me. He and I have grown apart over the last few years, but having a friendly face in front of me instantly eases the tension in my gut. "What are you doing here?"

"Helping you, I hope. I know I might not be your favorite person, but this really isn't the time to address our personal matters, is it?" He takes a seat and picks up a pen, spinning it across his thumb, an old trick we used to do in college to intimidate our competition during debates. "I got a hold of Bowen, by the way. She's out of the country."

I inhale sharply through my teeth. "Shit. That's why they're sending over a baby lawyer."

He shrugs. "Be that as it may, let me give you some free legal advice. Word on the street is, you have no alibi —which I'm assuming is true, otherwise you wouldn't still be in custody. So it's likely you'll be in here for a while. You want to rethink that? A solid alibi would go a long way toward clearing your name."

"No. I never laid a hand on Natasha. My whereabouts that night are nobody's business."

Ford looks at me searchingly, and I feel a flash of guilt. Does he know what's going on between Abbie and me? He isn't the type to believe everything the media says, and Abbie isn't exactly close to him, but...he surely has to at least wonder if there's any truth to those rumors.

"The judge might not grant bail at all, Graham. You're rich enough to be a flight risk. You could be in prison for weeks or even months while this gets sorted out. "

All I can do is brood. The same thought has already crossed my mind.

"And if you're locked up," he goes on, "what do you expect Abbie to do?"

"She'll be taken care of. In fact, I need you to do me a favor," I say, lowering my voice. "I added her as an authorized user on my bank account when she started. Standard operating procedure for nannies, for emergencies. Which, if this isn't a fucking emergency then I don't know what is. Point being, there's a debit card with her name on it at home. Top drawer of the desk in my office, in a sealed envelope from the bank. There was obviously never a need to tell her about it before now."

He nods. "Okay. I'll get it to her. What else?"

"I have urgent paperwork that needs to be signed *today* for a business deal. It's a merger with a bank in Dubai—they have over 23 billion dollars in assets, which should keep my Board of Directors and our shareholders feeling secure enough to ignore any dips in the company stock if this murder charge ends up going sideways. I swear to God, Ford, I'm innocent. But the public won't know that. And if people start offloading shares en masse, the business could go under like that. My whole empire is at stake."

I study his face, defeat weighing heavily on me. I have no one else to turn to, no one else I can trust. I'm going to have to rely on our decades-old friendship to get me through this.

"I understand. Completely," Ford says, nodding slowly. "I'm just going to need a power of attorney so I can sign off on that paperwork on your behalf. Do you want me to draw up the POA docs?"

"Please. Right away. And one last favor—will you help Abbie handle things? Stay with her and Jude at the estate for a bit? I need to know they're okay, both of them."

That same knowing look crosses his face, but he nods. "Whatever you need, old friend. I'll take care of everything. You can trust me."

Chapter Four

Abbie

IT's BEEN forty-eight hours since Graham was taken away. And I've gotten exactly nowhere.

Meanwhile, Jude is busy shuffling from one lesson to the other, trying to keep a smile on her face even though she misses her mom and her dad. Cassie's been helping me keep Jude distracted, having her assist with caring for the horses in the stables, braiding manes, and taking trail rides through the property. In fact, all of the staff are focused on keeping Jude preoccupied right now—so she still has no idea what's actually going on. Graham's history of dropping everything for business matters helps us keep the lie afloat. But I'm not sure how much longer we can maintain the charade before Jude starts to question it.

It's exhausting, all this uncertainty. The knots in my stomach won't let up, leaving me anxious and nauseated as we go from one tutor to the next. I know my dad is supposedly handling things, but I haven't received an update from him either, and now he's the one avoiding *my* calls. I don't even know if I can trust him. Maybe I shouldn't have asked him for help.

After tennis, I take Jude to the kitchen for lunch. Mary and Esmeralda are waiting there, regaling her with tales from when she was little and trying to sneak into the pantry for extra cookies. Jude's giggles lift my spirits, even if temporarily. For her, it's just a regular day in a regular world, where her dad is off on another business trip and her mom is...more or less out of sight, out of mind. Not that Jude has stopped asking me when she'll be able to visit Natasha again. But I have a good excuse for that, and it isn't even a lie, really—Graham is the one who needs to take her to the hospital. The doctors are doing everything they can. We just have to think positive and wait for more news.

I'm sitting at the island eating an apple with almond butter when my phone rings. I fully expect it to be my dad, but instead it's a number I don't recognize with a New York City area code, which sends my heart into rapid palpitations. It's got to be Graham, or maybe even his lawyer. I hurriedly make up a lie about needing to talk to my dad and then rush out to the front steps of the estate to have a private conversation.

"Hello?" I ask tentatively, heart in my throat.

"Abbie." He breathes my name in such a way that reinvigorates my entire soul.

"Hey." Tears cling to my lashes. "I didn't think they'd let you talk to me."

"Nothing can keep me from you. Not even this," he assures me, but I can hear the stress in his voice. "You and Jude are the only thing that keeps me going in here."

"How are you?"

His laugh is bitter. "It's a regular picnic here. You'd love it."

I try to match his laugh, but it falls flat. "I'll just bet. God, I've been so worried. I tried calling and they wouldn't let me talk to you. I'm losing my mind."

"I'm okay," he promises. "How's Jude?"

"We're keeping her busy." I swallow down the lump in my throat. "She thinks you're on a business trip, but she still asks about you every five minutes. She's trying to be brave."

He takes a deep breath, and I can only imagine the guilt he's feeling.

"I'll bet she is. My little warrior. Just keep doing what you're doing and don't let her know otherwise. I don't want to scare her. She's got enough to worry about already."

"Of course. The whole staff is taking excellent care of her, I promise."

"That's my girl." Hearing him call me his sends a shock of warmth through me, but it quickly turns back to tensions and nerves. I hate this so much. He should be here, home with us. Before I can stop myself, I'm choking back sobs.

"Shh. Listen to me, Abbie. It's going to be okay," Graham soothes. "Your father came to see me and he's going to make sure you're taken care of. The other thing is...the police are probably going to interview you soon. I need you to do something for me."

"Anything."

"When they ask you about the fight at Piatto, tell

31

them the truth—how we fought like that often, the both of us, and even when it got ugly, the threats were empty ones. You've heard enough arguing between us, so don't feel like you have to hold back on the details. Okay?"

"Okay. I can do that."

"Good." He clears his throat and takes a pause. "I need to go, but there's one more thing. Most of all, just... just remember that I love you. No matter what happens. I'll love you until the day I die, Abbie Montgomery."

"Graham." My voice cracks, and my tears have returned in full force. "I love you so much. You'll be out of there soon, and back with us where you belong. I love you."

"I love you. Give my love to Jude."

And then he's gone. I sink down on the steps and dig my palms into my eyes, trying to stop the flow of tears. I have to get it together for Jude. Go back in there and act like everything's fine, like the world isn't falling apart.

Suddenly I hear gravel crunching, and I look up to watch as a black car comes up the drive. The car slides to a stop in front of the porch, and a driver slides out to open the back door.

My father steps out, sunglasses hiding his expression, dressed in a nice suit despite the heat. As he waltzes toward me, I stand up and swipe at my wet cheeks, trying to keep the panic off my face. Is he here to take me away?

"Dad? What are you doing here?"

"Sweetheart." He embraces me, but I stay stiff in his arms. He never calls me that. It's purely for show, though I'm not sure who this performance is for. "Are you okay?"

"Obviously not." I pull away with a glare. "Why are you here?"

"Graham sent me."

That's when it hits me—Graham just told me that my dad was going to make sure I was taken care of. I had assumed that meant...well, I guess I didn't really have time to even think about it. But I definitely didn't expect him to just show up here on the doorstep.

I shake my head. "What for? I don't know what you can do from here, Dad. I thought you were going to get ahold of Bowen and help with all the legal stuff."

He nods. "I've been in touch with the team at Bowen and Ellis, though Elise is still out of town. But Graham asked me to stay here for a few days and keep an eye on things, so that's what I'm going to do."

My mind is boggled. Did Graham seriously ask my dad to...babysit? To nanny the nanny? What the hell is going on?

Just then, the driver hands my dad his overnight bag and fancy leather laptop case. Dad slips him a tip and then gestures for us to walk inside.

"How's Jude?" he asks, setting his things down in the foyer.

"She's holding up, I guess. We're keeping her busy."

"Good. Keep doing your job. That's the most important thing you can do right now."

"Wait. How did Graham seem, when you saw him? Is he...okay?" I ask, whispering.

My dad shrugs. "He's a fucking mess. But I told him I'd handle everything, and I will."

That makes my stomach churn, but before I can ask

any more questions, Esmeralda comes down the hall. She freezes when she sees us huddled together in the foyer, a look of surprise on her face. My dad immediately unleashes his trademark charm.

"Esmeralda! What a pleasant surprise. Look at you, you haven't aged a day."

Her eyes dart between him and me and his luggage as she says, "Hello, Mr. Montgomery. Are you...here to see Abbie?"

"That and more. I'm here to be of service, however I can. Graham sent me." He takes her hand and kisses her knuckles. "How have you been? Really."

"We're all stressed right now," she admits quietly. "Your help is appreciated. I'll have a guest room ready for you right away."

"Thank you, dear. I'm just glad I can lend a hand to my best friend. He's lucky to have you, too."

Dad's really laying it on thick, but Esmeralda doesn't seem to notice how smarmy he's being. He rubs his hands together and looks around. "Now where is my goddaughter hiding?"

"She's having lunch in the kitchen. Can we get you something to eat?" Esmeralda asks.

"Just a whiskey, if you please." He twinkles at her, and I suppress an eye-roll. "Think you can manage it?"

"Of course." She whisks off down the hall, still smiling over all his shameless flirting.

I take Dad into the kitchen. Jude looks up from her lunch curiously.

"Hi," she says hesitantly.

"This is my dad," I tell her. "He's here to visit us. Do

34

you remember him? It's been a few years since he was here last."

"Of course she remembers her uncle Ford," my dad says, moving toward her. "Gosh, you must've grown four feet since the last time I saw you. You still love horses?"

Jude smiles shyly. "Yeah. My horse Desi, she's a British Vanner, and we won three ribbons at my last exhibition."

"Wow, that is incredible. You know, I'd love to meet Desi sometime," Dad says.

My heart aches watching them interact. He was never like this with me when I was little, and even if he's just playing a part right now, he's doing a damn good job of pretending he actually has a heart. I was rarely granted the same courtesy. But my bitterness has no place here—this is about keeping Jude calm and supported, so I bite my tongue.

He tells Jude, "So, I'm going to be staying here for a few days. Is that okay with you?"

"Sure!" she says. "I can even take you riding, if you want?"

My dad laughs. "I'd love that."

Esmeralda returns with a glass of whiskey, neat, and he takes it graciously.

"Thank you, dear. You're a godsend. Abbie, would you join me in the office for a moment? We need to talk."

I battle the sinking feeling in my gut as Esmeralda assures me she'll make sure Jude gets to her next lesson on time, and then follow my dad to Graham's office. Once we're inside, he shuts the door and pours another finger of whiskey into his tumbler.

"Whatever it is, just tell me. Don't sugarcoat it," I say impatiently. I'm terrified that something bad is going on behind the scenes with Graham's case, that my dad has been hiding the worst of it from me.

"Abbie, relax. I didn't bring you in here to give you bad news."

Relief pours through me. "Okay. So...what, then?"

My dad ignores me and starts rifling through the desk, and something about it strikes me as incredibly invasive. "What are you doing?"

"Aha." He pulls out a white business-sized envelope and rips it open, unfolding the thick paper inside. "Graham told me he got you a debit card, for expenses, in case you needed to take care of Jude. You're an authorized user on his account, so go wild."

I take the debit card from my dad as if it's a precious thing and carefully put it in my pocket. I'm touched that Graham thought of me, even in the midst of dealing with his life imploding. "Thank you for helping, but what exactly do you plan to—"

"Don't worry your pretty little head about it." He waves me off and takes a long sip of his drink. "I'm going to handle everything, okay? You just keep your head down and take care of my goddaughter. It'll all work out."

I want to believe my dad, so I do. He might be an asshole sometimes, but he's also smart, incredibly cunning, and a freaking lawyer, so if he says it's going to work out, he must be telling the truth. This is the first time I've felt the weight of this whole situation lighten up even the tiniest bit. Thank God.

We spend the rest of the day together. Jude even

takes him on that trail ride she promised, Cassie and I following along a little ways behind them as my dad catches up with Jude. Dad tells her lots of stories about the old days when he went to school with Graham, making all of us laugh. Their college days were wild, and I always liked hearing the stories, but now they're a balm to my soul. I was nervous about my dad showing up here unannounced like he did, but he's been true to his word so far—he's here to help. I'm glad Graham sent him.

Thanks to the debit card, I'm able to sit with Mary as she puts together an online grocery order and arrange for the estate's weekly delivery, and then I volunteer myself and Jude to help cook dinner. Partly because both of us so desperately need to keep busy, but also because I've found myself relishing Mary's company and I know Jude does, too.

After we've all eaten and retired to the living room, I finally get the call—the one I've been dreading. I step outside to answer it, trying to keep my voice steady as I say hello.

"Hello Miss Montgomery, my name is Detective Krohl. I'm handling the Ratliff case. We'd like to have you come down to the precinct tomorrow to answer a few questions. Would you be able to do that?"

"Yes. Of course." I can barely breathe, even though the detective has a kind, soothing voice. "Anything you need."

"Great. Can you be here at 9:30? We can send a car to get you, if you're in the area."

"9:30 is great, and I can get a ride. Thank you."

"Thank you. Just ask for me when you get to the front desk. We'll see you tomorrow."

When I hang up, I realize my hands are trembling. That call lasted less than two minutes, but it felt like an eternity.

There's no way I'm going to sleep tonight.

Chapter Five

Abbie

THE NEXT MORNING, I get up early to have coffee and toast in the kitchen with Esmeralda and Mary. I filled them in last night after I spoke with the detective, and even though my dad had offered to keep an eye on Jude while I'm in the City, Mary insisted that she'd be happy to do it herself. Which will work out for the best anyway, since it means my dad can do work on his laptop all day while Mary basically gets to spend hours reading romance novels in between escorting Jude to her lessons.

"We'll make cookies this afternoon, too," she tells me as I carry my dishes to the sink.

"Jude will love that," I say, trying to sound normal. But my guts are churning, and I'm still freaking out inside about this interview.

Esmeralda must notice I'm not doing well, because she pats me on the shoulder and says, "Just keep your head on straight and your answers direct. There's nothing to worry about."

I nod and shoulder my purse and then head out to the

driveway, where I find my dad chatting with Ronaldo next to the waiting town car.

"You're going to be fine, sweetheart," my dad says performatively, pulling me in for a quick hug. Lowering his voice, he murmurs in my ear, "Don't fuck this up."

"I won't," I say, jerking back with a glare.

Ronaldo opens the car door for me, and I slide into the back seat. Here goes nothing.

When I step out onto the curb at the police station almost two hours later, all I can do is stare up at the gritty brick building with a lump in my throat. I try to remember Esmeralda's pep talk from earlier: stay calm, give direct answers. But how am I supposed to do that when the man I love is literally behind bars, and the one thing that could free him—a legitimate alibi—is a secret that I'm supposed to be keeping?

"Miss Montgomery?" a voice calls out.

My head snaps to the left, where I see a man in a well-cut charcoal suit and designer glasses smoking a cigarette. He's young, maybe in his late twenties, but he also looks slick, polished in a way that instantly tells me he's a lawyer. I'm instantly on my guard.

"Yes?" I say hesitantly.

He comes over and hands me his business card. "I'm Brooks Farris, a junior attorney at Bowen and Ellis. We represent Mr. Ratliff, and we'll be representing you as well."

"Are you the junior attorney with whom I spoke the other day?" I ask, eyes narrowing at the memory of how I was treated. "The one who called me Nancy Drew?"

"Pardon?" He looks confused for a second, and then

winces. "Oh. Wait. I bet I know who that was. An unfortunate case of nepotism at its finest. I apologize sincerely, Miss Montgomery."

If I'm not mistaken, I believe I just caught the slightest hint of a Southern twang—it reminds me of my mom's accent, and I find myself warming to the guy. And missing her.

"Well, it's nice to meet you, then. I'm glad you're not him." I hold out my hand and we shake. "No offense, but...why isn't Miss Bowen here?"

He laughs. "You don't beat around the bush, do you? I like that. Bowen's out of the country, consulting on a high-profile case that we're not at liberty to discuss. I'll be handling things temporarily, just until she returns. And if it makes you feel any better, I got my J.D. at UNC and I've been at the firm for four years. I'm not as inexperienced as my title implies."

"I didn't mean it that way, I just...I've never done this before."

"You'll be fine. This ain't my first rodeo," he says, still looking amused.

Even so. Why didn't the firm send Ellis, then, or at least a more senior attorney? And how can Bowen possibly still be out of town with all of this going on? I was under the impression that she and Graham were old friends, and that as a lawyer she was both damn expensive and damn good. Who the hell is more important than Graham? The Queen of England? An Arab prince?

Farris checks his watch. "Why don't we do a little prep before we go in? We have some time. Does that work?"

"Actually, that'd be great," I say. "I'm so nervous."

He motions me over to a bench, and once we're seated he starts talking me through what to expect.

"I know it seems intimidating, but they're just going to want to corroborate information they already have, try to get a sense of the players and all the moving parts, what happened when, fill in some blanks, that kind of thing."

I nod. "Okay. I can do that."

"It's possible they'll try to get you to implicate Mr. Ratliff in some way, maybe by poking holes in your story or getting you worked up, seeing if they can trick you into saying something that hurts his case. But we're not going to let them push you around. That's why I'm here." Gone is the smile from moments earlier; now he's all business. "So if at any point you get uncomfortable, just defer to me. Okay?"

"Got it," I say. "And thank you."

Minutes later, after Farris has given me a few more pointers, we head toward the station's front doors, but as we go up the steps I grab his sleeve.

"Just so you know—Graham's innocent," I tell him, desperation washing over me. I need him to understand this more than I need air in my lungs. "I mean, she OD'd. You can't force someone to overdose. He shouldn't be in there at all. This whole thing is—"

"I understand, Miss Montgomery. And we'll be sure your testimony conveys that. It's going to be okay," Farris reassures me for what seems like the millionth time.

But I'm still a total emotional wreck as we make our way inside.

SITTING IN A TINY, freezing cold room on a plastic folding chair isn't as much of a thrill ride as it looks on television. The second the detectives sit across from me, that same wave of fear comes tripping down my back again. I take a drink of the crappy coffee they provided to steady myself and look over at Farris, who nods reassuringly. I can do this.

As the two detectives get their notes and their voice recorder sorted, I study their faces. The older man looks tired but kindly; he's the one who Farris and I met at the front desk—the same detective I spoke to on the phone last night. Detective Krohl. The woman beside him is younger but somehow harder looking, like she's seen too much on the job; her name is Detective Hernandez. They haven't been cruel or pushy, but suddenly my heart is in my throat.

I have to get Graham out of this. I might be his last hope of getting out of police custody.

Krohl goes through the formalities of stating the date and time and location into the recorder before having me state my name and age. Then things start rolling for real.

"Let's talk about your relationship to the Ratliffs," he says, leaning back with a hand clamped around his cup of coffee. "How long you've known them, what your job is with the family, your duties, everything that you do day to day."

"You want me to...talk about my job?" I ask, blinking back the surprise. What does that have to do with anything?

Next to me, Farris leans forward. "What do the details of her employment have to do with this investigation?"

"It's standard protocol," Hernandez answers. "We're just trying to understand her relationship to the Ratliffs, establish how she fits into their lives."

I look over at Farris for guidance.

"Keep it simple. Just the basics," is all he says.

"Well?" Hernandez prods.

"Um. I guess I've known the Ratliff family for about three years now? Well, wait, longer than that. See, my dad got his MBA at Harvard when Graham—Mr. Ratliff, I mean—was there for undergrad. They were best friends all during college. I was just a toddler then, but I've always known *of* the Ratliffs, like from my dad's stories and stuff. But. Sorry, I'm rambling."

"You're doing fine. Go on," Detective Krohl says, nodding.

I can feel beads of sweat rolling down my back already, but I continue. "Anyway. The Ratliffs were always traveling the world, I guess, so they weren't really part of my family's circle of friends growing up. Mr. Ratliff was...more of a character that my dad talked about. But then, about three years ago, the Ratliffs moved back to New York from abroad, and my family spent the summer with them in the Hudson Valley, and so that's when I got to know them all a bit better. And I met their daughter, who I got along with really well. She was five at the time, she's eight now. And so, when Mr. Ratliff needed a nanny for her this summer, my dad suggested me to Mr. Ratliff for the job. And I took it. So that's...how I became the nanny."

Jesus, Farris told me to keep it simple and all I can do is sit here and word-vomit.

"Is this a full-time job?" Hernandez asks, jotting something in her notepad.

"Yes. Well, for now. During the school year I'll be back at Cornell, so the job is actually almost over. I mean, unless they wanted to arrange some kind of weekend position when Jude goes back to school in Manhattan or something, but we haven't really discussed—"

"That's enough background, I think," Farris says softly, cutting me off. "Your duties?"

I clear my throat. "Right. So the job is...I look after their daughter. Babysitting essentially, but she has a lot of lessons and tutors and things so I accompany her to those as well, make sure she eats, bathes, goes to bed on time. Mr. Ratliff works a lot and Mrs. Ratliff lives and works here in Manhattan. So that's why they need help. Is that —does that explain it enough?"

Krohl nods. "And the daughter's name?"

Do they...seriously not know? I look to Farris, who nods for me to answer. "Uh, Jude Ratliff."

"Is it true that Mr. Ratliff believed his daughter was fathered by another man?" Hernandez says.

"What? That's ridiculous," I blurt. Farris clears his throat and I try again. "I mean, no. Nobody would think that. She's like a miniature version of Graham. They look the same, similar mannerisms, they put marmalade on their toast the same way. There's no question."

Detective Krohl nods, but Hernandez stares at me

like she's waiting for more. I just stare right back, trying to slow my breathing and get my racing pulse under control.

"Are you currently living with the Ratliffs?" Hernandez asks pointedly.

"Yes."

"And where is that?" Krohl adds.

"The Ratliff estate, in the Hudson Valley. Mr. Ratliff and Jude are there for the summer, but Mrs. Ratliff has mostly been at the family's apartment in Manhattan. She has a show on Broadway at the moment, and um...I guess she's been living there pretty much exclusively since the divorce. Mr. Ratliff and Jude have their own bedrooms at the apartment, of course, and they stay there during the week when Jude's school is in session, although...I believe Mr. Ratliff is looking for his own place as well. So he and Mrs. Ratliff won't have to be under one roof going forward, and Jude can take turns staying with each of her parents. Maybe that's not relevant?"

I had no idea I was prone to so much babbling when I get nervous. This is awful.

"So basically, you travel with the family as needed," Hernandez says, waving her pen impatiently.

"Yes. Sorry."

"Let's talk about Graham and Natasha's fight at Piatto on the night of August first," Krohl says briskly. "Eyewitness reports say you were there with the family for dinner."

"Yes. I was there to help with Jude. It wasn't really a family-type restaurant." I shrug.

"Is it common for you to go to dinner with the family?" Detective Hernandez asks sourly.

I look at Farris, who nods again. "We usually eat at home, but yes, I do attend the majority of the meals with the family. My job hours are flexible, depending on their needs."

"What happened during that fight at the restaurant?" Krohl asks. "Can you tell us in your own words?"

I hesitate. That fight was ugly and loud, and on paper, I know it makes Graham look abusive. Not only that, but it was very public. All I want to do is just skip to what happened later that night—give these detectives Graham's alibi, tell them that he was in bed with me until the next morning, that he couldn't possibly have had anything to do with Natasha's OD. But I can't. Because I have to do what Graham asked me to do.

Which is to tell the police the truth about the fight at Piatto and all the other fights he and Natasha have gotten in. It's the only way to downplay the way he threatened her that night. To make it seem like it was something ordinary, quotidian, mundane. Harmless. Which, it was.

So I do. Babbling as I go, I recount how the Ratliffs squabbled after Jude told the waiter she didn't want pasta and Natasha called her "bitchy." How I'd rushed Jude to the restroom to keep her from witnessing the argument, and as a result had missed most of what the Ratliffs had allegedly said to each other. This must match some of those eyewitness accounts, because Krohl nods as I speak, flipping through his notepad and making little checkmarks in it with a pencil.

Then I mention how often I've overheard the Ratliffs fighting at home, how the verbal abuse they volley back and forth is basically just par for the course. I add that

Natasha usually seems intoxicated during the fights, that both of them have occasionally broken things or made physical threats—but that it has never amounted to anything.

When I'm done, Detective Hernandez glowers at me. "We have reports that Graham Ratliff threatened to *kill* Natasha Ratliff at the restaurant that night. Would you say that that sort of threat was...how did you put it...*par for the course?*"

I force a laugh. "That's what you're keeping him here for? Seriously? Graham Ratliff is all bark. He says stuff like that all the time! Like he told me he was going to kill the gardener who planted some flowering shrub he's allergic to, but guess what? That gardener is alive and well. So is the cook who oversalted the scallops. He never actually *does* anything, he just comes across a little over the top when he's mad sometimes. But it's meaningless. It's just...hyperbole."

Hernandez and Krohl exchange a glance.

Krohl clears his throat. "Would you say—"

"Actually, I think you have all you need from Miss Montgomery," Farris interrupts. "Have a good day. Miss Montgomery, please come with me."

I take a deep breath and say goodbye, following Farris out the door.

And then, for the first time in a long time, I pray.

Chapter Six

Abbie

I'VE BEEN a ball of nerves ever since I got back from the police station yesterday.

Even though Farris reassured me that I did fine during my interview, I still can't help obsessing over the answers I gave to all the questions, worrying I might have inadvertently revealed something that could get Graham into more trouble. I tried so hard to do exactly what he asked and downplay the fight at the restaurant, but I have no idea if it swayed the detectives at all. That Graham was even arrested to begin with remains completely inexplicable to me.

After returning home, I'd faked a migraine and let my dad take over my nanny duties for the rest of the afternoon. Stomach in knots, I couldn't eat the beautiful salmon dinner Mary made, I barely slept, and on top of feeling physically and mentally drained, I've been expending what little energy I have trying to pretend everything is business as usual for Jude's benefit. I hate that I don't have any solid answers for her, hate having to lie about where her dad really is, about whether I think her mom is going to die in the hospital. I just want this nightmare to be over for all of us.

But I know I have to swallow down my anxiety and do my best to give Jude as many great days as I can. Because if everything blows up, she probably won't have any of those for a while. In fact...if Graham stays in prison, and Natasha remains in a coma, Jude could very well end up in her godfather's custody. The last thing I'd want is for Jude to grow up with literally the same dad that I did, even if it would mean I'd get to see her on my visits back to Connecticut.

When the hell is Graham coming home?

Knocking on the door to the study, I poke my head into the room with a, "Hey."

My dad has set up camp in here for the second day in a row, fingers flying over his laptop as he takes endless calls and drafts legal documents and does whatever else lawyers do.

Instead of answering me, he just nods, brow furrowed as he types away at his keyboard. I step into the room and close the door behind me, standing there until he finally looks up.

"What is it?" he says a little impatiently.

"I just wanted to see if there's been any progress made with Graham's case yet."

"Bowen and Ellis are working on it. You know that." He drops his gaze and resumes typing, but his dismissive tone has me bristling.

"Bowen's not even in the country, so I don't know if I believe that," I say coldly. "Is anybody at the firm doing anything at all? Or am I the only one who gives a shit?"

"Look, can we talk about this later? I have a lot of client calls today."

An angry laugh bursts out of me as my worry and frustration boils over. "Why are you even here, Dad? You're supposed to be helping, but you've barely done a thing. At minimum, I thought you'd at least keep me in the loop."

"There is no loop. Everyone's doing the best they can to secure his release, trust me. But the legal process isn't instantaneous, kiddo. There's a lot of red tape and bureaucracy to get through and a lot of nuance at play that you don't understand," he says. "So just calm down."

"Calm down? Graham's in *fucking jail* for a bullshit charge he couldn't have possibly had anything to do with, while his legal team is charging him what I'm sure is highway robbery to sit around with their thumbs up their asses, and now you're telling me—" but I abruptly break off as I realize how loud my voice has gotten, how my eyes are starting to sting.

Jesus, I really am losing it. I can't let myself fall apart, and I definitely can't have Jude overhearing this conversation.

My dad grabs a handful of tissues off the desk and holds them out to me. "Clean yourself up, for God's sake. Throwing a temper tantrum isn't going to fix anything."

I say nothing as I swipe angrily at my tears. The worst part is, I'm not just angry at my dad for being an asshole—I'm angry at myself for acting like a child. Especially in front of him.

"The minute I hear something, I'll let you know," he says more gently. "Until then, your job is to stay out of the way and take care of that kid. That's it. You think you can manage?"

Clenching my jaw, I give a curt nod. Then I turn on my heel and storm out. Why did I think that talking to my dad was a good idea? I don't feel better at all. If anything, I feel worse.

Up in my room, I fix my makeup and pull my hair back. After collecting Jude from the tennis court, I have her change into her riding gear so we can head to the stables and see if Cassie will join us for an afternoon trail ride. It's the one thing that never fails to boost Jude's mood.

The second we get there, the girl is off like a shot.

"Cassie!" she calls out, racing to the office in the back. "Let's go riding! Girls only!"

"Girls only, huh? Unlike most other days we ride?" Cassie teases as she appears in the doorway, an amused smile on her face. "How can I say no to that?"

The look she gives me is full of sympathy. She's the only one at the estate who knows about Graham and me, all the bullshit we've been through. She understands better than almost anyone except maybe Amanda, although my best friend still thinks I've been sleeping with an attempted murderer. But Cassie has known Graham for years. She knows he would never.

Once we all tack up and mount, Cassie leads us toward the hills at an easy trot.

"Where do you want to go today, Jude?" she asks. "Sky's the limit."

"Let's go down to the creek! Maybe we can pick blackberries."

"I love blackberries," I chime in. "That's a great idea, Jude. Maybe we can even bring some back to the house for Mary so she can whip up something yummy with them."

"Ooh. We could have blackberry pie. Or jam! Or shortcakes," Jude says excitedly.

She takes off, and Cassie and I have to nudge our horses to keep up. I'm so glad Jude has this distraction. She needs this.

We come to a stop under some shady trees and tie up the horses so Jude can play in the creek. It's a hot day, but the water is still too ice cold for me to even consider joining in, so Cassie and I sit on the grassy bank and just watch her splash and squeal.

"How's it all going? Have you heard anything from him?" Cassie asks quietly after a few minutes go by.

"We talked for a minute the other day, he called me from jail, but I have no idea what's going on with his lawyers or when he might be released. I'm a mess." I exhale slowly so I don't start crying.

"And Jude?" Cassie says. "Is she holding up okay?"

"Off and on. I mean, she's worried. She won't stop asking about her dad. And how long can we keep lying to her? At some point she's going to realize that he isn't on some business trip. I'm so stressed out. And having my dad here isn't helping. I know he seems charming, but he's seriously the worst. I had a breakdown earlier and he said I was 'throwing a tantrum.'"

Cassie shakes her head. "That's so hard. God. I'm sorry."

"And then Natasha—Jude is dying to go back to the hospital to see her mom, but I don't even know if she's doing better or worse. I've tried getting the nurses to talk to me, but they won't tell me anything because I'm not family and there's this whole investigation going on."

"No wonder you had a breakdown—you've got the world on your shoulders, girl. I don't blame you. Between Graham and Natasha and Jude and your dad and whatever the hell else is going on, you're a damn superhero as far as I'm concerned," she says, and I love her even more.

"I'm doing my best. Trying to keep it together for Jude. Everything just...sucks."

Cassie nods. "It does. I have no words of wisdom for you. But I get it."

I try to smile. "God, I'm sorry for whining like this. I just hate that I feel so helpless. There's like, nothing I can do. I'm so worried about him, and Jude, and even Natasha."

"You're not whining. You have every reason to be upset right now," Cassie assures me, giving me a quick side hug. "This is all just so wild. I mean, there's no way Graham had anything to do with that OD. How can anyone think that? The justice system really is broken."

"Yeah." I sigh. "I hate the media, too. They're making everything worse. Painting him as the villain now that Natasha's sick, and it's all just to be as salacious as possible."

"Vultures."

Jude splashes over to us and tells us she's ready for

some blackberry picking, so we join her. We all eat so many that our lips get tinged purple, and then we saddle up again and ride out.

I'm in the process of brushing Lucy down at the stables when my phone buzzes in my pocket. My hands are busy, and I figure it's probably just Amanda texting—hopefully to apologize for being so unsupportive the other day—so I ignore it. It's not until Jude and I are walking back to the house, sweaty and pleasantly exhausted, that I remember to check my texts.

My heart starts to pound when I see the text is from Graham's number.

I've just been released due to lack of evidence. Meeting with my attorneys first—will be home directly after. Please keep Jude up until I get there. Love.

I have to read it three or four times in a row before it really hits me. He's been released! He's coming home! Thank fucking God. I guess my performance really was convincing.

"Abbie? Are you okay?" Jude asks, glancing between my face and the phone in my hand, her voice tinged with fear.

"Oh, sweetie, I'm fine. Better than fine," I say, tucking my phone away and finally letting myself feel all the joy and relief. In that moment, I decide not to tell Jude—to let her dad's return be a happy surprise tonight. "Let's get these blackberries to Mary and then shower up, okay?"

I put my arm around her shoulder and ruffle her hair a little, my pulse still racing.

The second Jude goes to her room, I give Mary the good news. Her eyes light up, and she immediately starts pulling out recipe books so she can get to work on a welcome back feast. Then I track down Esmeralda and tell her to start preparing for Graham's return. Well aware of how much she loves being the queen of all things gossip, I give her permission to let the rest of the staff know, so long as everyone keeps it hush-hush around Jude.

Lastly, I try to find my father, but come up empty-handed. When I bump into Esmeralda, she tells me he took the afternoon off to golf at Graham's country club. I give him a call on his cell to relay the news, but he seems unsurprised.

"Wait, did you already know?" I ask.

"No," he says. "But I did think it would take at least another day before Bowen and Ellis were able to secure his release."

"Oh. So...are you going home now?" I ask, hoping his answer is yes.

He laughs. "In a hurry to get rid of me, eh? I'll leave tomorrow. Ran into an old friend here, so we're having dinner and drinks. I'll be back at the estate later tonight."

"Okay. See you then."

But after I hang up, I can't help worrying about how weird it will be to have my dad around when Graham returns. I'm already sick of all the tiptoeing around, having to hide our relationship even when we're at home. I just want to be able to hold Graham's hand without getting anxious about prying eyes, sleep in his bed without fearing the possibility of gossip, be able to act like myself fully with the man I love. It's not only my dad's fault that I can't, either. The whole staff is supposed to be in the dark about me and Graham as well. And the more I think about it, the more I realize: I can't live this lie forever. I want to be with Graham for real. For always.

I can only pray he feels the same way.

GRAHAM MAKES it home just before dinnertime, though my dad is still out for the evening. Jude and I are in the kitchen, helping Mary finish up with the feast, when we hear the front door slam shut. Jude freezes, her head instantly tilting to the side, and Mary and I share a look.

"Who is that?" Jude whispers.

"Where's my baby girl?" Graham's voice bounces off the empty halls.

"Daddy!" Jude squeals, bolting out of the kitchen with a spoon still clutched in her hand.

I follow behind her, heart pounding, making sure to walk just slowly enough that Jude can have him all to herself for those first few precious seconds.

When I reach the foyer, I see Jude in his arms, Graham's face buried in her hair. He was probably as scared as I was, not knowing when—or if—he'd ever see his child again. If he'd ever get his life back.

As I stand there, tears pricking my eyes, Graham lifts his head and gazes at me over Jude's shoulder.

"Thank you," he mouths to me.

All I can do is nod. I don't want to start crying. Especially since Jude is already wriggling out of his grasp, asking questions about his "work trip" and why it took so long. Graham deflects by telling her he wants updates on all the horses, which Jude is more than happy to provide.

We spend the rest of the night together, the three of us. Graham and I share long looks across the table during dinner, and then he takes a very long shower that I'm a bit devastated I can't join him in. Afterward, he finds me and Jude in the living room and convinces Jude to pick out a movie on Disney Plus for us to watch. I can barely pay attention, though, because I'm so distracted by the heat radiating off of Graham's arm that's stretched across the back of the couch.

Every now and again he'll brush his thumb across the nape of my neck or tug my hair, giving me goosebumps and making my scalp tingle. I want him so bad, it's driving me crazy. I look over at him, and I swear I can almost see the electricity crackling in the air between us.

When we finally put Jude to bed, Graham picks up where I left off reading *Black Beauty* to Jude until her eyes drift shut. We're tiptoeing out of her darkened room when her little voice murmurs, "G'night, Daddy and Abbie. I love you."

"Love you too," we whisper back in unison, our fingers already intertwined.

It's the most perfect evening we've had in what feels like an eternity.

Chapter Seven

Graham

I CARRY Abbie into my bedroom, her soft lips on my neck stoking the combination of love and torrid lust that's threatening to overtake me. The last few days are a shadow, a blur of desperation and darkness crowding my every waking thought. But I push it all back. The only thing I want to focus on right now is this woman, legs spread wide, surrendering herself to me.

When I throw Abbie on the bed, she stays on her back gazing up at me, chest heaving with her heavy breaths. I stand over her as I pull off my shirt and pants, cock straining against the fabric of my briefs, unwilling to let her out of my sight for even a second.

"I missed you," she whispers. "I was so scared. I didn't know if I'd ever see you again..."

Her voice breaks, and she can't finish. She looks away, and I freeze. It kills me to see her trying so hard to keep it together, trying to hide her emotions.

"Abbie," I say softly.

A choked gasp escapes her lips, and she squeezes her

eyes shut as the tears start to fall. But she doesn't stop fighting it. Instead of giving way to sobs, she stays silent, taking slow, steady breaths. Fighting it, fighting the pain, fighting herself. All I can do is drop onto the bed, climb over her, cover her trembling body with mine.

I whisper her name over and over as I kiss her collarbone, her neck, her throat, her jaw. Her legs wrap around my hips, arms circling my torso. We're locked together so tightly, the hitching of her chest almost feels like it's my own.

"Shh, love. Don't hold back. Let it out. Let it out. Everything's going to be all right," I soothe her, praying it's not a lie, kissing away the tear tracks at the corners of her eyes.

Her lips find mine, and her tongue probes into my mouth hungrily, aggressively, little moans issuing from her throat. I'm instantly hard all over again.

I twist a lock of her hair around my fingers and tug. She moans louder.

"I missed hearing you make that sound," I tell her between kisses.

"I missed making it," she says, reaching down to squeeze me through my briefs.

Now it's my turn to moan. Pulling away, I roll to the other side of the bed. "Sit up," I say. "You're wearing far too many clothes for my liking."

With that, I slowly slide the straps of her tank top down her arms, trailing kisses over her shoulders as I go. She shivers at the attention, and I move my mouth over her neck again, making her breath come faster. Then I pull her top off over her head, make quick work of removing her bra, and take her right nipple in my mouth. I ease her back down on the bed as I suck greedily. Fuck, I've missed this. The feel of her pert, pebbled nipple in my mouth. How her body arches as I lavish her with my tongue. When I move to her other breast, she drags her fingernails through my hair and I let loose a groan.

"I missed your taste," I murmur. "I missed your scent. I missed everything about you."

"Don't make me cry again," she whispers. "I need you. Don't be gentle."

I oblige. I kiss my way down her torso, tugging her skirt off roughly, and find her bare pussy waiting for me. She opens her legs and I lick my lips, eager to dive into her. To devour her. Because tonight is for getting lost in Abbie's body, for erasing the past few days and forgetting where I've been. It's my homecoming.

Her center is as sweet as I remember, her clit just as sensitive as it's been in my dreams. As I swirl my tongue around the small nub, she claws at my scalp and lets loose another deep moan. I love the sound of her coming undone, the way she pulls my hair harder and harder, her voice soft and breathy as she urges me on. I begin lapping her all the way up and then back down, slow at first and then faster.

"Graham," she pants.

The way she says my name like that goes straight to my cock. With a growl, I dive into her opening, tongue plunging inside as deep as I can go. She gasps in pleasure and starts grinding against my mouth. I'm so turned on I can't help thrusting against the bed myself, turning animal. Abbie's getting closer by the second. I can sense it. The way she's pulling my hair, her moans pitching higher, her thighs squeezing my ears.

"Wait. I don't want to come yet," she says, lifting my head in her hands and shifting just out of reach. "I need to feel you inside."

She tugs me toward her and I crawl up the bed, dropping kisses from her hips to her breasts along the way. Abbie's in such a hurry to have me, she doesn't even get my underwear all the way down before she has my throbbing cock in her grip, pumping it in her hand as she thumbs the slick of precum over the head.

I give her nipple one last hard suck and then fall into her arms, burying my face in her hair. "I'm going to fuck you silly," I rumble against her neck, feeling her shiver at my words.

"Good. Because that's exactly what I need."

She gives my shaft another firm squeeze, and I groan at her touch.

"Get on your hands and knees," I order in between kisses.

She obeys, spreading her knees wide, thrusting her ass toward me, her pinkness exposed. I think about burying my face in it, getting a second round of her taste on my tongue, but I can't hold back any longer. I'm desperate for her, desperate to feel the tight, wet silk of her cunt wrapping around me once again.

Abbie is mine and mine alone. I'm going to make her remember that.

After dropping my briefs to the floor, I get back on the bed to join her. On my knees, I position my tip against the soft lips of her pussy and tease her with a few quick dips in and out. Her hands fist in the sheets as she waits for me to destroy her, her entire body trembling with anticipation. I tease her some more, enjoying myself. Pushing just a little deeper with every pump, lengthening each thrust bit by bit before I finally glide all the way in, hard and deep. Both of us moan, and I force myself to go completely still. I'm buried inside her to the hilt, eyes shut, reveling in the feel of her. So tight. So wet. So hungry for more. This is my heaven.

"Fuck me, Graham," she murmurs, squeezing her walls around me.

At her words, I let the animal loose. My hips smack against her ass with satisfying slaps, and I gather her hair into a ponytail in my hand, holding it tight as I thrust faster and harder, like tomorrow will never come. But she feels too good, and I'm nowhere near finished with her yet.

Pulling out, I flip her onto her back and drag her to the end of the bed, so her ass is almost off the mattress. Then I pull her ankles up to rest on my shoulders and slide into her again, feeling her clench around me as I pick up where I left off. I pound into her like I have something to prove—and maybe I do. If there's a way to communicate my love to her with my body, this is how I'll do it. I look down into her lust-hazed eyes and slow my rhythm, letting her feel every inch of me inside of her as I move. Mouth falling open with her groans, Abbie slides a hand between her thighs, toying with herself as I fuck her.

"God, that's hot. Good girl. I love watching you do that," I encourage her.

"Mmm," she answers.

I turn my head to nibble her ankle, and then she pulls her legs down so she can wrap them around my waist.

"Come here," she says, holding out her arms to me.

I lean over her chest, and she starts to suck my neck as I continue spearing into her steadily, not missing a beat. The bouncing of the mattress works in my favor. As I increase my pace, Abbie tightens her legs, locking her ankles together at my back, pulling me even closer.

"Yes," she whispers in my ear. "Yes, yes, yes."

She hugs me tight, lifting her hips to match each of my thrusts. She's so wet, her cries becoming more wild, more feral, and soon it feels like she's letting her pussy take control of her body. My balls tighten, and I sweat with exertion. But I won't stop until she gets her fill. And God, I can tell she's close again. So close. Moaning my name like a mantra, teeth on my earlobe, fingernails digging into my back, urging me to go faster. Maybe I can sense that she's about to come before she does, because the orgasm seems to take her by surprise.

Cupping her face in my hands, I cover her mouth with mine, and we kiss as she rides out her climax. I groan in encouragement as she writhes under me, pussy contracting so hard around my cock that I know I won't last much longer myself.

"I'm about to come," I tell her.

We search each other's eyes, a question in mine, both of us knowing what I'm asking.

"Stay inside me," she whispers.

That's all I need to hear. I throw my head back and let loose a growl, fucking her like she's my life source. All the while, I allow myself to be as loud as I like. I've spent days in lockup. Tonight I will be as loud as I please, and I very much please.

Abbie matches my moans, so loud I think she's coming again, but before I can ask I'm exploding into her, filling her with everything that's been pent up inside. The climax rolls over me in waves, getting me so high so fast that my eyes water as I watch her through my orgasm. As we gaze at each other, gasping for air, a warm feeling takes hold. It's somehow more than lust, more than love.

Afterward, we get comfortable on the bed and remain locked there in each other's arms for what feels like hours, saying everything we haven't been able to say since I was taken away.

"I was so scared you'd never come back."

"Nothing could ever keep me from you and Jude," I reassure her, kissing the top of her head. "Especially not a bunch of baseless accusations and false imprisonment. I'm so sorry you had to go through that."

She laughs, but it's humorless. "How can you say that? You're the one who went through hell." She swallows so hard I can feel it. "God. I just...don't know what we'd do without you."

"And I you," I tell her. "Your love kept me sane."

Abbie kisses me, and then looks up with a teasing grin. "You're telling me you think you're sane? I don't know. I've had my doubts."

I have to smile back. Sometimes the only way to process the most difficult challenges in one's life—death, divorce, separation from loved ones, being arrested and subsequent jail time, dubious mental health—is with humor. Even if it's the darkest kind of humor. I know that Abbie understands this. It's just one more reason why I can't imagine my life without her by my side.

"I'm so grateful for you," I tell her quietly. "And your father. He came to see me at the precinct and handled everything I asked him to, assisted my legal team 'round the clock to make sure they could secure my release. Thank God I had the foresight to authorize you on my account. If I'd been away any longer—"

Abbie cuts me off with a kiss. "Shh," she whispers. "Let's not think about it."

"You're right. It's over. Let's put it behind us." I pull her to me even more tightly. "We have nothing to worry about now. Nothing to hide."

Abbie goes still for a moment, and then says, "Nothing except us."

I tilt her chin and kiss her deeply, pouring my apology out through the kiss. "Only for now, my love. I promise you that."

It's a promise I intend to keep.

Chapter Eight

Abbie

I STRETCH IN BED, snuggling closer to Graham and sighing as he runs his hand down my naked back.

"Can we just stay like this all day?" I mumble groggily.

"I wish, love. But Jude will be up soon, and I've got to see what my email inbox looks like. The past few days have undoubtedly wreaked havoc on the business."

"Boo. But I get it."

He squeezes me tighter and drops a kiss on my temple before easing himself out of my arms and sliding off the bed. I enjoy the view of his ass as he makes his way to the bathroom.

"I'd better head back to my room," I tell him, picking my rumpled clothes up off the floor and tugging them on hurriedly. "Need to get showered and dressed before someone sees me looking like I spent all night getting fucked by the master of the house. See you at breakfast?"

"Not a moment later," he says, toothbrush at the

ready in his hand, watching me smooth my skirt down with a smirk on his face.

I give him one last goodbye kiss, one last squeeze of his cock, and then leave him there semi-hard as I whisk myself out the door. I can only hope nobody's around to witness my walk of shame. Because despite Graham's reassuring words—and the very real hope that I have for our future together—in reality, we're still hiding our relationship. It would be a scandal to get caught leaving his bedroom the morning after, especially looking the way I do.

In the guest wing, down the hall from my room, is the room my father is staying in. I never heard him return last night, but I can hear him moving around in there now—undoubtedly hungover and still stinking of gin and tonics, if I know him at all—as I quietly open my door and slip inside. I'm surprised he didn't try to find Graham to share a celebratory whiskey whenever he got home from the country club last night, but I'm glad he didn't. Having Graham all to myself last night was the stuff of dreams.

After a quick shower and outfit change, I put on a little makeup and pull my hair into a ponytail, anticipating another trail ride with Jude at some point in the not-too-distant future.

There's a firm knock at my door just as I'm finishing up with my hair. With a grin, I fling open the door, fully expecting to see Graham waiting there to escort me down to the dining room. But the person I find standing in the hallway is my father.

Without a word, he walks into my room and shuts the door behind him.

"Uh, good morning?" I say, noticing that he looks fairly bright-eyed and bushy-tailed for someone who was out late drinking with an old friend.

"Just wanted to let you know I'm leaving today, as discussed. Everything seems like it's going well between you and Graham, so there's no need to linger. I'll get out of your way."

I nod, suddenly feeling incredibly awkward. Dad's not stupid—he must know I spent the night with Graham. That is, if he hadn't heard the audible evidence himself. How embarrassing.

Cheeks on fire, I clear my throat and try my best to act normal. "Well. Thanks for showing up, Dad. It meant a lot to Graham. And to me."

"Don't mention it. That's what dads are for." He gently nudges my chin with his fist.

My jaw clenches, even as I force a smile. Did he *seriously* just say that? Because honestly, my dad has no idea what dads are for. In fact, I'm still not entirely sure what made him step up this time. Presumably the possibility of me not being able to marry into Ratliff money and thus save his ass—which doesn't exactly put Dad in the running for Father of the Year.

"Should we go down to breakfast, or are you heading out now?" I ask.

"I'll stay for breakfast, hit the road after. But actually, there's one more thing I wanted to discuss first," he says. "Regarding the arrangement."

"Okay..." I say hesitantly, already expecting the absolute worst.

Really, I should have seen this coming. My dad

doesn't do anything for free. Including, obviously, coming to his daughter's aid in times of extreme duress.

Is he going to blackmail *me* now? Threaten to tell Graham the truth about how I was originally sent here to seduce and extort him this summer? Unless I...what? Push Graham to loan Dad money, or take part in some joint business venture requiring a large investment on Graham's part? My father is a devious man. Whatever he has to say, it won't be good.

He interrupts my racing thoughts with, "I just wanted you to know that whatever happens with you and Graham, you have my blessing. I can see how much you care about him and how much he cares about you, too. Makes an old man's heart happy."

It's difficult to keep my jaw off the floor.

"Really? You don't want me to keep trying to...get something out of him?"

Dad laughs. "What a little cynic you've become. But no. You can forget that whole plan. You did your job, but I'm calling it off now. I have some good things of my own coming up on the horizon."

"Okay," is all I can say in response. I'm in shock. I can't wrap my head around this.

I've been agonizing all summer long trying to follow Dad's orders. Beating myself up over my failure to succeed at blackmailing Graham, while desperately trying to hide the fact of my hopeless teenage crush morphing into a full-blown, head-over-heels infatuation. Yet here my father is, suddenly absolving me of all the guilt I've been feeling about the whole situation.

Something in my chest expands, and it's like the

weight of an anvil gets lifted off my shoulders. I'm free. Free to love who I love, to pursue my relationship with Graham without hiding or constantly looking over my shoulder and stressing about my dad's next demand.

"I just want you to be happy," he goes on.

All I can do is nod. "I am, Dad. But what about our house and everything? You said—"

He waves me off. "Don't worry about me and your mom. I mean it, Abbie, things are looking up. We'll be okay. It's not your place to worry about it anymore."

A lump forms in my throat. Of course I'm still going to worry about my parents anyway, but I had no idea how badly I needed to hear my dad say those exact words. As he pulls me into a hug, I have to blink back tears. When I start to sniffle, Dad lets me go and pats me on the back.

"All right now, enough of that. Let's go see what Mary's got on the table for us. I don't know what it is, but I can definitely smell the sausages from here."

When we get to the dining room, we find Jude and Graham already in their seats. Jude's chattering away happily, showing her dad all the pictures she drew for him while he was gone, and Graham looks like he's fighting his emotions as he carefully looks over each one.

"These are so good," he's saying. "This one's Desi, isn't it? You captured her perfectly."

"Thanks, Daddy. But that's not even the best one I did of her! Hold on, it's right here."

"Morning," my dad says, announcing our presence.

Graham looks up from the sprawl of sketches with a smile as his eyes meet mine. Meanwhile, Jude waves at us from her chair and practically yells, "Good morning, Abbie and Uncle Ford!"

"Wow. Did someone give you sugar already?" I tease, taking the chair across from her.

"Nope. I'm just happy we're all here together," Jude says.

"Now that, I can agree with," I say. "Breakfast smells delicious. What are we having?"

"Mary's making a full English breakfast. It's Daddy's favorite!"

"A good ol' fashioned fry-up, eh?" My dad takes the seat next to me and immediately starts fixing himself a coffee. "Sounds like exactly the thing I need."

Moments later, Mary bustles in with her arms loaded down by plates of food for us. There's buttered toast, fried mushrooms and tomatoes, eggs, two different kinds of sausages, bacon, and of course, baked beans. Which are not necessarily my first choice for a breakfast accompaniment, but that's the English for you.

We all talk lightheartedly and make jokes, while Jude continues to regale us with tales of horses and tennis lessons and more horses. She's happier than I've seen her in days.

Once we've finished, Graham and my father decide to head to the study for a quick chat while I help Jude get ready for the day. While she's brushing her teeth and getting dressed, my phone buzzes with a text—from Amanda. My pulse jumps. She and I haven't spoken since Graham first got arrested and she was convinced he was guilty. Maybe this is the apology I've been waiting for.

I heard Graham got released due to lack of evidence.

Yes, I type back hesitantly. *He's home now. We're glad to have him back.*

The ball is in her court.

So...you're still staying at his place? she responds a few moments later.

I try to push away my annoyance. *Yes.*

I see a bubble of ellipses pop up, which means Amanda is typing something, but then it drops away. It happens again, but still she doesn't send whatever it is she's trying to say.

Finally, my phone buzzes again. *I think you should go home, Abbie. Or come stay with me. Just to be on the safe side. At least until this all gets figured out.*

I text back in a fury. *Amanda, he's innocent. I told you that. I'm not going anywhere.*

Unable to be proven guilty is not the same as being innocent, she replies.

I clench my jaw. Is she serious? Still doubting Graham, still refusing to support me?

I'm just worried about you, she adds.

Well don't be. I let my anger out as I type, *TBH, I've really needed you during all this, but you haven't been there for me- at all. And now that Graham's back home, you're just giving me more shit. You're supposed to be my best friend. But I'm starting to feel like I don't know what you are anymore.*

She doesn't reply. Which is fine. Just fucking fine. I swipe away my tears and knock on the bathroom door, telling Jude to pick up the pace.

By the time we get back downstairs, Dad and

Graham are standing in the foyer saying their goodbyes. The front door is wide open and my dad's bags are waiting at his feet.

"I can't thank you enough, old man," Graham is saying, grasping my dad's hand in a firm shake. "You really saved my ass."

"Don't mention it. That's what friends are for," Dad says. Then he turns and gives Jude a pat on the head. "I'm heading home now, kiddo. You promise to be good for Abbie?"

"I'm always good." Jude beams. It makes everyone laugh, and I force a smile even though I'm still upset about my text-fight with Amanda. "What? I am!"

"You are, love." Graham puts his arm around her and pulls her close. "We hope to see you again soon, Ford."

"Bye, Dad." I give him a quick hug, my emotions a tumult. The last few days have been such a whirlwind, and now I'm fighting with Amanda again. I can barely process it all.

"Bye, princess." He gives us a two-fingered salute, picks up his bags, and heads outside, where I can see Ronaldo waiting next to the town car to drive Dad to the airport.

As soon as the door closes, I feel a wave of relief wash over me. Not that it wasn't a good visit...but I still can't shake the feeling that my dad was acting a bit out of character, and besides, it's nice to be here with just Graham and Jude again. Like we're our own little family. Amanda can cast doubt all she wants—but I know this is where I belong.

Graham turns to Jude. "How would you like...to have

the entire day off?"

"Yes!" she shouts, giving a little fist pump.

"Good. Because I already canceled with all your instructors."

"Can I watch cartoons?" Jude asks.

"Of course. In fact, I'll join you. Let me just have a private word here with Abbie first."

She gives a whoop of delight and takes off running toward the living room. I'm still smiling at her boisterous retreat when Graham lifts my hand to his lips for a soft kiss. It's barely the strength of a butterfly's wing, but it instantly has me weak in the knees.

"I believe in open lines of communication, so I want to be transparent—and let you know I paid your father for his services," Graham says quietly. He gently kisses each of my fingertips. "Bowen came through at the end, but at that point it was a matter of too little, too late. Ford's the one who really saved the day. He liaised with my lawyers, got the paperwork going, arranged the bail funds. Without him, I never would have gotten out so fast."

"I'm glad," I tell him.

Graham is a generous man. More than generous, from what I've seen. It eases my worries about my family's finances completely, and I know my parents will be taken care of for a while.

Finally, everything's coming together. My family has money, my dad is supporting me, I have Graham back, and for the first time in far too long, I feel like things are going to be okay.

If only I hadn't lost my best friend in the process.

Chapter Nine

Graham

Today is the day I reclaim my life.

And God knows it's time.

I woke up with Abbie in my arms this morning, her breath soft and even on my chest, the first rays of the rising sun spilling through the window, painting her a warm gold, and suddenly I knew exactly what I needed to do. Every challenge I've faced, every setback I've endured, every dream I've worked to achieve up until now has led me toward this path. This woman. This day. Everything is crystal clear.

Today is the day I ask Abbie to marry me.

There are preparations to be made and conversations to be had, but I've already set things in motion. There's not a doubt in my mind that this is what I want. My life has been radically changed by this woman—all for the better—and there is nowhere else I belong but at her side.

Before I can even think about pulling together a grand gesture, however, I need to get Abbie out of the house. I decide to enlist Cassie's help, as I've noticed they seem to be friends. I go into my office and make the call. Without me revealing too much about my reasons for needing Abbie to be gone, Cassie happily offers to take her out for a girls' day.

Yet Abbie doesn't seem excited when I track her down to tell her she's got the day off, and it takes some convincing to get her to agree.

"But you just got home," she protests, brows furrowing. "I don't want a day off."

"Shh, love. You've been through so much." I kiss her fingertips. "Take the day to relax, please. Besides, I want to give Jude my full attention today. She deserves some one-on-one time with me after my...unplanned absence."

Which is completely true, if I'm honest.

It seems to do the trick, because Abbie lets out a sigh. "You're right. She could use some daddy time. Maybe you two can go for a trail ride with Cassie."

"Actually—"

But before I can finish my sentence, as if on cue, the doorbell rings, echoing down the hall. Abbie's eyes narrow at me suspiciously.

"I believe that's for you," I tell her with a smile.

Seconds later, she's racing up to her room to change into a bathing suit and sundress. I keep Cassie company in the foyer until Abbie comes back. After Jude pops in for a quick hello, Abbie and Cassie head out the door. I watch them go, listening to them chatter about the local Italian deli where they're going to stop en route so they can put together a picnic lunch for their day at the beach.

It's good to see Abbie looking so lively again. God knows she's earned it.

With that first obstacle out of the way, I call out for Jude.

"I'm in my room, Daddy!" she yells from upstairs.

I steel myself for the conversation I'm about to have with my daughter. My heart is already racing, but all I can do is hope for her blessing. Here goes nothing, as they say.

When I reach Jude's room, I find her reading *Misty of Chincoteague* in her beanbag chair, using her gigantic stuffed horse from FAO Schwarz as a footrest. I lean against the doorjamb for a moment, just watching her. She's a remarkable child. Smart and resilient and kind-hearted, but with a spine of steel underneath it all. I've never been more proud of anything I've created.

"Hey, little warrior," I interrupt gently. "Can we talk?"

"Sure, Daddy. About what?" Jude's face scrunches up as I drop onto the floor beside her, and I smile to let her know this isn't going to be something scary.

I take her hand. "I have something important to tell you, Jude, and I hope you'll be as excited about it as I am. But if you aren't, it's perfectly all right to say so, or to ask questions or to discuss it more—so don't think you have to react a certain way just to please me. I love you very much, and this affects you just as much as it does me. We're in this together. Okay?"

Her eyes dart back and forth as she searches my gaze, looking for clues. "Okay."

She gives my hand a squeeze, as if she's expecting this to hurt, and I take a deep, steadying breath.

"So here it is. I've given this a lot of thought, and...I've decided I want to ask Abbie to marry me."

Jude gasps, and then looks confused. "But what about Mommy?"

I was prepared for this initial response, but it still feels like a knife in the gut. "Do you remember the talk we had, about me and your mom? We love you, Jude, and we'll always be your parents, but we're simply better people when we're apart. So it's going to stay that way."

Her face falls a little, but she nods slowly as she appears to mull it over. "Does this mean Abbie would be my...stepmom?"

"That's exactly right."

"Wow," Jude says wonderingly.

I can't help but smile. "Here's the thing, Jude. Even though I know this is what I want, I still need to make sure *you're* okay with it before I talk to Abbie. Because it's important that you and I agree on what's best for our family. So if you feel like you're not ready for me to ask her to be a part of our family, I need to know. I'm not going to change my mind, but I am willing to wait a bit if you're not comfortable with the idea yet. I know it's a lot to take in all at once."

And then I hold my breath as Jude looks off into the middle distance, pondering everything I've just dumped in her lap.

"I love Abbie," she finally says. "And I think she'd make a really good stepmom. But..."

"But?"

She chews on her lower lip. "I want to ask Mommy if it's okay. I don't want her to think I won't love her anymore if I have a stepmom. It's important for her to know she's still my mom."

Jude's request is not at all surprising, although the idea of going to see my ex-wife sours my stomach. Still, I can see how important this is to Jude. And the last thing I want to do is make her feel that she has no agency, that she isn't a part of this decision. So I won't deny her. If it's important to my daughter, it's important to me.

"Why don't we go to the hospital to see your mom now?" I offer.

"Okay! And then maybe I can help you propose to Abbie."

"You know what? That's exactly what I wanted."

Jude beams.

I call Ronaldo and tell him to bring the car around, and Jude and I are on our way to Manhattan a few minutes later. The entire drive down, Jude babbles nonstop about the wedding.

"We can have it at the house! And Desi and Lucy can be the flower girls. I mean, flower horses. Actually, I've never heard of flower horses, but it's totally a thing now."

"I think it's brilliant," I tell her with a smile. My little horse-obsessed daughter and her wild ideas.

When we pull up to the hospital, my grin instantly becomes strained. I don't want to go in there. I don't want to see Natasha. But this is for Jude. And for her, I would do anything.

As soon as we step off the elevator on Natasha's floor, the RN at the nurse's station glances up, his expression immediately going stern and guarded. I tell him that Jude and I are here to see Natasha, and he personally escorts us to the room with a scowl.

It's not hard to guess the reason behind the chilly reception. My face has been splashed all over the globe thanks to the media, and being painted as an attempted murderer of a celebrity actress doesn't earn one many kindnesses. Even still, for the duration of the short walk, I can feel the eyes of the other nurses hot on my back. I'm accustomed to getting side-eyed, but I hope that Jude doesn't notice. I don't want her asking questions that I'm not prepared to answer.

"I've got my eye on you," the RN warns me before heading back to his station.

A young nurse is tending to Natasha, scribbling something on a clipboard. She shoots me a glare before offering a much more pleasant expression to Jude.

"How are you doing this morning, sweetie?" she asks.

"Okay," Jude answers shyly, moving toward the bed. "Is my mom any better?"

"She's stable," the nurse says, sidestepping the question.

Jude looks back at me, and I try to arrange my face into a reassuring smile. But it's difficult.

"Can we talk to her?" Jude asks the nurse.

"Of course," the nurse says, stepping back to allow Jude some space.

Natasha is surrounded by a halo of wires and IVs and

beeping machines. I know she's sick, but even with the sickly fluorescent lights overhead, she looks almost angelic in her repose, her brow smooth, her hair in a long plait that one of the nurses has laid over her shoulder. Jude hovers at the bedside, watching her mother with an expression of intense worry and intense love.

"We need some privacy," I tell the nurse, who doesn't seem to be able to read the room.

"Not as long as you're here," she says in a mock-friendly voice, clearly for Jude's sake.

This is not what I had in mind. This nurse could run straight to the press after she hears what Jude has to say to Natasha. It could cause another shitstorm before I've even finished dealing with the last one. But before I can say anything, Jude climbs onto the bed next to her mom and gently strokes her cheek.

"Hi, Mommy," Jude says softly. "I really miss you. I wish you weren't still sleeping."

Natasha doesn't move, of course.

"I wanted to ask you something," Jude goes on. "It's important. But first, I want you to know you'll always be my mom. I love you so much and I always will, no matter what."

Jude glances over her shoulder at me, and I nod to show my encouragement. She's got such a pure spirit. My entire chest aches, as if it's caving in. Even this glowering troll of a nurse in the corner can't take away the tenderness I feel for my daughter right now.

"Daddy told me today that he wants to marry Abbie, and...I want him to. She won't replace you though, she'll just be my stepmom. I hope that's okay. You already saw how Abbie takes really good care of me, and I know she'll be good to me. Maybe all of us can even be a family together sometimes, if you want." Jude takes her mother's hand in her own and gives it a squeeze. "So what do you think? Would that be okay?"

She sits very still, fastening her gaze on her mother's face. I don't want Jude to be disappointed, but before I can work up the courage to gently remind her that her mom is in a coma and won't be able to respond, Jude lets out a gasp.

"Mommy said yes!" she exclaims.

My gut tightens. "Oh sweetheart, don't let your imagination run away with you—"

"But her finger moved! I felt it!"

The nurse and I exchange a look, and then she rushes over to check Natasha's vitals.

"I'm sorry, honey," the nurse says to Jude. "You need to leave now. We're going to run some tests on your mom."

Jude climbs off the bed, buzzing with excitement.

"Can't I stay a little longer?" she begs. "I want to be here when she wakes all the way up."

"The doctors will need to see her alone," the nurse says gently. "Go on. You can wait in the waiting room if you like."

I hold out my hand. "Come on, love. We have a lot of preparations for today. I'm sure the nurses will call us as soon as they know what's going on."

Jude looks back at her mom. She leans over the bed

rail to kiss her cheek one last time and then tucks her small hand into mine. As we make our way down the hall, Jude virtually skips at my side, convinced that what she felt back in the room was a sign.

But I can't help but wonder: is this a good omen, or a bad one?

Chapter Ten

Graham

THE ENTIRE DRIVE back to the estate, I keep my phone gripped so tightly in my hand that my knuckles turn white. I don't know which impulse is stronger—the hope or the fear that I'll get an update from the hospital. But by the time we arrive home, hours later, I've still heard nothing.

Meanwhile, Jude has been buzzing nonstop with over-the-top proposal ideas and fantastical wedding planning suggestions, buoyed by the conviction that her mother is just as excited as she is for me to marry Abbie. I certainly won't disabuse my daughter of that notion, but if Natasha really does wake up any time soon, Jude is going to find herself facing a very different opinion from her mother regarding my future nuptials.

And while I'm doing my best to match Jude's enthusiasm, the shadows of my past continue to loom. Part of me can't stop thinking that all of this is going to blow up in my face in spectacular fashion. But dear God, I hope I'm wrong. Because being with Abbie, even for such a short while, has already made me a better man. Thanks to her, I've narrowed my focus in a way that has completely rearranged my priorities and my life goals. All for the better.

No longer do I feel the burning fire of ambition driving me the way I once did, nor the need to prove myself to the world. In retrospect, I was never ignorant of my true motivation, either: attempting to remedy the perceived failures of my youth and the disappointment I felt knowing that I'd never live up to my father's expectations.

It's difficult to believe I spent so many years measuring my own success solely against the success of others, putting the acquisition of power and financial ascendancy above all else. Now, all that matters is my family. My daughter and my future wife. As long as I can love and cherish and provide for them, the rest is all just a bonus.

And I'll ensure my family knows how much they mean to me, too. Because I want nothing more than to continue making indelible memories with them going forward. We'll ride horses more, laugh more, play more, experience more. Together. I've made sound investments and my stock portfolio is both diverse and strong—if I didn't loathe the idea of early retirement, I could walk away from the banking empire I've built and be comfortable. It would require a change of lifestyle, and I'd probably need to sell a few properties, but I could manage it. So even if my business doesn't bounce back from this PR nightmare with Natasha, I know I'll be okay. Which is why I've decided that I can afford to slow down on the career front and let myself truly live, do more of what I love with Abbie and Jude at my side. And that is exactly my plan.

Starting right now.

First stop is the kitchen to talk to Mary. Jude bursts into the room ahead of me, practically bursting at the seams with excitement.

"My mom said it's okay for Daddy to marry Abbie!" she announces, beaming from ear to ear.

When I step through the door, I find Mary and Esmeralda sitting at the island drinking tea, both shooting me raised brows. That's when I remember that Abbie and I have been keeping our relationship under the radar for so long, I now have to start filling in the blanks.

"We've tried to be as discreet as possible," I explain. "For the sake of both Jude and her mother. It seemed prudent to see how things played out before making any grand announcements. I also didn't expect to come to this kind of decision so quickly, but what's that saying? The heart wants what it wants."

"You think I didn't see what was going on, Mr. Ratliff?" Esmeralda says with a smirk. "Congratulations. She's a fine young woman. And Jude adores her, of course."

Mary's excitement almost matches Jude's. "A wedding! Goodness! How exciting! Have you two chosen a date yet? And what about the venue? Of course, I'm sure Abbie has an idea—"

"I haven't actually—" I start.

"He hasn't proposed yet!" Jude cuts me off.

When Mary and Esmeralda look at me aghast, I nod sheepishly. "I'm planning to do that tonight."

Despite this whole plan seeming last minute, I've had the ring for ages—it's an heirloom piece that belonged to my grandmother. I never considered giving it to Natasha, since she's definitely not the antique jewelry type, but now that everything is aligned, I finally see how right I was to hang onto it all this time.

Jude adds, "We're going to take Abbie on a picnic and then Daddy's going to ask her! Can you help us?"

"A picnic? Are you sure that's the way you want to propose?" Esmeralda asks hesitantly.

"I think it's terribly romantic," Mary says. "Picnics are romantic."

"Abbie loves it here, and so do I," I say. "The mountains, the trees, the asters and lilies and butterfly bushes all over the property this time of year. I can't imagine any place she'd rather be proposed to, especially not some fancy restaurant or anywhere public."

Esmeralda just laughs. "Well. Look at you. Taking a leap of faith and going after what really makes you happy. It's about time, Mr. Ratliff, if I do say so myself."

"I appreciate the vote of confidence," I tell her. "I know it must seem sudden, but I've never been more certain about anything in my life."

"Leave the food to me, and I'll make sure it's a picnic to remember," Mary reassures me.

"What can I do?" Esmeralda asks kindly. "Or shall I just help Mary in here?"

"I would love it if you could help Mary," I tell her.

"And thank you both. Jude and I are going to go prepare the proposal site."

"It's going to be so pretty!" Jude says, hopping up and down. "We're going to have lights and flowers and horses and cupcakes! Oh yeah, don't forget the cupcakes please! Abbie likes salted caramel the best."

"Absolutely. I'll even volunteer to taste test them first." Esmeralda cracks a grin.

I smile back at them, gratitude washing over me. Their support means everything. Mary and Esmeralda have been with me longer than anyone else I've ever employed. They were here before Jude. They were here before Natasha. They've seen my highest highs and lowest lows. They've helped care for my daughter and run my house. Their opinions wouldn't change the outcome of today, but it helps to know I have their support and that they are with me on this.

Suddenly, Natasha is nothing more than the ghost of lives past. I have my whole life ahead of me with the woman I love and the daughter who brings my life such deep meaning. Natasha doesn't hold power over me anymore. She never will again.

"Let's go, Daddy!" Jude tugs at my hand. "We have so much to do!"

"You heard the little lady." Mary snaps her towel at us. "Go make the place beautiful for Abbie."

We make our way to the stables, where Jude fills up boxes of lights and ribbons, going on about how perfect everything is going to be. As she picks through the decorations, I call a local florist and order enough flowers to open my own shop, paying an exorbitant fee to have them all delivered immediately. When I tell the florist what I need so many flowers for, she promises the most glorious blooms I've ever seen. I'm pretty sure I've cleaned out her entire inventory.

We take Lucy and Desi to Abbie's favorite spot on the grounds, under the massive old tree by the creek. It holds so much significance for us that I cannot picture proposing anywhere else. This is one of the first places I took advantage of her ripe, willing body, where we slow danced under the stars, where our love was cemented. There is no place more perfect on the estate to ask Abbie to be my wife.

As we start decorating, my excitement grows. It's almost a foreign feeling, this elation. I'm prone to brooding, an Englishman to the core. I do not get excited, I do not express my emotions, but Abbie makes me want to be more present, to allow myself to feel things. In a way, I feel like a child again. The child I was before my father taught me to repress myself and bury my emotions. Now, I'll never look back.

"This is going to look like magic!" Jude crows as she wraps the tree trunk with ribbons. "The most magical place in the world!"

As I'm stringing the lights, the flowers arrive. Ronaldo must have jumped in the van with the delivery person to direct him here; once the van is parked, they get out and start unloading, Ronaldo winking at me all the while. There are hundreds, thousands of roses, lilies, and sunflowers, dahlias and hydrangeas and many more I can't even name, an explosion of color and scent. Jude runs around happily, making bouquets. She even makes a crown for herself.

We spend what feels like hours getting everything ready. Eventually, it looks like a young girl's fantasy has exploded across the grass. Jude is positively enamored by the entire thing, and I can't help but feel a surging sense of pride. This place looks...truly enchanted.

My phone rings in my pocket, and suddenly my stomach drops. But it's not the hospital calling about Natasha—it's Esmeralda.

"Cassie just pulled in the driveway. Better get back!" she tells me.

I grab Jude and we race back to the house, stopping only to drop the horses at the stables. When we finally burst into the foyer, we find Esmeralda and Mary standing there chatting with Abbie and Cassie, clearly stalling to keep Abbie there. She and Cassie look perfectly sunbaked and relaxed after their beach date. Jude runs to Abbie, buzzing with excitement and energy.

"Hey, you," Abbie says to Jude, wrapping her in a hug. "Where'd you just come from?"

Jude opens her mouth and I place my finger to my lips to remind her to keep everything a secret, and she grins widely, though I can tell it's killing her not to say anything. "Nowhere."

Abbie glances over at me and I walk over, cup Abbie's face in my hands, and kiss her. She steps out of my grasp, her wide eyes flitting from person to person around us, knowing full well I've just tipped our hand. But I reassure her with a broad grin.

"It's okay, Abbie. Everyone knows."

"What? But why—"

"We have a surprise for you!" Jude blurts, unable to keep mum.

"Well, that secret lasted all of thirty seconds," Mary says.

All I can do is laugh. I'm just as excited as my daughter is. I don't want to wait any longer than necessary. I want this ring on Abbie's finger, I want her committed to me.

"A surprise for me?" Abbie smiles, quelling the shock on her face.

"Yes!" Jude looks at me. "Can we now, Daddy?"

"Abbie just got home. Let's let her have a few moments."

Abbie gives me a questioning look before turning back to Jude. "Let me go upstairs and change real quick and then you can show me, okay?"

"Okay!" Jude nods.

"Is this...what I think it is?" Cassie asks the second Abbie is out of sight.

Jude goes over to her and whispers in her ear, and Cassie's face splits into a huge grin.

"I'll leave you to it, then," Cassie tells me with a wink. "Good luck."

Mary and Esmeralda go to the kitchen to finish packing up the food, and Abbie comes down minutes later in her riding gear.

"I figured if Jude was involved, horses were also involved," Abbie says. "Was I wrong?"

"You're an excellent guesser." I rest my hand on her lower back and kiss her cheek.

"Here's your picnic," Mary says, bustling over to me with the heavy basket.

Abbie grins. "Picnic? I'm liking this already."

"Come onnnnn." Jude grabs our hands and leads us to the stables, where Lucy, Desi, and Daisy are all outfitted with fresh ribbons that Jude braided into their manes for the occasion.

The whole ride to the tree, my stomach is in knots. I know this is what I want, but I can't help wondering if it's also what Abbie wants. My self-doubt only gets stronger as we ride up to the tree, and Abbie gasps at the sight of all the flowers, lights, and ribbons surrounding us.

"Oh my God. What is this?"

Jude dismounts from Desi and claps her hands. "It's magic!"

I tie up the horses and help Abbie off her horse, taking her hand. "Do you like it?"

"I love it. This is a dream," Abbie says. She looks up at me. "You did all this? For me?"

"Jude did most of it." I grin. "I helped."

I lead her to the center of all the flowers, right under the tree, and clear my throat.

"Abbie Montgomery, you mean the world to me. You are my sun and my stars. You are the very air I breathe." As I say the words, my nerves recede. Everything fades away until I can only see Abbie. Well, her and Jude, who stands next to us watching, jumping up and down with her hands clasped into excited little fists. "You've brought joy and love to this house again. And now, we can't imagine it without you."

I drop to one knee and withdraw the ring from my

pocket. It's a classic, late Victorian daisy ring, comprised of a 3-carat antique cushion cut diamond set in a halo of smaller diamonds.

"This was passed down to me by my grandmother. I've held onto it my whole life, hoping I'd someday find the right woman to wear it, and I can imagine no one else but you."

Abbie gasps, hands going to her cheeks, staring at the pair of us Ratliffs in shock.

Smiling, I ask her, "Abbie Montgomery, will you marry me?"

Chapter Eleven

Abbie

I'm standing in the middle of a dream come to life, surrounded by my favorite people and my favorite flowers, in my favorite spot in the world. My heart is in my throat and my eyes are starting to mist over with tears and every inch of me is floating off the ground just *thinking* about what Graham has asked me. Heaven. I'm in literal heaven.

The man I love rests on one knee at my feet, a gorgeous diamond ring glittering at me from its velvet box, his usually stern face laid bare in love and trust. Jude bounces behind him, a flower crown on her head, clapping and grinning like we're at a horse show. And then there's me, surrounded by all this love, struck speechless with overwhelm.

Is this really my life right now?

"Say yes, Abbie," Jude coaxes. As if I need to be coaxed.

The euphoria inside me is bubbling over, and I have

to let out a laugh. "Oh my God, Graham. Yes. *Yes*. Of course I'll marry you!"

I've barely gotten the words out before Graham scoops me up in his arms and kisses me, twirling us in a slow circle amidst the blooms. Our first kiss as an engaged couple. It's delicious.

Behind us, Jude cheers and starts dancing around. I start laughing again, because I can't help it. This is the most magical moment of my life and I never want to forget it. I want these images imprinted on my mind for all time.

"I love you," Graham says, his voice cutting through my reverie. He sets me down and gently slides the ring onto my finger and it feels so official now, I can feel my heart racing. Graham and I are *engaged*. "I love you so much, Abbie."

"I love you," I murmur against his lips, almost afraid to look at the ring again because it means so much to him, and is such a magnificent display of love, that I'm afraid I'll start crying. "I love you more than anything."

"Except me!" Jude chimes in, rushing us for a hug.

I throw my arms around my tiny bestie and give her the tightest squeeze I can. In the twinkling lights, with the sun hanging low over the horizon, my ring lights up like a carousel on the boardwalk, and it steals my breath away. Jude wriggles out of my grasp and grabs my hand to look at the ring.

"It looks like a princess ring," she breathes.

"I think you're right," I agree. "It's the most beautiful ring I've ever seen."

"It suits you perfectly," Graham says, pulling me in for another kiss.

It's so surreal to stand here and be openly affectionate with Graham in front of anyone, much less his daughter. There's no way the two of them pulled off all of this on their own, which means they had help, which means we're no longer a secret. And that feels so good.

"Do you know what else this means?" Jude suddenly asks, tugging on my shirtsleeve. "Do you know what marrying my dad means?"

I think I know, but it seems so important to Jude, like she's just dying to say it, so I pretend to think it over. "Let's see. Getting married to your dad means I get to wear this incredibly shiny ring. And it means you'll have to help me pick out a dress. And I guess it means I'll also have to move into the house permanently. What else could that mean?"

"You're going to be my second mom!" Jude blurts out, unable to contain herself any longer. "You're going to be my new other mom!"

"Oh my gosh, you're right!" I gasp, my hand going over my heart as if I'm in shock, but I'm hit so suddenly with the pure force of Jude's love that I almost can't keep up the act because I'm blinking back tears again. "Is that okay with you?"

"Better than okay." Jude throws herself into my arms and I hold her tight, kissing the top of her head and letting a few silent tears fall into her hair. "You'll be the best second mom in the whole wide world."

"I can't wait," I tell her.

And that's when it really hits me: Not only I am

finally getting Graham, but I'm getting Jude, too. Forever. I'm so happy, I don't even know what to say.

"Are you okay?" Graham murmurs gently in my ear.

"Yes!" I sniff, wiping up the rogue tears on my cheeks. "Are you kidding me? This is the happiest I've ever been in my entire life."

"But you're crying." Jude looks up at me, her brows furrowing. "Are they happy tears?"

"Oh my sweet girl, the happiest. The happiest tears imaginable."

We settle onto the picnic blanket and Graham starts unloading the picnic, laying out a sumptuous feast that only Mary could have assembled. She made all my favorites—crab cakes, avocado and citrus salad with white balsamic dressing, lobster rolls on crusty bread, fresh strawberries with Chantilly cream and slices of sweet green honeydew melon. I am going to have to thank her profusely for this later. We eat and laugh and take silly selfies with the flowers and the food and the horses, my ring finger featured in every single one of them, until it's full dark out and Jude nearly falls asleep surrounded by zinnias, her flower crown askew.

"I made all the bouquets," she murmurs. "Daddy said I should be a florist."

"You did such an amazing job." I pull Jude in so she can rest her head on my shoulder. "Girl, you really could be a florist. This is gorgeous!"

"Can you be a horseback-riding florist?" she asks.

"You can be absolutely anything," Graham says. He fixes Jude's crown and gently runs his knuckles over her cheek. "Come on now, love. I think it's time we get back to the house."

"But I want to stay here," Jude protests in voice only. She lets her dad scoop her up and settle her on Desi's back, where she instantly straightens up. "We aren't done celebrating yet."

"I think for now we are. We can pick up where we left off tomorrow, okay?" I kiss her hand and let Graham help me up onto Daisy's saddle. "For now, we need to get you back before you fall off Desi!"

"She would never let me fall." Jude pats her horse's neck and stifles a yawn. "Okay, maybe I do need to go to bed soon."

We all laugh, together, like a real family. Graham gives me a large bouquet of flowers before we ride off, and I spend the whole ride back to the house dreaming of happily ever after. Homemade waffles in bed. Horseback-riding competitions. Lazy summers in the pool. Decking the halls in the winter and jumping into leaf piles with Jude in the fall. By the time we get back to the house, I'm a mess of tears and elation.

Jude climbs right into bed and drifts off quickly, gripping my ring hand as she slides into a heavy sleep. I can't believe this is actually going to be my life. It's one thing to work here, but another to become a part of the family. I can barely breathe through it.

"Would you care to join me in my bedroom, or are you too exhausted to continue the celebration?" Graham teases as we leave her room.

"Never too exhausted to celebrate with you," I tell him, letting my eyes rake his body.

In the hallway, Graham gently presses me against the wall and places a line of kisses across my jawline. "I've never seen you so happy. I do believe it's turning me on."

I giggle, both at his words and at his stubble tickling me. "Is that so?"

"Mm, it is. I want you out of these clothes as soon as possible," he whispers in my ear, his hands slowly sliding down my back to cup my ass. "So I can properly propose."

My mouth falls open. "You call all of that out there an improper proposal? It was stunning. Seriously."

"That was mostly for Jude." He gazes into my eyes, giving my ass a firm squeeze that has my insides turning to liquid. "Are you ready for your second proposal, Miss Montgomery?"

I shiver at his words and the hunger etched on his face. "Lead the way, Mr. Ratliff."

Soon, I'll be Mrs. Ratliff, spending every night in the same bed with Graham. With no consequences. We'll be able to do what we want, as long as we want, as loud as we want. The thought has my heart pounding hard again as we walk to his bedroom, our fingers intertwined.

When he opens the door, I see there are flowers here, too, and lit candles all over the room, giving it a gorgeous, romantic glow. I shake my head slowly, awed at the effort he must have put in. The man who has everything and wants for nothing did all of this for *me*.

"Graham, this is incredible."

"You are incredible," he says from behind me, gently nuzzling my ear.

With a contented sigh, I close my eyes and relish the

feel of his hands all over me, making quick work of my clothes, dropping them to the floor one piece at a time.

"You are compassionate and kind and you bring out the best in everyone," he says, kissing each newly exposed part of my body in between his words. "You brought me back to my daughter. You brought me back to life. You have the gentlest hands and the sassiest tongue and the most tantalizingly perfect breasts I have ever laid eyes on."

With that, he spins me around in his arms and dips his head to kiss a trail down my chest. His hot mouth covers each nipple in turn, sucking just hard enough to make me groan, my knees going weak. I can feel how hard he is through his pants, his length digging against my hip. It makes me ache for him as he slips a hand between my legs, where I'm already soaking wet.

"Are you ready for me?" he asks, though I'm certain the answer is obvious.

"Mmm." I lean back against the wall and widen my stance to give him better access.

His fingers immediately find my clit. He toys with me, squeezing gently, his lips pressed to my ear. "I want to give you the world, Abbie."

Before I can respond with *exactly* what I want to give him in return, he slides a finger inside my aching cunt and I gasp, all thoughts of dirty talk fleeing my mind.

"You will want for nothing," he goes on, adding another finger and pumping into me slowly. "Everything you desire will be at your fingertips. Including me. Body and soul."

He stops to claim my mouth, sucking my tongue until I'm moaning and riding his fingers.

"If you will have me," he finishes.

"Yes. Now."

I have him unzipped in seconds, dropping his pants and briefs to the floor so I can wrap my hand around his thick, hard shaft. But he's still fingering me, the curl of his fingers drawing hot bursts of pleasure from my center, and it feels so good that it takes all of my willpower to push him away so I can trace my wet opening with the tip of his cock.

"Have all of me. Take me. Marry me," he whispers in my ear, forcing his body against mine so the wall is supporting me fully. He takes the lead, feeding his dick into my pussy, stretching me wider with every hard inch that fills me.

"Yes," I pant, grabbing his ass with both hands, trying to pull him deeper inside. "*Yes.*"

I grind against him, but I can't get enough from this angle, with both of us standing up. When I cry out in frustration, Graham grabs the backs of my thighs and lifts me so I can wrap my legs around his waist. Then he spears up into me, pinning me even harder against the wall.

"Marry me, Abbie, and make love to me for the rest of my life."

"Yes," I whisper, my face pressed into his chest as he fucks me into the wall.

"Say you'll be mine forever," he demands, his thrusts finding a rhythm.

"*Yes.* I'll be yours. Forever and always."

With every declaration I make, he moves faster, pumping into me more frantically by the second. I whimper, gripping his shoulders tightly, electricity rocketing through me. *Yes.* My eyes close. I give in to the sensations, the heat building inside me. Every thrust is perfect, sending me higher, my moans getting louder, until suddenly I'm coming so hard it takes my breath away.

"Fuck me, fuck me, fuck me," I cry, clinging to him as my body trembles with bliss.

Graham lets me ride it out, then tips up my chin to look me in the eye.

"My wife," he growls, picking up his pace once again. "You will be my wife."

I nod, trying to catch my breath as he pounds into me. "And you will be my husband."

He groans, lifting me off his dick to set me back on my feet. "Get on your knees," he commands, stroking himself feverishly. "I'm going to watch you swallow down every last drop of cum like a good fiancée would."

I drop to the floor, my mouth open, ready to be a very good fiancée indeed.

Chapter Twelve

Abbie

I'm ready to move into Graham's room now, but he says we need to wait until we're legally married. Not because he's the old-fashioned type, but because we need to respect Jude and the staff by easing into things. We've only been together for the summer, after all, and we don't want to ruffle any feathers, he said.

Not only that, but the news of our alleged affair has already been splashed all over the tabloids, as well as his arrest on attempted murder charges—and the power of bad press can't be ignored when his daughter's custody and well-being is at stake. We need to play by the books.

Still. I feel like we've been two planets destined to collide this entire time. Now that we're finally together officially, I'm anxious for our new life to begin.

"Won't the tabloids have a field day when they find out about our marriage anyway? It won't stay a secret forever," I muse over my coffee, sitting on the couch in his office.

"Oh, naturally. They'll shit themselves. I can already see the headlines now: 'Ratliff abandons ailing wife to marry teenage nanny in clandestine ceremony,' etc." Beside me, Graham lets out a rueful laugh, tapping away at a work email on his laptop.

"But you've been divorced for over a year," I point out.

"Natasha liked to blur that line publicly as often as possible." Graham gives my knee a comforting squeeze. "Regardless, we'll get through it. The bad press will blow over eventually. Maybe they'll even decide they like us once we're official. Not that I'm holding my breath."

I nod, feeling more assured by his casual use of the phrase "we" than by my faith in the press to let go of a particularly juicy story—factual or not—before it has entirely run its course. If the media's behavior this summer is anything to go by, they'll bleed our story dry, and then they'll squeeze it some more. I doubt they'll work too hard to fact check the details if people are still buying magazines and letting themselves be taken in by clickbait.

"Maybe they'll be kinder once we're married," I say hopefully.

"I think they will have less to talk about, yes. It's boring once you're happily married. The controversy is gone."

"Even though I'm so much younger than you?"

Graham closes his laptop and sets it on a side table so he can turn to face me.

"Abbie, my love. You are a remarkably mature young

woman." He takes my hand and kisses it. "And you are exactly what I need. Exactly what my daughter needs. What this family needs. Hell, what this house needs. Your age is inconsequential to the magnitude of your impact. You belong here. Don't ever doubt that."

I lean across the couch and kiss him gently on the lips. "Thank you. I think...I think I really needed to hear that." I try to force a smile, but it fails miserably.

"What is it?" Graham asks.

"Nothing. It's just...something's been weighing on me. That we haven't really talked about yet." My anxiety suddenly hits me like a kick in the gut, and I drop my eyes.

"So talk. I'm listening," he says softly, his warm hand still wrapped around mine.

Taking a deep breath, hoping I'm not about to completely ruin everything, I look up and say, "What happens when I go back to Cornell? The fall semester starts next month. It's a three-and-a-half hour drive from here, which isn't a commute I can make on a daily basis. Obviously I'll have my dorm apartment, but how...how are we going to make this work?"

This whole summer, I've been avoiding the subject, barely even allowing myself to *think* about my inevitable return to school—and that was before Graham proposed. I was already dreading the fact that I'd have to spend the upcoming school year in campus housing, only seeing Graham and Jude on weekends and holidays, if they'd have me. So what happens now that Graham and I are going to be married? I've never even heard of a long-distance marriage. What if this changes everything for him? What if he'd assumed I would just drop out and live here full-time? I'm not giving up my degree.

Graham cups my cheek and draws me in for another long, slow kiss. When he finally pulls away, he says, "I've already been looking at real estate in Ithaca, love."

"Y—you have?"

"I have. And my agent has a few places lined up that might work, smaller houses and condos with outdoor space that I think you and Jude would like. We're going to video-tour them this week. I was going to have you sit in on the call and help me decide. After all, it's going to be yours. And you won't be needing a dorm room once you've got your own house."

I start laughing, the knot in my chest dissolving at Graham's words. He's really thought of everything.

He pulls up the listings on his phone so I can see photos of the properties he's considering, and tells me all about his plans to stay with me at the new place as much as possible over the next few years while I finish my degree program. But the thought of maintaining a long-distance relationship still makes me anxious. And I hope to God I won't be so distracted by my yearning for Graham and Jude that my grades start to suffer. I'm going to need a strong support system.

Speaking of which...

Amanda has always been my support system. My go-to. My partner in crime, though I think that term has lost some of its humor for me as of late. But we're still on the outs after our text-fight the other day. She never texted me back and hasn't even tried to call. Not that I've tried to call her, either. But it completely sucks. We've never really fought before, and not talking to my BFF for the last few weeks has been eating away at me. At the same time, it's not on me to reach out to her and apologize when she was the one in the wrong. Or am I just being petty?

Then again, why *hasn't* she reached out yet? If I'm being petty, Amanda is, too. Except what if she's thinking the same thing? I don't know how to deal with this.

Graham finally tucks his phone away. "So when shall we wed? I was thinking this weekend," he says very seriously, as though planning a wedding takes all of five minutes.

"Sorry, what?" I laugh.

"This weekend," he repeats. The look on his face doesn't change. He's not joking. "I want you protected. I want you cared for. And I want to be able to stop hiding. Don't you?"

"Yes, but..." I'm speechless for a moment, torn between how sweet it is that he's so ready to be married, and how inane he sounds, this powerful man who can buy an island if he wants, thinking a wedding is something that can just be thrown together in a few days' time.

"But planning a wedding takes time," I finally say. "Months, usually, if not years. We've got guest lists and cake tastings and I've got to find a dress and a venue—"

"Do you want a huge wedding? Something extravagant? Because if you do, I'll make that happen," he says, "but to be perfectly honest...Abbie, love, I've done it all before. Five hundred guests, a bar tab the size of Manhattan, an exclusive venue that you have to know someone to book. Not to mention the press eating it up like a five-course meal from the sidelines. I've had *that* wedding, complete with the bridezilla. It was a nightmare. One I'd happily endure again if it would please you, love, but for God's sake, think hard about what you want."

Graham clasps his hands before him like a child begging for candy, and I smile.

"Okay. This weekend," I say, my heart racing, because *ohmygod I'm getting married in a few days.* "We'll keep it low-key. I'd prefer something intimate anyway, here on the estate. And if I change my mind later, we can renew our vows with a bigger ceremony in the future. Deal?"

"Absolutely a deal." He kisses me again. "Tell me exactly what you want and I will make it happen. I'm a man with a lot of income and power at my disposal. You want an abundance of flowers? I'll buy out a whole shop again, two shops if necessary. An elaborate cake? Mary was trained at one of the best patisseries in Paris. Live music? I'll get a few members of the New York Phil to play violins as you walk down the aisle. Just say the word, and it's yours."

I stare at him. "*Graham Ratliff.*"

"What? You don't like violins?"

"You've been planning our wedding!"

He looks sheepish, and it's so cute I could die. "No, I just—those are just examples of things that can be done."

"Examples that you already have in mind because you've been planning it!"

He has no response to that, and I laugh and kiss him hard. In this moment, my heart feels like it could explode with joy.

But then I remember that I have to choose a maid of honor, and I know that person could only ever be Amanda—and it hits home all over again how lost I've been feeling without her voice in my ear or her texts in my pocket, without our FaceTime chats where she teases me about Graham or helps me choose my outfits.

My eyes start to well up, and I can't stop the tears from spilling down my cheeks.

"Don't cry, love. Am I pushing too hard? We don't have to rush," Graham says.

I shake my head. "I want to rush. It's just that...I had a fight with Amanda...and we haven't made up yet." I don't want to tell him why, and I'm glad when he doesn't ask.

"Why don't you reach out today and extend the olive branch?" he suggests. "Inviting her to the wedding is the perfect excuse."

Yeah, it would be—except that this is a wedding she'll never get behind. She still thinks he's guilty. If I marry Graham, does that mean I'll lose Amanda forever? All I can do is let him pull me into his arms, leaning into him for support while I brood.

"Try to relax. We can talk more about the wedding later," he says, rubbing circles over my back. "But first, I want to show you something. Or, well, a lot of somethings."

When I nod, he eases me back onto the couch beside him, retrieves his laptop from the table, and opens it. Then he clicks around until he finds what he's looking for and turns the screen to me. I see a spreadsheet full of charts and graphs, numbers clicking in real time.

"Um, wow. What...exactly is this?" I ask.

"This is our net worth." He points to a number. My jaw drops. "The cumulation of all the stocks, bonds, real estate, and investments tied to my estate and my business."

I don't even have words to describe that number except: *holy shit.*

"What's mine is yours, from my heart to our properties. All of it," he says earnestly.

Guilt rises in my chest. This was exactly why my dad sent me here to begin with. He needed money to get my very broke family out of debt, and his plan was for me to extort his best friend in order to get that money. I abandoned the plan already, but now, the fact that I agreed—that I came here with the worst of intentions—is killing me all over again.

And there's only one thing I can think of to make it better.

I swallow hard. "I want to sign a prenup." Graham raises his brows, but before he can say anything, I go on, "Because honestly, as much as I'm looking forward to sharing your life and all the fancy stuff that comes with it, I'm not a gold digger. And I don't want to look like one in court later, if anything were to happen to you, or if we...split up."

"Nothing's going to happen to me, Abbie, and we won't split up. But I'm happy to honor your wishes. I'll have my lawyer draw up a document this week," Graham says kindly.

"Can we do it now?" I push.

I'm not just doing this for my reputation, or to prove

to myself (or anyone else) that I'm marrying Graham for all the right reasons—I'm doing it to stick it to my father. To get back at him for sending me here under false pretenses, for pimping me out, for using me without a second thought. This prenup will show, once and for all, that I'm with Graham for love. That my loyalties lie with him.

My future husband pulls out his phone again. "I'll call Bowen."

While Graham gets on the phone with his lawyer, I scroll through the list of properties and companies Graham owns. I knew he owned a banking empire, and that he probably had some decent investments, but my God. My. God.

Minutes later, Graham gets off the phone. "Bow is sending the documents over now."

"Good. Thank you. And one more thing..." I trail off, thinking over my words carefully. "I called my parents to tell them about the engagement, but it turns out they're on vacation. In the *Bahamas*. It's the first time they've taken a trip together in years, and I couldn't stand the thought of making them feel like they had to fly back home just for me. So...I didn't tell them."

His eyes widen, and he whips out his phone. "You're their only daughter. Of course they'll come home. I'm sure they'll be happy to—"

"No!" I bat the phone away. "It's better this way. I wasn't even sure I wanted them at the wedding to begin with. Honestly, I don't know how they'll react to the news. Or if they'll support us at all. I was thinking I'd tell them afterward. What do you think?"

I don't tell him that even though my father absolved me of my guilt, seeing him on my wedding day would remind me of why I came to the estate in the first place—the awful plan I agreed to before my whole world changed. All I can think is, *thank God I signed that prenup.*

"Don't you want your father to give you away?" Graham asks.

"No. I mean...I guess I hadn't really thought of that part, but no. It's not something I've dreamed of, ever. I'm not an object to be given and taken. I'm not a piece of livestock that's getting a transfer of ownership. I don't need anyone to give me away, except for me."

I've gotten myself all worked up, and I know it. But Graham just searches my eyes, nodding slowly.

"Okay. If that's what you want. We'll tell them afterward." He pulls me into his arms. "Now. Have you started practicing your new signature yet? The double f can be quite the challenge if you aren't used to it."

A grin tugs at my lips. I love this playful version of him. "Is that so?"

"It is, indeed."

I go to his desk to grab a pen and a legal pad, and then come back over and sign the name Abbie Ratliff, complete with swirls and dots. It looks impeccable, and Graham starts to laugh.

"If I didn't know any better, I'd think you've been practicing that signature a fair amount already, you little minx."

"Maybe I have," I tease, tossing the pen and paper aside and crawling into his lap.

Graham tilts my chin so we're staring directly into each other's eyes, and says softly, "I can't wait to make you my wife."

Joy overwhelms me. Pure, unfiltered joy. "I can't wait to make you my husband."

Chapter Thirteen

Abbie

WITH THE WEDDING only days away, Graham and Jude and I fall into a whirlwind of last-minute planning. Flowers, cakes, dinner menus. Who we're actually going to invite. Graham had no problem honoring my request to keep the guest list small, and it didn't take much effort to prune down everyone in my life. Besides my mom and dad, there's really only one person I need there, standing at my side, no matter what.

Amanda.

But we still haven't made up yet. It's been nothing but radio silence between us. Is this stupid fight really the end of our friendship? It can't be. And yet...what if it was? What if Amanda truly wants nothing to do with me (and my relationship with Graham) anymore? There's only one way to find out, though. I can't just sit here thinking the worst.

So after I fortify myself with another round of coffee and almond croissants, I go out to the pool—a place that always instantly relaxes me—and deposit myself in a lounger under an umbrella. Then I take out my phone and go to Amanda's contact. My finger trembles over the call icon.

Deep breath in, deep breath out. This is it. We'll either make up and she'll accept my invitation to be my maid of honor, or we won't, and she won't...but either way, I'll have my answer. I'll know where we stand. No more endless agonizing over it.

She picks up in the middle of the first ring. My heart is pounding wildly in my chest, my stomach clenched, my eyes squeezed shut.

"Abbie Abbie Abbie, I'm so sorry, I was wrong, I love you, don't hate me," she blurts.

I'm so wound up, all I can do is let out a breathless laugh.

"Is that a...'you are a ridiculous human and there's no way I'll ever forgive you' laugh?" she asks. "Or a 'you are a ridiculous human and there's no way I won't forgive you' one?"

"The second one, you silly goose," I tell her, swiping at the tears gathering in my eyes. "Definitely the second."

"I've been following the news some more, and yeah. I jumped too soon. I'm so sorry about what happened to Graham, and I should have believed you. I just wanted to protect you, and I was fearing the worst. I've read too many domestic thrillers with evil husbands, I guess. I'm an ass."

"No, you're really not," I tell her. "I know how bad it looked. I just wish it had played out differently, but...life's like that sometimes."

"So you forgive me? I'll never pull that tough love

bullshit on you again, I swear. I should have stood by you, and I wanted to call you, but I was scared you hated me."

"Never. And of course I forgive you," I say.

"Good. We've been friends for so long now that I forgot what my life was like without you. And it really, really sucks. Now catch me up on all the things, and I'll catch you up on mine."

"Okay. But I have a favor I need to ask you first. Something really big."

I'm nervous all over again, so I walk over to the pool steps and sit down to dip my feet in the cool water. It's one thing for Amanda to say she was wrong about Graham, but entirely another to expect her to support me in marrying someone accused of attempted murder. I take a deep breath, but I can't make the words come out.

Off my hesitation, Amanda gently says, "Hey. Abbie. I'm your best friend. Whatever it is, just ask."

So I tell her about the fairy-tale proposal Graham and Jude arranged for me, how we're in the midst of planning a quickie private wedding, how I haven't even found a dress yet, and how I can't imagine anyone else in the world as my maid of honor—

"Yes, yes, a thousand times yes! I'd love to!" Amanda jumps in. "God, I'm so happy for you! I can't wait!"

"Me either." I wipe my cheeks and take a steadying breath. "Graham already arranged a private car to pick you up tomorrow morning. The dress code is, wear whatever you want, as long as you feel fancy in it. You'll stay here at the house with us and we'll have so much fun."

"It's going to be so good to see you again!" she gushes.

"I've missed you so much this summer. Seeing you once isn't enough."

"I know. It hasn't been the same without you."

"Okay, I better go pack. Tell Graham I said thank you for the ride and text me the details when you get a minute. Mwah!"

We say our goodbyes and part of me feels sad when we hang up, but I know I'll see her soon. She'll stand by my side as I marry my love, and everything will be perfect. Except for one tiny little thing. I still need a dress.

I find Jude in the kitchen, chatting away with Graham and Mary about the flower crowns she's going to make for the horses to wear at the wedding. Graham greets me with a quick kiss on the temple, and Jude lets out a cheer. Mary laughs and tells her to calm down.

"I'll leave you ladies to finish up planning the menus, then. I'm going to be swamped in meetings for the rest of the day, I'm afraid," Graham says.

"That's actually perfect, because today we need to go shopping to find the perfect dresses." I crook a finger at Jude, who squeals with glee. "We're on a tight timeline, after all."

"Yes! Dress day!" Jude exclaims. "Can we go now? I'm already ready."

Graham arranges for Ronaldo to pull the car around front so that Jude and I can be driven into town, and then excuses himself. Jude runs to get her shoes.

"Do you want to come with us?" I ask Mary, suddenly feeling very overwhelmed. "My mom and dad are on vacation, so my mom can't make it, and my best friend won't be here until tomorrow. I'd love another opinion. Of course, I completely understand if you're too busy."

Mary flushes. "I would be honored, Abbie! I don't have any children of my own, so I never thought I'd be able to experience this. Let me go change and fix my hair, so I don't look like a mess while you try on those stunning dresses. I'll be quick."

She hurries off and meets me and Jude in the foyer a few minutes later, tugging at her hair. Glancing down at her jeans and checked shirt, she asks, "Do I look okay?"

"You look like a regular person!" Jude says, staring at her. "I've never seen you in real clothes before. You look great!"

We laugh our way to the car waiting outside. Ronaldo takes us straight to a local boutique, full of beautiful dresses for all occasions. I tour the entire store with a very helpful staff member, and soon enough, Jude and I each have a dressing room full of dresses to try on.

Jude volunteers to go first. Mary and I settle into the plush couches before the tri-cornered mirror as the employees fuss and coo and hand us mimosas. When I start to protest that I'm only nineteen, Mary shushes me with a wink and raises her glass to mine in a toast. It feels like a magical afternoon, full of lace and all the trimmings topped with champagne.

"I don't like it," Jude says for every one of the first six dresses she tries on. Mary stifles a giggle as Jude makes faces in the mirror. "I look old."

"Okay, well let's find something you *do* like." I bite

my lip to keep from matching giggles with Mary. "How many dresses do you have left to try on?"

"One more," Alice, one of the associates, tells us. She holds open the curtain to the dressing room for Jude with a smile. "We can always look for more after this?"

"Maybe number seven is the lucky dress," Jude says hopefully. I undo her zipper for her, and she skips into the dressing room, ready to get changed again.

Mary beams. "She has *really* taken to you."

"Not as much as I've taken to her," I say truthfully, suddenly feeling gratitude instead of anxiety. "She's one of my favorite parts of the house."

"Besides Graham." Mary winks at me with a knowing smile.

I can't respond, only blush.

"Guys! What do you think?" Jude asks, throwing back the dressing room curtain and doing a twirl.

"Wow," I say, drawing out the word. "That is something."

It's a classic princess dress, nothing but ruffles upon ruffles and a full tulle skirt. Sparkling aurora borealis crystals adorn the top, flashing pastel rainbows and making Jude look as glittery as a disco ball. Mary starts clapping excitedly.

"You look like a one-girl party!" she says.

"I love it, too," I chime in, encouraging Jude to do another twirl. "You look amazing."

"It's the perfect unicorn dress," Jude announces. "It's the one. Now it's *your* turn, Abbie."

Alice holds open the curtain to my dressing room, packed to the gills with dresses of various lengths and silhouettes. That tight feeling in my chest returns as I run my hand over the dresses, trying to find which one to start with. There are full-length dresses, shorter dresses, dresses with embroidery and lace and sequins. How do I know which one to choose?

I pick up a full-length mermaid number and pull it on. Alice helps with the zipper when I step out of the dressing room, and I make my way over to the mirrors to finally look at myself in a wedding dress for the first time ever. My face must be its own kind of mirror, because Mary immediately comes to my side and places a reassuring hand on my shoulder.

"You look beautiful," she soothes. "The dress is such a small part of the day. All that matters is that Graham will be waiting for you at the end of the aisle, waiting to take your hand and say 'I do.' The dress is just the icing on the cake."

I nod slowly, taking in her words, tears clinging to my lashes. "It's just...a lot."

"I know. Getting married is a lot." Mary smiles at me in the mirror. "But as for the dress? You could walk down the aisle in a paper bag and he'd be happy. And so would you."

I stare at my reflection and this gorgeous dress. It's too much. It makes me feel like I'm too old, too grown up all of a sudden, like my life is changing too fast.

I hurry back to the dressing room and flip through every gown until I come across the perfect dress, the one that makes my heart sing. I slip it on and make my way out to the mirror.

Mary and Jude both gasp as I walk out. Jude starts

bouncing in her seat, and Mary beams like she's the proud mother I so desperately needed. I take my place in front of the mirror and it just feels *right*. The dress is classically beautiful, done in ivory satin, with an A-line skirt, a V-shaped neckline, and delicate lace cap sleeves embellished with tiny seed pearls. It feels mature, but also youthful, like me. Like the woman Graham sees. I can't keep the smile off my face.

With Graham and Jude at my side, I have faith that everything will work out exactly as it's meant to.

I'm about to live happily ever after.

Chapter Fourteen

Graham

Morning rises on my wedding day. I wake with the sun and go for a run, attempting to diffuse the adrenaline that's been pumping through me since last night. Perhaps I shouldn't have insisted that Abbie and I sleep in separate beds after we made love. Her presence might have calmed me.

It's not that I have cold feet in the slightest—if anything, I've been counting down to this day since before the ring was ever placed on her finger. It's more that I can't shake the sense of doom that's been hanging over my head ever since Natasha overdosed and went into a coma. Between the bad press and the false arrest and the jail time, I've had one bad turn after another. And who's to say that Abbie herself won't be the one to change her mind at the last minute? All of this has happened so quickly for us.

Can I really put my faith in a happily ever after? Should I?

Maybe I should.

Maybe it's finally time to trust that things will work out exactly as they're meant to.

I wonder when the relationship changed for Abbie, from infatuation to something more. Hell, I wonder when it changed for me. The second she set foot on the estate at the beginning of the summer, there was a ripple effect. But I couldn't take her flirting seriously. Not at first. My plate was full. I had too much drama with my ex, a sullen child, and I was drowning in work. Abbie was merely a staff member, albeit a dangerously tantalizing one, and an inconvenience.

Even as she trotted around my house, half dressed, clumsily attempting to woo me, I fought my attraction to her. I knew there was no way she'd be able to keep up with my needs. Not only that, but she's the daughter of one of my oldest friends. She was my nanny. She was too young, too needy, too inexperienced for my tastes. Everything about her screamed *off-limits*.

But God, how I craved her. So I gave in. Little by little, and then all at once, I gave in.

And now, I can't imagine my life without her.

My run takes me through the property, and I push myself harder than I have in a long time. I want to sweat out the fear, sweat out the insecurities, so there is nothing but pure love left inside me when I watch Abbie walk down that aisle toward me. Time and again, I've proven myself to be a man who gets what he wants because I push myself until there is nothing left but assurances. That's what I need right now.

My fit tracker buzzes on my arm to let me know I've hit the two-and-a-half-mile mark, so I finish my trek up to the top of a steep hill and then start to make my way back home. Air burning my lungs with every breath, I take in the stunning view of the dawn sky, alight with countless warm colors. I tell myself that everything will be perfect, that Abbie is destined to be at my side because I feel it in my gut. I ignored all the warning signs with Natasha, chalked the red flags up as me being young and wild at heart, resistant to settling down for all the usual reasons.

Now? I'm older. Wiser. More experienced than I ever could have imagined. Things have changed. I've changed. As I crest another hill, I search my mind for any doubts, any second thoughts, any hesitation—and find nothing. Nothing but excitement for my wedding day to unfold. To see my new wife walking toward me. To kiss her in front of God and everyone present. To make her mine. Forever.

Picturing our wedding night has me achingly erect, so as soon as I get back to the house I bolt upstairs to my room and jack off in the shower, head pressed to the wall, thinking only of Abbie's perfect mouth and the love in her eyes. I come fast, and so hard it takes my breath away, but it isn't enough. I get out of the shower still hard, still desperate for her as I think about our life unfolding together.

The house is silent. Mary and Esmeralda should have only just arrived for the day, which means my bride-to-be is likely asleep, waiting for the scent of the day's first pot of strong coffee to coax her out of bed. The urge to wake her overtakes me, and I throw on my robe, then slip out of my room and head to the guest wing.

I knock gently at Abbie's door as a courtesy, but I

don't wait for an answer. The door opens silently, and I find her curled up on the bed asleep, her breathing even, slow, and deep. Just as I suspected. One long, bare leg is kicked free of the sheets, and her golden hair lays spread across the pillow like a halo around her head.

She looks angelic and perfect, but I feel no hesitation about the fact I'm going to wake her. This is our wedding day. I'm going to give her the gift of an orgasm.

So many times in our history, I have taken what I want from this woman and left her aching in return. Not today. I drop my robe to the floor and slide onto the bed gently, spooning her so my body conforms to hers. Abbie stirs a little under the blankets and shifts herself back into me. Even in her sleep, she hungers for my touch. I have to admit, it's an ego boost.

I pull down the sheet just enough to expose her shoulder and kiss it. That's when I notice she's wearing nothing on top. Intriguing. Sliding my hand down her body, I find my love completely naked, as if she's been waiting for me to arrive. I press my hard length against the crack of her ass, through the blanket, and find myself groaning.

"Graham," Abbie mumbles drowsily.

"Good morning, love," I whisper in her ear, tugging the covers up so I can get underneath with her, nothing but skin between us. "I wanted to see you first thing."

"Mmm," she murmurs, pushing her bare ass into me again.

I slide my hand down her side, tracing the curve of her hip, giving her thigh a firm squeeze. She responds like a cat, arching and all but purring as her eyes remain closed. My fingers find her center, hot and slick, and Abbie moves her legs to give me better access to the deliciousness I want. Lazily tracing her vulva, I whisper in her ear.

"So wet, you naughty girl. Were you dreaming about me?"

"Maybe." Her voice is still thick with sleep, but I can hear the sauciness coming through loud and clear.

"Tell me about it."

She hesitates. Owing to her lack of experience, she's still learning to navigate her sexuality, still learning how to tell me what to do, or what she likes. I'm as encouraging as I can be, but getting her to open up can take a little extra effort—effort that's always well worth it in the end. I squeeze her nub between my thumb and forefinger and bite down on her shoulder to get her attention, my dick jerking when her breath catches in her throat.

"Tell me," I growl.

"You didn't say please."

I grin at her attitude, loving the pushback I get from this cheeky woman. Loving how she doesn't kiss my ass.

"Tell me. Please." I slip my hand farther down to toy at her opening and she hisses with pleasure. "Tell me what made you so wet in your sleep."

"Mmm," she moans as I slide just the tip of my finger into her, using my thumb to continue rubbing her clit. "I was dreaming about our wedding night."

"You mean tonight?" I prod.

"*Yes.*" She breathes the word out, so sexy and sultry. There is something exceptionally delicious about the way she's both half asleep and aroused. It makes her throaty and lusty.

"Tell me more." I suck gently at her earlobe. "Or should I guess?" Her response is only more moans as I continue to play with her, getting more aggressive with her as she gets louder. I drop my voice to match the huskiness in hers. "Let's see...I assume it was something naughty, and something you like very much. Was I going down on you?"

"Mmm." She nods slightly.

"You like that, do you?" I slip another finger into her and plunge deep, watching her jaw fall open slightly. Her eyes haven't opened, but her body is fully awake now as she grinds into me and my hand.

"Yes. Fuck, yes," she whispers.

My cock is raging now, the precum at my tip wetting the crack of her ass, but I exercise restraint. Even though I know I could easily enter her from behind, then roll her onto her stomach and fuck her until we're both coming our brains out, this isn't about me feeling good. This is for Abbie. So I slide my other arm underneath her and give her nipples some much-needed attention as well.

"I can't wait to marry you," I whisper in her ear. "I can't wait for you to be mine."

She shivers. "I'm already yours. And you're mine."

Her breath catches in her throat as I pinch her nipple hard. She's so turned on, so on edge. My poor cock is throbbing, but I enjoy this so much.

"Always," I agree.

She reaches behind her under the blanket, trying to get a grip on my cock. I shift so she can get her hand on it, and she murmurs her approval as she finally achieves her goal.

"Shh, enough of that," I say as she starts stroking. "This is about you getting off, love."

"Where's the fun in that?" she whispers, giving me a squeeze.

I let out a moan before regaining control of myself. "You're plenty of fun enough."

Abbie laughs softly, but it quickly turns into a throaty sound as I shift our bodies so that she's on her back and I'm on my side next to her, my fingers still thrusting into her. When she spreads her legs, I add a third finger, pumping into her harder and deeper by the second. I don't know if she's ever been this wet before.

"Yes," she pants, her head tilted back in ecstasy.

I dip my head down to suck on her right nipple, and it's the magic key that unlocks her. She grips my forearm with both of her hands for support and rides my fingers faster and faster, gasping and moaning until she breaks. Just the sound of her coming breaks down my walls.

"You're beautiful," I tell her. "I love you."

Her eyes snap open. "Let me suck you off. Please. It's our wedding day."

Who am I to deny my future wife such a request? Abbie is still coming off her high, but she rushes at me, taking in every inch of me with her hot, hungry mouth. I'm already so turned on that it's barely a minute later before my orgasm rockets through me, so much more powerful than the one I just had in the shower. I paint the back of her throat with hard spurts of cum, gritting my teeth as each wave threatens to send me reeling.

When I finally come down, she sucks me clean and licks her lips with a devilish grin.

"You are going to make a remarkable Mrs. Ratliff," I tell her, pulling her in for a kiss.

"I'm counting on it," she replies.

Chapter Fifteen

Abbie

I HAVE NOT SPENT my entire life planning my wedding. Honestly, I didn't think I'd actually ever get married. Growing up, my parents weren't exactly shining examples of marital bliss, and almost everyone I know has divorced parents. Even my future husband has been divorced. I'm not opposed to the idea of marriage, of course, but it wasn't something I thought I'd want for myself.

But now that I'm sitting here mere feet away from my wedding dress, Esmeralda curling my hair to make it look like a 1940s film starlet's, Jude at my side, everything feels so immensely different. The idea of marrying Graham just seems so *right*. So natural. When he got down on one knee and proposed, I didn't even have to think about my answer. Of course I want to spend the rest of my life with him and Jude. I never dreamed it would happen so fast, though.

Jude spins in the vanity chair next to me, babbling a million miles a minute about eighteen different things:

horses, the wedding, how pretty the cake is, her dress, if I think she can wear lip gloss for the ceremony, more horses. She's talking so much I can barely think straight, which is actually a blessing. All the excitement and anticipation is making me jittery, but her upbeat chatter helps to keep me distracted.

What does a happy marriage look like? What do I want it to look like? For me, I think it's about love that lasts, and emotional stability (though I know having financial stability is also a really big factor, thanks to witnessing my parents' issues), and mutual support for each other's personal and professional endeavors. With those things in mind, I cling as tightly as I can to the image of me, Graham, and Jude living happily ever after, and take slow, deep breaths, focusing on what's most important today: my new family.

"I just think it would be better if we all rode in on horseback," Jude says, interrupting my thoughts while pawing through my makeup. She picks my favorite palette and holds it up. "What about these colors? It looks like the sunrise."

"Perfect!" I tap her on the nose and grin. "Is this for me or for you?"

She squinches up her face. "Both? I like the sparkly pink."

"Even more perfect. I think you're allowed a little eyeshadow for a special occasion."

Esmeralda steps back with the curling iron in her hand. "What do you think?"

I turn to inspect my hair in the mirror, loving it. "It's perfect. Thank you so much."

"It was my pleasure. I'd better go get changed myself." Esmeralda smiles and clears away the hair products crowding the vanity, then leaves me and Jude to finish getting ready.

Jude picks up right where she left off. "So, about riding the horses down the aisle..."

I have to laugh. "You know, Jude, if you ever decide to get married, you can have whatever you want. You can even say your vows on horseback if you want."

"Really?" Jude gasps. "Why don't you and Daddy do that?"

"I'm not sure we like horses quite as much as you do, sweetie." I kiss her on top of her head and take the makeup palette from her. "Ready for your eyes?"

Jude sits perfectly still as I do her makeup. She carefully closes her eyes as I swipe on the pale pink eyeshadow and blinks as instructed for the layer of clear gel mascara. I keep it as subtle as possible, because as much as I want to be a cool stepmom, Jude is still only eight years old.

"What do you think?" I ask.

Jude stares at herself in the mirror, adjusting her crown of braids and posing a little. "It looks good. What about the lip gloss?"

"You are relentless," I tease her. "Let me see what I have."

I rummage through my lipsticks, then lay out a selection of tinted lip balms and clear gloss that I think are appropriate for her.

"Make your choice," I say. "But I must warn you, that lip gloss is super sticky."

Jude claps her hands and carefully sorts through the pile until she settles on a small round tin of rose lip balm. "This one. It smells the best."

"Well then I'd say it's perfect for you, don't you think?"

She nods and I tell her how to apply it with a Q-tip.

"What about you?" Jude asks, upping her posing game in the mirror. "Which one are you going to wear?"

I pull out old reliable, Teenage Fantasy. "Your dad likes this one," I tell her and layer it on carefully. "So, it's my favorite."

"Do you have a favorite that no boys like?" Jude asks.

"Ooh, asking the real questions today." I laugh. "This was actually already my favorite, and your dad just happened to like it, too. But even if he didn't, I'd still pick it for today. And you know what else, Jude? Your makeup, just like your clothes and hair and everything else, is something that is totally up to you. In fact, you don't even have to wear makeup unless you want to. So choose what you like and don't worry about what anyone else thinks. Do it for you, missy. No one else."

Just then, someone bursts through the door without knocking, and squeals loudly, "I'M HERE, BITCH."

"Amandaaa!" I exclaim as we tackle each other in a joint hug. "You're here!"

"Oh my God, your hair looks amazing. Is that your dress hanging up? It's so gorgeous. I'm going to cry. Shut up, I'm going to cry. Give me a tissue before I ruin my makeup."

Jude hops up and runs a tissue over to Amanda, who

takes it graciously and dabs her eyes. "Oh my God, are you Jude?"

"I am!" Jude curtsies in her fancy new dress and bats her eyes.

"Aren't you the cutest?!" Amanda gushes. "I missed you when I came here to visit Abbie a few weeks ago—I think you were at your horseback-riding lesson? But I've been super excited to meet you. And this time we'll totally get to hang out! You look stunning, by the way."

Jude preens. "Abbie did my makeup. She let me wear her rose lip gloss, too."

"It's definitely your color," Amanda says. Then she turns her attention back to me. "So what's the what? What can I do to help? Should I change now or wait?"

"First of all, sit your butt down and take a deep breath," I say with a laugh. "We have plenty of time. I still have to do my makeup and get dressed. I mean, obviously."

I gesture at the dress, hanging from the bathroom door, and Amanda runs over to inspect it close up, cooing over the fabric and the lace and the cap sleeves.

"Agghhhh, I can't believe you're getting married!" She gives me another quick hug and then perches on the edge of the bed like I told her to, though it doesn't seem to be calming her down any. "God, this whole thing is like a fairy tale. Or a movie. Can I do your makeup?"

"Since you clearly cannot sit still for five seconds, I suppose I'll allow it," I tease.

Jude leans over on the vanity, already grabbing for my lipstick. "Me too! Can I help?"

I have to laugh. The two of them combined is just too

much, and I'm loving every second of it. "Of course. What's a wedding day if someone doesn't do the bride's makeup?"

"You do your lashes, though, because I don't want to poke your eyes out," Amanda says. "But don't you worry. Jude and I will make you the most gorgeous bride of all time."

And honestly, they do. Amanda gives me the perfect subtle cat eye, then works some inexplicable magic with my unruly brows, and Jude helps me blush up my cheeks until they're as rosy as apples. It's not a huge transformation—I just look more like *me*. I feel amazing.

"Dress time!" I announce.

Amanda takes mine off the hanger and unzips it for me. There's a knock on the door just before I slip out of my silk robe.

"One second!" Jude calls out. "My other mom is getting dressed!"

Amanda looks at me with wide eyes and a grin, and I feel so happy I could fly.

"We brought a quick snack for the bride," Mary calls through the door.

With Amanda's help, I hurry into my dress and nod to Jude to open the door. Esmeralda gasps loudly, pushing her way into the room.

"Oh, my sweet girl!" she gushes. "You look like a dream."

"She looks better than a dream," Mary says, setting a tea tray on the end of the bed. "I thought you could use a little sustenance before your big moment."

"I'm starving!" Jude announces, diving for the tray

laden with sliced fruits, cheeses, bridge mix, crackers, fresh croissants, a bottle of ginger ale, a bottle of prosecco, and a few fancy sparkling waters. Mary's thought of everything.

"Thank you. Except I don't know if I can eat. I'm having major butterflies," I admit.

Mary pats me on the shoulder. "You're going to be fine, I promise. We can't stay, but we wanted to wish you luck."

"We're making sure everything is perfect. The judge who's officiating just got here," Esmeralda adds.

"I can't thank you both enough." I take their hands and give them a squeeze. "You've all been so good to me."

Esmeralda beams. "It's our pleasure. Now Jude, would you like to come downstairs and help us with the flowers? I hear you're very good at that."

"I am!" Jude jumps up, strawberries in her hands. "But what if Abbie needs me?"

"Then I will come find you as quickly as possible," Amanda reassures her.

"Perfect. Let's go, little miss." Esmeralda holds the door open for Jude, who skips out of the room, holding her dress in both hands. Esmeralda and Mary both grin at me as they follow her, shutting the door behind them and leaving me in silence with Amanda.

"Sooo." Amanda picks up the bottle of prosecco. "Quick drink before you go on?"

"Please." I giggle. She pours us both a half glass and we hold our stems up in a toast.

"To my best friend, who is growing up way too fast. To the girl who joined the nerdy-ass debate team with me in high school, who helped me find the most respectably slutty prom dress senior year, who always supports me and is always there, no matter what life may bring. May she have the best life with the best husband. May she make an awesome and totally cool stepmom. May she never forget her friends."

"I'll never forget my friends." I wipe a quick tear from my eye and clink her glass. "You're the best, and I'm nothing without you."

We spend the next hour reminiscing about our high school days, our least and most favorite college classes, all the fabulous vacations we're going to take in the future. I help Amanda get dressed, too, and we're just putting our shoes on when there's a knock on the door.

"Abbie?" I hear Esmeralda's voice. "It's time."

Excitement thrums through me so hard it takes my breath away.

"You going to be okay?" Amanda asks gently as she adjusts the strap of her lacy yellow dress.

"Better than okay." I give her an honest smile. "I'm elated. And a little scared. But mostly elated."

"I think that's exactly perfect." Amanda threads her arm through mine. "Come on, let's get you married."

We walk down the hall together until we come to the top of the stairs, where Jude stands with her hands clasped in excitement. The sweet floral scent hits first, and I peek down to see that the entire foyer has been decked out in a profusion of roses in warm summer colors—pale and deep pink, peach, lavender, golden and buttery yellows. Mary and Ronaldo and Cassie sit on folding chairs before an archway of cream-colored roses, where Graham stands beside the judge, waiting. For me.

He's so handsome standing there in his suit, looking happier than I've ever seen him.

"Do you love it?" Jude asks, sweeping her arm to encompass the foyer below.

"I love it so much," I tell her, pulling her in for a squeeze.

Esmeralda hands bouquets of wildflowers to Jude, me, and Amanda, and I hear violins start playing from somewhere within the house. Real ones. Live ones. Amanda gives me a side hug and whispers, "You've got this."

Watching Jude—soon to be my stepdaughter—walk down the stairs first, toward Graham, is surreal. I can't believe this is my life, I can't believe this is my present, I can't believe this is my future.

She gets to the end of the aisle, a creamy white runner flanked by the folding chairs, and takes her place next to Graham on one side of the arch. Then it's Amanda's turn to go down and take her place on the opposite side.

"Ready?" Esmeralda whispers.

All I can do is nod.

The music changes and Esmeralda gestures for me to go ahead.

With my heart in my throat, I begin the slow descent down the stairs, toward my new husband, toward my new life. Everything feels like it's moving in slow motion as I soak up every feeling, every flower petal, the joy on Graham's face.

I've just started down the aisle when suddenly the front door bursts open and uniformed police officers flood into the foyer. Behind them, on the porch, paparazzi in dark clothes crowd each other for the best angles, their camera flashbulbs going off like strobe lights.

I freeze, unsure what to do, and look to Graham, who appears as shocked and confused as I am. All our guests, few as they are, start murmuring. Someone with a camera darts into the house, snapping photos, and I feel my bouquet slip from my slack hands. Have they come for Graham again? Is that even possible?

"What is the meaning of this?" Graham demands.

"Abigail Montgomery?" One of the officers heads straight toward me, handcuffs at the ready. "You are hereby under arrest for the attempted murder of Natasha Ratliff."

Chapter Sixteen

Graham

ALL I CAN DO IS watch and seethe as my beautiful bride is escorted out of my house in handcuffs. Paparazzi fill the front drive, stepping on the hydrangeas to get a better view of Abbie being tucked into the back of a police car. The press is about to have a fucking field day.

Incendiary tabloid headlines are sure to come swiftly and cruelly. Abbie will be on the front page of every single magazine and celebrity gossip website—yet again—except this time she'll be in a wedding dress and that fiery red lipstick. This was supposed to be one of the best days of my life, but instead it has spiraled into a complete and utter shitshow. What in bloody hell is going on?

Esmeralda comes up behind me and places a hand on my shoulder. I know she means well, but I shrug her off with a scowl as the cops clear out. They made it abundantly clear they weren't talking to me as soon as they entered my home, and no amount of heckling them made any difference. There is no point in putting up any more of a fight right here, right now. Because I know better.

Causing a scene, particularly with so many cameras around, is a death sentence. The tabloids will spin the story even more than they did when I was arrested. Is there any safe move for me? Not really. I'll be pegged as emotionless for not interfering, but I'd be labeled much worse if I caused a scene.

Anger and confusion pump their lead into my bloodstream. Abbie guilty of attempted murder? Are the police so desperate for leads they're just grabbing anyone? I still don't understand why there's an ongoing investigation at all. Natasha overdosed. Fact. She's in a coma due to her own actions. Fact. Neither Abbie nor I went near Natasha that night. Fact, fact, fact.

How can this possibly be happening?

The police cars clear out, but the paps are slower to move. I don't know if they got any clear shots of me, but I keep our few guests and my daughter as far back from the windows as possible. Everyone convenes in the kitchen, talking in low, worried voices. Jude sits on the counter, tears streaming down her face as Mary tries to soothe her.

I've done my best to keep myself poised as insanity rained down on my household. I remained calm when they cuffed my bride. I remained resolute when the press trespassed on my property to take incriminating photos of Abbie being led out in her wedding dress. I've kept composure as my guests, few though they are, mill around sending me pitying looks.

All this I've done, but I'm about to break.

"I need to go call my lawyer," I say to no one in particular. I catch eyes with Mary and tilt my head toward Jude, asking her to keep watch. Mary nods her understanding, and I go.

My self-control is crumbling the entire way down the hall, and I slam the door, hard, as I enter my office. I pour two fingers of Scotch into a tumbler and throw the alcohol back without a second thought. Then I pull my phone from my pocket and dial Bow.

"What the fuck is going on, Bowen?" I demand as soon as she answers the phone—after her MIA act the last time I had legal troubles, she's been keeping extra tabs on me, picking up all my calls instantly, checking in every day. "Why did my bride just get arrested and dragged away from our wedding ceremony in handcuffs? The cops wouldn't tell me anything. Start talking."

"Shit. Looks like Natasha woke up this morning. I've been in fucking meetings all day, this is the first I'm hearing about it." I can hear her fingers flying across her keyboard in the background. "Apparently an 'unidentified source' has been leaking nonstop to the media, and Natasha's blaming the whole thing on Abbie. It's *trending* now. Jesus Christ."

A bark of a laugh escapes me. "That's preposterous. It was an overdose!"

"Well, whatever this alleged source is saying has cast enough doubt for an arrest to be made. I'd bet you anything it's Natasha herself talking to the press."

"Whoever it is, you need to stop them." I pour another finger's worth into my glass, my hand shaking. I don't know what to do with this rage, and it's becoming dangerous.

Bow huffs in frustration. "I'd love to. But we've been

over this, Graham. I can't interfere with an active police investigation. Due process can't be sidestepped. All we can do is sue their asses after the fact, which we will, especially since they're now two for two on the false arrests."

"Fuck the legal system," I hiss and swallow down my second drink. "I need you to get to that police station as soon as possible, Bow. That's my wife."

"You made it official? Congratulations," she says, sounding genuinely pleased.

I wince. "Almost wife. They hauled her off before we could exchange vows. Look, just head over now and I'll meet you at the station as soon as I can."

"Absolutely not." Bow is firm, which makes me bristle. "You showing up will cause more harm than good. And besides, Jude needs you right now. Stay home, Graham. I'm the lawyer, let me do my job."

My lip curls hard. "Like you did last time?"

"That's not fair. I was on an urgent case for a client in Monaco. I know the timing was shit, but I promise I will spend the rest of my career making it up to you, okay? Starting now."

I let out a long breath. "Fine. Do what you must."

"I'll call you as soon as I have some answers. Sit tight."

We hang up, but I'm still pacing my office, boiling over with pent-up anxiety and anger. If I can't be with Abbie, there's only one other place for me to go: the hospital.

I return to the kitchen and find Esmeralda, pulling her to the side for a private chat.

"I need to leave."

"Of course, Mr. Ratliff," she says. "What can we do?"

"I need someone to take care of Jude."

She offers a wry smile and gestures to the table by the window, where Abbie's best friend is currently painting Jude's nails, the two of them having what appears to be a very animated conversation.

"I don't anticipate that being a problem. Amanda already offered to help however necessary. I'll handle the guests myself," Esmeralda says.

"Thank you."

I kiss Jude goodbye and promise to be back as soon as possible.

"Are you going to get Abbie?" my daughter asks, looking terrified. Amanda squeezes her shoulder reassuringly.

"I'm going to do my best," I promise.

There are no more paps outside by the time I peel down the driveway in my car, and for once, I'm disappointed not to see them. Hurling one of their cameras across the grounds would have been immensely cathartic.

I spend the entire two-hour drive to Manhattan making calls on my Bluetooth, trying to find ways to help and coming up frustratingly short. Is this what Abbie felt like while I was locked up? Something that feels like grief overwhelms me as I picture her sitting in a cold cell, listless and confused. I have to do something. They can't keep her there.

Getting through the hospital takes no time at all, as I've been here entirely too often already. The same bitchy nurse Jude and I saw last time we visited follows me to Natasha's room, where I find my ex-wife sitting up in full makeup, watching TV. A tray of half-eaten soup and crackers is on the table next to her. When she sees me, she grabs the remote and hits mute.

"There's my husband!" she coos. Her eyes are glassy, probably from the drugs they have her on, but she seems very much like her old self. Pity.

"Ex," I remind her, burying my anger under years of practice. I walk over to the bed, the nurse watching me from the doorway. Lowering my voice, I hiss, "What the fuck did you do?"

Natasha places a hand dramatically over her chest, her eyes going wide. "Don't yell at me, Graham, I'm so weak."

I clench my jaw, entirely unmoved by her display. "Funny, you're looking remarkably well recovered to me. *Start talking.*"

She looks at me serenely, like she isn't trying to ruin my life. "You should be thanking me, darling. I stopped you from marrying a murderer."

"You did this *to yourself.* And believe me, there will be consequences for your actions—my lawyers are already on the case. What the hell were you even thinking?"

Despite the fact that I'm not buying her innocent act in the slightest, Natasha pushes on with her dewy eyes and trembling chin.

"When I woke up and the nurse told me about your proposal plan, I knew I had to save you and Jude. I had the police brought in immediately. Abbie tried to *kill me,*

Graham. She wanted to get me out of the way so she could take your money. And she almost succeeded!"

Behind me, the nurse makes a sound of disapproval—obviously, she's completely fallen for this whole fucking charade. Which, of course she has. Natasha is playing her part perfectly. She's a great actress. But I know what she looks like when she's acting.

And she is lying through her goddamn teeth.

She's so full of shit, sitting here in the bed she's made, playing the victim. Always the fucking victim.

"Don't look so angry, Graham. Can't you see I'm just doing what needs to be done? It's not your fault she bamboozled you, a pretty young thing like that. Of course you fell for it."

That's the final straw.

"You fucking *hag*," I hiss. "You miserable, manipulative—"

"Don't get angry, now," Natasha says in a singsong voice.

"Should I call security, Mrs. Ratliff?" the nurse behind me asks loudly. "Do we need the police to come and remove him?"

"Maybe we do," Natasha muses, looking me dead in the eye, her gaze cold and calculating. She could never lie through her eyes. "Maybe I need a restraining order against you, Graham. You clearly don't believe me. Or maybe you planned this whole thing with the nanny so you could off me and steal my daughter. Jude needs to be safe. I'd better call my lawyer..."

I turn on a heel and storm out of the room before my temper truly shatters. My ex-wife is a vile human, and so help me, I will do whatever it takes to keep her out of my life for good. I've just turned the corner, the nosey nurse still chasing after me, when I see a familiar figure walking toward me.

It's none other than Quinn. Quinn fucking Dempsey.

Chapter Seventeen

Graham

My former fucking stable hand.

I square my jaw and stand my ground as Quinn continues walking my way, the gap between us shortening until we're all but facing off in this hallway like two gunslingers in an old western, each unwilling to make the first move.

"*You*," I sneer.

"Mr. Ratliff," Quinn says good-naturedly, but his body language betrays his voice. He has his hands stuffed in his pockets, his brow furrowed, like a child who knows he's in trouble. "Didn't expect to see you here."

My phone rings, so I hold up a finger to hold him there and answer the phone.

"This is Graham."

"Graham, this is Daniel."

I smile. "Perfect timing, my friend."

"Bowen told me to call you. She said you might have another job for me."

Daniel is my private investigator, the same PI who

dug up all the evidence that revealed *Quinn* was the rat who sold the story of my alleged affair with Abbie to the tabloids. The very evidence that enabled Bow to put together a very intimidating lawsuit against Quinn for libel. Now, I trust Daniel with my life.

I didn't have a need for these kinds of things, once upon a time. I used to be able to handle my own business and not worry about someone sneaking around in the dark to get answers. Natasha changed all of that. She and her little boy toy standing here in front of me.

"Yes. As it happens, I do have need of your services again." I square off my shoulders and keep a stern eye on Quinn, who looks around so casually he may as well be modeling checkered shirts. He's even whistling.

It disturbs me how quickly and easily he gets under my skin, when I've taken on more powerful people than a goddamn stable boy, but he's managed to make himself a pawn in a very dangerous game. A game that I apparently can't stop losing. At least, not yet.

But Quinn has no idea how deep this goes. How his involvement has already doomed him to a very unhappy fate. He still imagines he's going to drive off into the sunset with my ex-wife when all the legal dust settles between me and her. Quinn Dempsey is in for a very rude awakening. Because if there's one thing I know about Natasha, it's that she devours men once she's through squeezing them dry, and she spits their bones out afterward. The damage wrought by my legal team will be nothing compared to what Natasha has in store for this boy.

On the other end of the line, I hear Daniel flipping through some pages.

"I've got my notes here from Bowen—as I understand, this concerns Abigail Montgomery and the attempted murder charge?"

"That's correct. I need you to help build a case in support of her innocence."

The evil nurse has finally departed, and now Quinn makes like he's going to try stepping around me as well, but I stop him with a fierce look. He shrugs and puts his hands back in his pockets. The urge to destroy him grows.

"I'm on it, Mr. Ratliff."

"Excellent. Clearing her name is paramount. I'm prepared to be *very* generous if you can help my team accomplish that quickly," I tell him, hoping the offer of a monetary bonus will grease his wheels even more.

"Understood, sir."

I hang up and tuck the phone away, giving the weasel another death glare as I turn my attention back to him. "What are you doing here?"

"It's a free country, last time I checked. I should ask you the same thing, though. As far as I know, you aren't exactly welcome here. That whole attempted murder charge and all."

As I stare at the shit-eating grin on his face, I can't help but wonder what Natasha has on him, or what she's offered him, that makes him so cavalier. The boy could barely look me in the eye when he worked in my stables, yet he somehow managed to screw me six ways to Sunday at my ex-wife's bidding and now acts as though we are on the same level.

"I suppose someone needs to explain the judiciary system to you? They had nothing on me. They have nothing on anyone. Natasha overdosed," I remind him.

"Did she?" Quinn cocks his head to the side. "She's been very sick for someone who 'just' overdosed. It's no wonder people suspect foul play."

"Yes, it's very curious, isn't it? Natasha begins to lose control over the press and our child and then all of a sudden, tragedy strikes..." I trail off, watching a nurse scurry down the hall, giving me the side-eye. I'm sure Natasha has the entire floor hanging on her every word.

Sometimes I forget her charms, because I've become immune to them. I was susceptible for a long time before I learned my lesson. Quinn will have his moment in the sun, just like I did, and then one day he'll be forced to realize what he's gotten himself into. How truly fucked he is.

Unless I can get to him first.

Natasha isn't the only person in this hospital with resources at their disposal.

"We need to talk." I clear my throat and offer the little shit my most serious expression. "I am willing to offer you a bargain."

"Oh, really." Quinn pulls himself up to his full height, wearing what I like to think of as his "collective bargaining" face, which is laughable at best. "Go on. I'm listening."

"I need you to tell the press the truth. Tell them what really happened to Natasha." Quinn opens his mouth to protest, but I hold up my hand to stop him. "You've made quite a stir telling lies for her, and I'm sure you didn't mind your minor celebrity status while you were at it. But if you do this, then in return, I'll drop the lawsuit against you. You can walk away from this free and clear. No court appearances, no hundreds of thousands of dollars in lawyer fees, no jail time or criminal record. It'll be like none of this ever happened. You'll be free to live your life. I just need you to come forward with the real story."

A beat passes, and I can see that he's thinking it over. I'm so tense I can feel it in my gut.

But finally, Quinn just shakes his head, smirking. "Well, well, well. How low you've sunk after all."

"Pardon?"

"Look at you standing there, trying to coerce a former employee in the middle of a hospital. You think I'd do anything to help cover your ass? You're really desperate, aren't you? I bet your little lawsuit won't amount to shit, either. In fact, if this does go to court, I'm gonna make sure *you* have to pay my lawyer fees."

The urge to tackle him hits me hard. I try to banish it with a tight smile. "It's not too late to do the right thing. Do you really want to end up in prison? Natasha isn't going to save you."

He laughs. "Don't you get it? You've already lost. We've got that shit in the bag—and I'm on the winning side! I have *Natasha.* With her comes all the legal help I need. And all the money, status, and comfort I'll ever need, too. And a sweet pussy, am I right? I don't know how you can get your rocks off fucking some naïve teenager with no experience when you've tasted the heaven that is Natasha Ratliff. My God, what that woman can do with her mouth."

I ignore his insult—to be fair, Abbie's lack of "experience" is something I've enjoyed immensely—and focus on staying as calm as possible. This hospital has eyes and ears everywhere, and the last thing I want is to send them running to call the police. Or the tabloids.

Speaking of which, I'd bet anything it was Natasha's bitchy nurse who sent the paparazzi to my house this morning just in time to witness (and document) Abbie's arrest.

"If you think I actually care what my ex-wife is doing with you or anyone else in the bedroom, you're very much mistaken," I tell him dryly. "I'll say it one last time. This isn't going to end the way you think. She's using you."

It's clear I'm not getting through to him. Quinn looks like nothing so much as a rooster, puffed up and cocky as he struts in front of me.

"She told me you'd say something like that. Try to sway me to your side. It won't work."

"You forget Natasha is the one who left our marriage to fuck her way around the globe. In fact, I'm not sure there was a time in our relationship where she *wasn't* messing around on the side. You think you can corral a woman like that with that limp noodle between your legs and the three brain cells you repeatedly rub together?"

Quinn's grin grows wider. "I wouldn't worry about what's between my legs. She likes it better than whatever you're working with, anyway. Maybe that's why your nanny likes it so much—because she doesn't know any better."

His jabs are puerile at best, but I'm still struggling to

bite my tongue. I've been losing control of everything lately—my life, my house, my respectability, my temper. I need to regain control. I need a win.

Unfortunately, Quinn takes my silence as an invitation to gloat.

"You're done, Ratliff. Natasha's about to get your house, your fortune, and full custody of your kid, thanks to the fact that you and that gold digger are both suspects in an attempted murder case. Soon enough, I'll have not only your wife and your money, but your daughter, too."

At the mention of Jude, I rear back in a fit of near-blind rage and punch Quinn square in the nose. Blood gushes between his fingers and he blinks back at me, first in terror, and then starts laughing. Laughing like a fucking maniac. That's when I realize he baited me. He did this on purpose.

"Looking forward to pressing charges of my own, old man. Did you know I have a contact at *TMZ* on speed dial? 'Bout to go give him a call. They are going to eat this up."

He salutes me with two bloody fingers and then heads off down the hall, toward Natasha's room, still laughing the whole way.

Fuck.

Chapter Eighteen

Abbie

THE ROOM IS FREEZING. Icy cold drafts blow from the vent in the ceiling, wafting across my bare shoulders and giving me goosebumps. Through the satin fabric of my dress, my thighs freeze against the metal chair and I try not to shudder because it'll just make me look pathetic.

These two detectives, the same two from my last visit to this interrogation room, stare at me from across the table. Gone is Krohl's awkward kindness from before, or what little of it he tried to offer me, replaced by a detached hardness that matches Hernandez's. Their cold looks hit me harder than the frigid room.

This was not how my day was supposed to turn out.

"Nice to see you again," I say, swallowing hard.

"Is it?" Detective Krohl asks, leaning forward on his elbows. "Do you think you're here for a pleasant little social visit, Miss Montgomery?"

"N-no. I was just trying to be..." Words fail me, so I shut my mouth and take a deep breath.

Dear God, don't let me cry. I saved up all my tears the entire way here and I won't release them now, or I'll fall apart. I don't understand what's happening. Why am I here?

"Let's get started. Talk to us about your relationship with Natasha Ratliff," Detective Hernandez says, tapping a pen on a yellow legal pad.

The affronted part of me is already formulating various sarcastic responses, about how we already covered this topic the *last* time I was here, but the terrified part of me wins out. Terrified of what happens when you sass two officers with guns who think you've impossibly tried to kill a woman who almost succeeded in killing herself.

"I don't know what else there is to tell?" Beneath my frozen fingers, my knees begin to tremble. "As I've said, I was hired on as a nanny for Graham Ratliff at the beginning of the summer. He's who I work for. Not Natasha. She moved back in briefly, but I always worked for Graham. I take care of their kid. That's all."

"Is it? Because it seems the situation is a bit more complicated than you've been pretending, isn't it?" Detective Hernandez cracks a sour grin at me and it turns my stomach. "In fact, the media seems to think it's a *lot* more complicated. What kind of dress would you say that is, Detective Krohl?"

The media. The tabloids, she means. Rancid rags posing as journalism aiming at nothing more than to exploit anyone and anything that can make them a red cent. And a police officer is seriously waving this in my face? This is why I'm suddenly a person of interest again?

I bite my lip hard, squeezing until the tears that prick my eyes are there for different reasons entirely.

"Well, Detective Hernandez, I'd say that looks an awful lot like a wedding dress," Krohl offers dryly.

Hernandez pushes on, goading me. "And would you say, Detective Krohl, that the scene we walked into at the Ratliff house looked something like a party?"

"A very fancy party," he agrees.

"A wedding, even."

Krohl nods slowly, as if he's only just now putting the pieces together. "Huh. Now that you mention it, it sure looked like Graham Ratliff was waiting at the end of an aisle."

They pass this exchange without once looking at each other, but keeping their eyes trained on me, as though they expect me to crack any second. It makes me feel like I'm on a stage and they are the audience, staring up at me, expecting me to put on a show for them. I don't know what they want me to say.

"I'm not sure what exactly you're implying, but I didn't do anything wrong," I say.

Natasha Ratliff overdosed. *She* is the one who mixed opioids and alcohol and nearly died, but now it's my life that's getting destroyed. Even though I had nothing to do with her OD.

I should be back at the estate right now, sipping champagne and feeding wedding cake to my new husband. Tossing my bouquet to my best friend and stealing kisses from Graham in between congratulatory toasts. Sharing dances with my new family.

Instead, I'm sitting here with my hands cuffed in my

lap in this freezing room as two idiot detectives berate me about my personal life.

Just because I was going to marry Graham doesn't mean I plotted to kill his ex-wife first. Is this seriously the best that can be expected from New York's finest? Buying into gossip rags and salacious headlines, chasing false leads, arresting innocent people left and right?

But as angry as I am, I still can't ignore the utterly helpless feeling lingering beneath, desperate for someone to just believe me.

Krohl takes a sip of his burnt coffee and sucks his teeth. "The thing is, Miss Montgomery, it appears there's a lot more to this story than you've let on."

I shake my head, clearing the fear from my throat. "There isn't. The story is, I was asleep in my room on the other side of the apartment the night Natasha overdosed. That's it. I had nothing to do with it."

"Why don't you take us through that night again, step by step?" Krohl jumps in. "Witnesses say the Ratliffs left the restaurant separately, without you or their child. Did you stay there at the restaurant after the fight?"

"Only for a few minutes. I was trying to distract Jude," I say softly, picking at my cuticles. "She was upset."

"And where did you go after that?"

"To an ice cream shop. We got sundaes." I remember it well. Jude loved having ice cream for dinner, and we sat in the purple booth and had ourselves a great rest of the evening, even though it had started out so shitty.

And then Graham came to me later that night, waking me with his passion. He came to *me* instead of

Natasha. Professed his feelings for *me*. We made love all night long. It was like—

"Miss Montgomery."

I blink, snapped out of the memory. "What?"

"I said, where was the ice cream shop?"

"It was a Van Leeuwen's. I don't know the address. I think it was on—"

Suddenly, the door slams open. A woman I don't recognize in a very nice suit storms into the room and slams her briefcase down on the table. "Abbie, shut your mouth."

I almost jump at her brusqueness. "Who—"

"Hush. Now." She flashes me a tight smile and turns to the cops. "Detectives."

"Elise Bowen." Detective Hernandez sighs heavily. "I suppose you're her counsel?"

Ignoring the question, Bowen says, "I see you've been interrogating my client without me present."

Hernandez shrugs. "She didn't ask."

"She didn't know to ask, and you know it," Bowen snaps.

"We read her the Miranda when we arrested her," Krohl says. "So technically—"

"Spare me the bullshit, Frank. I need to speak to my client. *Privately*," Bowen seethes.

Krohl doesn't look happy. "Look, we just have a few more questions to ask and then you two can talk all you need. You're here now, so she's got her counsel."

"She's entitled to her time," Bowen says. "Don't cross me on this. You and I both know you're already in deep shit for the way you handled the Ratliff interrogation."

"Fine." Detective Hernandez sighs heavily and stands, Krohl following behind her. "Knock on the door when you're ready. You know the drill."

"That I do." Bowen nods and turns her attention to her briefcase.

I stare as the two detectives get up and walk out. So this is the infamous Elise Bowen. The same Elise Bowen who left Graham to rot in jail because she was out of the country.

"You must be Bow," I say, keeping my voice neutral.

I may not be happy with her recent mishandling of Graham's case, but I'm still half scared to death being handcuffed in a chair here myself, and I'm relieved that Bowen showed up when she did. It's hard not to feel grateful when an avenging angel of law comes storming into an interrogation room with their briefcase ablaze.

She nods. "Pleasure to meet you and all the usual shit. Don't tell me anything right now. They'll be watching the room. CCTV, audio bugs, the usual."

"I didn't do it. What the hell is even going on?" It comes out more aggressively than I planned, and I find myself relishing the anger that comes with it. "Nobody is telling me anything, and I have no idea why I got dragged back here. I have nothing to hide."

"Then there's nothing to worry about." Bowen gives me a curt nod, but then her expression softens. "Look. The fact of the matter is, Natasha woke from her coma this morning and she's saying you're the one who drugged her. Her nurse has been talking to the press."

My heart drops. "What?" I choke out. "How could she say—that's not true!"

"It doesn't matter. The police have no real credible evidence. All they have are Natasha's accusations and media gossip. It won't hold up in court. That said, you are not to utter a *word* about anything related to this case unless I am present. Do you understand?"

I nod, to show her I'm serious about keeping my mouth shut. I'm still reeling from the revelation that Natasha recovered, and that she's accusing me of attempted murder and trying to ruin my life. Because, what? Because her ex-husband was interested in me? She didn't even want him, she just wanted his money and all the attendant comforts it could provide her. Even Jude, her own child, was merely a pawn in her game—something she could take and lord over Graham just to make him suffer more.

But what if Bow is wrong? What if her word is enough to sway a judge and jury? What if I end up locked up?

The lawyer interrupts my spiraling with a brief touch to my shoulder. "Come on. Let's get you out of here. Chin up."

She knocks on the door and the detectives come back in almost immediately, making it obvious that they were trying to eavesdrop in the hallway. They share a look with Bowen before taking their seats. It's like some sort of dance and I'm not privy to the steps.

"You know you don't have anything solid enough to keep her here," Bowen says. "There's no evidence, not even circumstantial."

"We have a witness statement."

"From Mrs. Ratliff?" Bowen shoots them a look. "We

all know that's horseshit. Especially given that your witness just came out of a *coma*, ergo her mental acuity cannot possibly be relied upon at present. Did you not bother researching the case studies regarding patient confusion and agitation after waking from a coma? No? What about the statistically significant prevalence of disorientation and paranoia? No? Hallucinations, delusions, is any of this ringing a bell? No? Pity. You're going to have a hell of a time making any of this stick."

Krohl and Hernandez just sit there staring at Bowen as she delivers her verbal lashing, the detectives' brows lowered, the tension in the room thickening. Not going to lie, I'm impressed. Bowen doesn't just talk the talk.

"I'll just need you to remove those handcuffs, now," she finishes with a smile. "My client is going home."

The detectives exchange a glance, and it's obvious that Bowen has won this round. *Yes.*

But as Detective Krohl unlocks my cuffs, he says, "Don't leave New York City. Your name is far from cleared."

Chapter Nineteen

Abbie

THE SECOND I slide into the back seat of the private car is the second my body chooses to release the dam of tears I've been holding back for hours.

I bury my face in my hands, wrists throbbing where the cold steel once rubbed. They didn't cuff me too tight but the very feel of it burned, leaving marks across my skin. All I can do is hide my face as I sob, hiccups wracking my diaphragm. I'm a mess and I know it; makeup running, hair a mess, eyes puffy and red. I probably look like a horror show in my dress.

Of course I'm relieved to be free, but I'm equally terrified that I'll end up back in police custody quicker than I can blink. I don't feel safe. I'm still on the brink of losing everything.

Bowen opens the back door and slides in next to me, briefcase first. After she closes the door, she digs around in her blazer pocket and then hands me a pack of tissues. For some reason, this makes me cry harder.

"It'll be okay," she soothes, somewhat awkwardly. I'd

bet anything that her usual clientele are power-hungry rich men charged with white collar crimes, not emotional young women wrongfully accused of attempted murder. "I wasn't bluffing back there—they don't have anything on you except a bunch of baseless accusations, which are questionable at best. They need actual evidence if they want to prosecute, and they won't get it."

I nod, blotting ineffectually at the black mascara tracks on my cheeks. "This isn't fair."

Her expression hardens again. "Fair is a bullshit notion. It doesn't exist. You can be just. You can be balanced. You can be considerate. But rarely is anything in life fair."

Wow. This woman really isn't one to sugarcoat things. I think I can see why Graham calls her a friend. He never did like being kowtowed to.

"I'll have you dropped off at the apartment in Central Park West." Bowen rifles around in her briefcase and produces a single key with a dark blue tag attached, labeled RATLIFF - MANHATTAN. "Natasha won't be there, obviously. She'll be under observation at the hospital for the time being. We'll be notified when the doctors say she can be released."

Staying in the apartment here in the city? Alone? My stomach drops. No way in hell am I going. That's Natasha's home turf, even if Graham technically owns the place.

"But what about Jude?" I protest. "I have to take care of her. That's my job."

Bowen is already shaking her head. "You need to stay

in the City until you're fully cleared by the police, so going back upstate is out of the question."

"What if Natasha gets out early and comes home?" I fret.

"She just woke up from a coma. That bitch isn't going anywhere. Pardon my French. "

That gets me to crack a smile. I think Bowen's irreverence is growing on me, too.

"In the meantime," she goes on, pulling out her phone and tapping at the screen, "we'll have to find a temp nanny for Jude. Maybe one of the staff up there can handle it."

"But she needs me," I protest.

Bowen lowers her phone and looks back at me, very seriously. "Listen to me, Abbie. You cannot leave New York City. As a suspect in an attempted murder investigation, there are procedures in place that you cannot sidestep. Part of proving your innocence is playing by the rules, irrespective of the fact that they're being implemented on the basis of false accusations."

"God. Do you always talk like that? I bet you're incredible to watch in a courtroom," I find myself blurting.

I wasn't trying to be funny, but Bowen throws back her head in a cackle. "I'm flattered. Maybe I'll invite you sometime. Let me just make a few calls and we'll get Jude squared away."

"Wait. We can hire Amanda. My best friend. She came up for the wedding, so she's already at the estate."

"Great. I'll get on it," she says.

A dagger twists in my heart as I think about how

much Jude has already suffered this summer. With her parents fighting, her mom being hospitalized, Graham's unexplained "business trip," and now my arrest, her entire life has been turned upside down over and over again. Knowing Amanda will be at her side is the only comfort I have.

Bowen starts to tell the driver where the apartment is, but then holds up a finger.

"Wait one second." She answers her vibrating cell, brows knit together. "This is Bowen... Mm. Fabulous. I'll be right there."

When she hangs up, she gives me a sympathetic look. I immediately think the worst.

"I have to go back in there?"

Smiling wryly, she says, "Nope. But I do. To get your husband."

"What?"

Bowen kicks open the car door with her red-soled Louboutin. "He's been arrested for assault and battery."

"Shit." I slump in the seat.

"Couldn't have said it better myself. Looks like you and Graham are turning into a real Bonnie and Clyde. A match made in heaven. Just sit tight."

With another strained smile, Bowen takes off.

As I wait for Bow to take care of the Graham situation inside the police station, I marinate in my rapidly growing indignation and outrage. I can't believe this is our fucking wedding day. Not only were we prevented from exchanging actual vows, but we've both somehow managed to get arrested. It might be funny if it weren't so goddamn awful.

Taking a deep breath, I resolve to put on a happy face for my groom. Well, as happy as I can make it. There isn't much I can do about my puffy eyes and red nose, but I run through the pack of tissues from Bowen in an attempt to wipe clean all of my ruined makeup. Then I roll the window down and pray that my teary eyes will be dry before Graham gets back.

Minutes pass, and I more or less stop checking the time because I'm driving myself crazy with anxiety. Not soon enough, I finally see Bowen and Graham walking toward the car. My heart squeezes in my chest at the sight of him. His collar is popped, the knot of his tie loose, and he's carrying his jacket with his sleeves rolled up. Disheveled as hell, but still devilishly handsome. And mine. Despite all of this, he's mine.

That's not nothing.

Graham gets into the car first. He takes my hand and kisses it, and as tame as the gesture is, it instantly lights my insides on fire, temporarily banishing my fear and grief. Our eyes meet and everything slows to a fading pulse. It'll be okay, I realize. We'll figure it out.

"Well, this is cozy," Bowen says, sliding in on Graham's other side and closing the door behind her. Graham looks over at her and Bowen grins. "What an honor to be packed into the back seat of a car like a can of sardines with the bride and groom on their special day."

"What's the status of Abbie's case?" Graham asks, not seeing the humor in the situation.

Bow huffs out a breath. "They have nothing besides Natasha's word. In my professional opinion, the prosecution would have a hell of a time trying to prove this overdose was at the hand of someone else. There is absolutely no evidence that supports that."

"So the case is closed," Graham says, sounding relieved.

Bowen frowns. "I didn't say that. The ball's still in their court."

"So we can't go home?" he asks, squeezing my hand.

"You can. But Abbie's bail stipulates that she can't leave the City. She's going to have to stay at the apartment here in Manhattan. Unfortunately."

I watch Graham mull this over, his jaw clenching. "Fine. Take her to the apartment. I'll go back to the estate to be with Jude. She's going to need me. And I'm going to have to tell her that her mother is awake. Jesus Christ."

As Bowen instructs the driver to take us to the address in Central Park West, every good feeling that was blooming in my heart withers and dies. I hadn't expected Graham to be able to stay with me, but hearing him so easily choose to abandon me on what should be our wedding night? It still hurts. I know he needs to take care of Jude, but what about me?

We should have exchanged our vows by now. We should already legally be man and wife. But instead of us spending the night together, I'm going to be all by myself in a large, empty apartment. It isn't fair. None of this is fair. I guess Bowen was right about that.

Swallowing down another round of tears, I clear my throat and ask Graham, "What happened with the assault? Who did you get in a fight with?"

"I ran into Quinn," is all he offers in explanation, avoiding my gaze.

169

My stomach does a slow roll. He punched *Quinn?* Why? Quinn is with Natasha. Why is Graham starting fights with the person his ex-wife is sleeping with?

Did he realize he still has feelings for her, now that she's awake? Does he...want her back? Does he regret moving so quickly with me?

What if he decides he doesn't want to reschedule our wedding?

"Graham?" I ask softly.

"I can't talk about it right now, love," is all he says. "I know you've been through hell and back, but let's just get you tucked away safe and sound. We both need rest."

He covers my hand with his, but it does little to soothe my worries. We spend the rest of the drive to the apartment in silence.

Chapter Twenty

Abbie

New York City's famous lights sprawl before me like a terrestrial galaxy, glowing warmly from countless windows and skyscrapers and traffic signals in the semi-darkness of the urban jungle. It should be beautiful, but it only makes me feel more trapped inside this apartment. A fucking glass box stuffed with luxury but no soul. But even the million-dollar view can't negate the harsh, relentless sounds of the horns and alarms and sirens out there. This city is so massive, so unknowable, so chaotic and bustling and full of life.

I hate it.

I want to go home. Back to the estate. I don't want to be in this fucking apartment, surrounded by couture furniture and cold modern art. Natasha's perfume lingers in the air, like it's being pumped in through the vents, and this whole place smells like her, feels like her. It's an extension of her being, and everything in it serves as a reminder that I can't escape her claws.

And then there's me, sitting illuminated by a single

lamp, my reflection emphasizing just how lonely I am. A lost little girl in a wedding dress, caught in the belly of the beast. It's almost midnight, which adds to the cursed ambiance of the place. Though I suppose the good news is that this day is soon to be over.

I press my forehead against the cool glass, closing my eyes to let myself mourn the loss of what today was supposed to be. What my life was supposed to be. Who knows what will happen now? I don't even know if Graham still wants to be with me. What my future holds.

My phone sits lifeless next to me. I've been here for hours, and still no texts from Graham. No calls from Jude. Nothing from Amanda, either. I'm truly alone in this horrible apartment, away from everything I hold dear. I'm debating a bath to drown my woes in when I hear the sound of a key in the lock.

I freeze, heart leaping in my throat, terrified it's Natasha. She might actually murder me if she catches me in here—especially wearing this dress. I bolt, and I'm halfway down the hall that goes to Jude's room when I hear a voice call out. It's Graham.

"Abbie?"

Slowly, I turn, and then make my way back to the living room on quiet bare feet. The second Graham hears my footsteps, he runs up to me and gathers me in his arms. I let him hold me tight, breathing the smell of him through his shirt as relief washes over me. He's here. He's really here. He came back for me.

"Are you okay?"

I can't respond except to shake my head silently. And then all of me starts shaking.

We stand there, pressed together, his palms warm against my back and my hands locked around his waist. Graham whispers soft, soothing words into my hair, and I melt into him, tears spilling down my cheeks. He only holds me tighter, letting me get it all out, until the shaking stops and I pull back to wipe my eyes.

"I'm sorry it took so long to get back," he says, leading me to the couch to sit down. "I wanted to see Jude, but by the time I got there she was already asleep, and then I had to meet with the staff to debrief everyone, and then the drive all the way back—"

I interrupt his explanation with a long kiss. "You're here now. That's all that matters."

"God. This whole day has been such shit." He sighs deeply, then laughs through his nose. "Well, not the whole day. It started off rather perfectly, if I do say so myself."

"That feels like it was days ago." It's hard to believe it was only this morning that Graham snuck into my room to pleasure me just before what was supposed to be our wedding. "I can't believe today was...today."

"I can't believe my wife is a common criminal," he says with a healthy dose of teasing to his voice.

"Future wife," I remind him ruefully, managing to keep the tears locked away. I don't want to cry anymore, not with him here. "Though I suppose I'll fit right in. You know what they say about the Ratliffs—common criminals, all of them."

"Oh, you have no idea," Graham growls, nuzzling my neck.

My sadness evaporates in an instant, replaced by

something else entirely, something more primal. Hungrier. When he sucks on my earlobe, my center runs hot and I let out a moan.

"I don't know if we should be doing this, Graham. We're not married yet," I tease.

In between the kisses he's trailing down my neck, he says, "Nonsense. I demand that you be my wife. Today. Now. This very second."

I laugh, just a little. "Do you know anyone who can get here now to officiate?"

"No. But I have a better idea."

"Which is...?"

Graham pulls me off the couch and walks me over to the window, then carefully spins me so my back is against his chest. Our reflections meld together in the glass, and I watch him drop a row of kisses across each of my shoulders, his fingers gently running down my arms. I watch him caress me in front of all of New York City, his hands expertly working my dress off, until I'm left standing there in my strapless corset, garter belt, and ivory silk underwear.

"I don't think this is going to make us married," I whisper, head falling to the side so he can kiss higher up my neck. "We've done this plenty and haven't been wed."

"You don't think so?" Graham murmurs, keeping himself very busy. I take a deep breath and goosebumps of pleasure break out across my skin. "Consummating the marriage is a very important step."

"But we didn't get to the marriage part," I murmur, the words dripping slowly out of my mouth like molasses. He is so very good at doing things to me. I can barely even stand, thanks to how weak my knees are. "We can't consummate what didn't happen."

"Who says we need someone else to marry us?" he says.

"Um, the state?"

Graham laughs. He wraps his arms around me and rests his chin on the top of my head. "There has always been marriage, my love, but the state is fairly new."

"The state has been around for hundreds of years."

"And people for a millennia. How do you think they celebrated unions?"

Something hot and heavy flares in my lower belly. "Naughty boy."

"Come with me." Graham takes my hand and leads me down the hall, into his bedroom.

Thank God he and Natasha had their own separate rooms. I'd die before I'd spend my wedding night in Natasha's bed.

As soon as the door closes, he cups my face and kisses me so hard it steals my breath. I melt into him, forgetting every horrible detail of the day as his tongue strokes mine, as he gently bites my bottom lip. All that matters right now is me and him.

"I've been dreaming of undressing you all day. But I never expected this," Graham murmurs, kissing my shoulder as he begins unfastening the hook and eye closures down the back of my lacy corset. "You look absolutely stunning."

"Want to leave it on?" I ask slyly.

"God no." He finishes with the corset and flings it away, pulling back to rake his hot gaze over my bare breasts. "You look stunning in lingerie, but you are impeccable in the nude. And that is precisely how I like you best."

"Are you sure about that?"

Locking my eyes on his, I slide my hand slowly down my chest, down my torso, over my belly, finally dipping my fingers beneath the waistband of my outrageously frilly and overly complicated garter belt. It's made of cream lace and pale blue ribbons, with double straps in the front and the back that connect to the thigh-high sheer stockings I'm wearing.

"You know...when I got dressed this morning," I tell him, slowly trailing my fingertips over the lingerie's straps and bows, "I made sure to put my panties on last, over the garter belt, in case you might enjoy leaving it on me during the...events of our wedding night."

Graham's jaw drops a little. "How are you so perfect?" he whispers throatily.

I grin. "I'm not. I'm just perfect for you."

"So it seems."

He steps back and undresses methodically, and I try not to drool at the sight of him getting more and more naked by the second. When he's finished, his cock standing at the ready, I go to him and wrap my arms around his neck, pulling him in for a long kiss. His hands slide up and down my back, then cup my ass, then move to my front to squeeze me through my panties. I have to push him away to catch my breath. My heart is pounding hard in my chest.

"Graham. I need you. Take me to bed," I pant.

Without a word, he lifts me into his arms and carries

me over to the bed, where he lays me down and peels off my skimpy underwear, leaving my garter belt and thigh-highs on. Then he climbs onto the bed, kissing his way up from my ankles to my lips, his hands stroking me as he goes. When he snaps the elastic straps of the garter belt against my thighs, all I can do is moan softly at the sweet mixture of pleasure and pain, clinging to the sheets, my core aching so bad I start grinding against the air. I feel his lips curving into a smile as we kiss, but I'm finding no humor in this. I'm on fucking fire. I need him inside me.

Emboldened by the sheer force of my desire, I grab his cock, squeezing hard as I use it to trace the wet mouth of my opening. I'm ready for him. I'm so ready. But before I can draw him into me, he moves his lips to my ear and whispers, "I, Graham Elliott Ratliff, take thee, Abigail Eileen Montgomery, to be my unlawfully wedded wife. I will live for you. I will die for you. From this day forward, for richer or for poorer. In sickness and in health. In blissful moments and in the hard moments. I will cherish you until the end of my days."

His words cut straight through me, instantly making me go still. With another kiss, Graham repositions himself so we're hip to hip, his thick cock pushing against my slit, and I spread my legs wide to take him in. He glides right into me, as easy as a hot knife through butter, filling me so perfectly that the world seems to go fuzzy for a moment.

"Oh my *God*, yes," I whimper, shivering as I reflexively clench around him.

"Abigail Montgomery," he goes on, "I will love you

when you smell like horses. I will love you when you talk back. I will love you on your best days and your worst."

He starts to thrust, his movements solid and sure as he rocks into me. I'm clawing at his back, gasping in his ear as he continues making his pledges into mine.

"I will love you when you are two hundred miles away at school or when I am an ocean away on business. I will love you when the sun sets and when the moon rises. Every day, I will love you more than the last. And that is my solemn vow."

He's been picking up his pace as he speaks, and now he's pumping into me so hard I'm crying out with every thrust, euphoria washing over me. He feels so good, so *fucking* good, it's all I can do to cling to him as he makes love to me. But now it's my turn to offer my vows.

"I, Abigail Eileen Montgomery, take thee, Graham Elliott Ratliff, to be my unlawfully wedded husband." I laugh with the pure joy of it, blinking back happy tears as I say the words that make our union feel so much more real, so much more unbreakable. "For richer or poorer, for better or worse, I give you myself, body and soul. I promise to be yours as long as I live."

We're moaning together, the heat of our bodies multiplying by the second, kissing and laughing even as it gets harder to breathe. Graham starts grunting, getting louder, more primal, the headboard knocking against the wall faster and faster. I claw my nails down his back and grab his ass to pull him even closer, as if he could ever get close enough.

"I'll love you every day of my life, Graham. I'll love you when you work too much or forget anniversaries. I will love you forever and never leave your side. That is my solemn vow."

Graham threads his fingers with mine over my head and gazes down into my eyes with love and desire and a steadiness I can't look away from. I can't describe what I'm feeling, how connected we are. This is more than love, more than sex. I've never felt so close to him.

"I declare us husband and wife," Graham says. "I may now kiss the bride."

He dips his head down and we kiss, and everything else in the world disappears. My body takes flight. An intense orgasm spills through me like liquid gold, lighting me up from head to toe, stealing my breath. I'm moaning my lover's name, letting out curses and cries of pleasure, and Graham buries his face in my neck and rapidly follows suit. We hold each other tight as we come, shuddering, squeezing every last drop of bliss from the high of marrying each other on our own terms. We revel in the moment, giving ourselves to each other, knowing we are safer and better together.

"Mine," Graham murmurs. "Forever."

"Forever," I agree.

We spend the rest of the night celebrating.

Chapter Twenty-One

Graham

Leaving Abbie behind at the apartment rips a gaping hole in my chest. I belong with her, she belongs with me, and both of us belong outside of this godforsaken city. New York was always Natasha's domain—Broadway, the bright lights, the never-ending buzz of eight-and-a-half million people, the sheer mad energy of the place. She's always thrived amid such chaos, fed off of it. Whereas my heart belongs in the country, with wide open spaces and fresh air to breathe.

I lived in London for years, so when we moved to the States, I wasn't unprepared for what city life would demand of me...but I hated it. My life flows better in the Hudson Valley; it's where my soul flourishes. It's home.

Now, though, home has a new meaning. Home used to mean the expansive grounds and the sprawling estate, the marble floors and high ceilings, the stables and tennis courts and pools and whatever other luxurious frippery my heart desired, all contained in one place. I can't even say the definition changed with the birth of my daughter, because she was, once upon a time, just another accomplishment to extol, another piece of art to display. Another worry to fret over.

But everything changed with Abbie. It shouldn't have. I'm old enough to not believe in fairy tales any longer. The veil has been lifted from my eyes, and I know I got where I am today because I didn't rely on rose-colored glasses. And yet.

Home is wherever her smile is. Home is wherever her hands find mine. Home is where I can bask in her presence and know that everything will be okay. Home is also with Jude, who owns more real estate in my heart than I own in the real world. And that's largely thanks to Abbie, too, and her insistence I get my head out of my ass and back into caring for my child.

I am the person I am today because of Abbie. But I don't know what it's going to take for us to get our happy ending. For us to finally be free and clear of Natasha's malicious schemes. It's all I can ruminate on as I stare out the window of the hired car on the drive from New York City back to the Hudson Valley.

When I arrive, I find Jude in the kitchen, baking with the women of the house. Amanda is still here, hired on as a temporary nanny until we can work out Abbie's legal woes. I appreciate having the extra help, but seeing someone else at Jude's side leaves a pit in my stomach. As if I need any further reminders that I need to get this fucked-up situation sorted once and for good.

As soon Jude sees me, she sprints around the island and dives into my arms.

"*Daddy*! Esmeralda told me you came home last

night, but when I woke up this morning you were already gone again. Why isn't Abbie with you? Why did the police come and stop the wedding?" Her questions tumble out of her mouth in rapid succession, her tiny hummingbird heart beating so hard I can feel it against my own chest. "When is Abbie coming home? Is it true what they said when they took her away?"

I feel Amanda's and Mary's eyes on me as I hold my daughter tight. I should have spent the drive here coming up with an explanation that wouldn't destroy her. Business associates are one thing, but the kindhearted girl who all but runs my house is a different animal entirely.

Still, Natasha brought this upon herself. There's nothing I can do now but tell Jude the truth about how beastly her mother is. It's time. This child deserves to know.

And yet something catches my tongue. Abbie wouldn't do this. There's no love lost between Abbie and Natasha, but Abbie still wouldn't decry Jude's own mother, knowing how painful it would be for a child to see their parent as a villain.

I feel the sharp gaze of Mary from across the kitchen, and realize I can't do it either.

But I can tell as much of the truth as possible.

"Let's sit, love," I tell Jude. "We have a lot to talk about."

"Is it bad stuff?" Jude says, her face falling.

"It's not going to be an easy conversation, love," I admit. "But it's important that you know what's going on. Ladies, may we have a few minutes?"

"Of course." Mary nods, motioning to Amanda.

"We'll be scarce."

Jude settles back on her stool at the island and looks up at me with big doe eyes, anxiety written all over her face. Anger overtakes me for a fleeting instance, where all I want is for Natasha to have her turn rotting in a cold jail cell for bringing this grief upon us. But I take a deep breath and try to clear my mind of everything but the needs of the worried girl before me.

"You know how your mum has been sick at the hospital?" I begin.

Jude nods solemnly.

"Well...she woke up from her coma this morning."

Jude's face lights up. "So she's better now? When can we go see her? Why hasn't she called—"

"That's just it, love. She's not all the way better yet. Sometimes, when people fall into a coma like your mum did, they wake up and they're very confused at first. Their bodies might not be sick anymore, but their mind can be muddled. So that's what happened. When your mum woke up, she wasn't feeling like herself. And..." I take a breath. "And she said that she thought Abbie tried to hurt her. On purpose. So that is why the police came here and took Abbie away."

Jude's mouth falls open, and she slumps on her stool. It takes her a moment to process everything I've just told her, and then she says, "I heard what the police said. They said 'attempted murder.' That's because Mommy said so?"

I forcibly unclench my jaw. "Yes. She's very confused and upset now that she's awake."

"But Abbie would never do that. Right?"

"That's right, love." I place my hands gently on her shoulders and look into her eyes. "But even so, the police are checking out every single possibility. They have to make sure that Abbie wasn't involved. That's their job."

Jude frowns. "But they can't arrest people if they don't have any proof, right?"

"They can't *keep* people without proof. And they did not keep Abbie. There is no proof."

"Then why isn't she here? Did she go back to Uncle Ford's house?"

"No. She's still in the city. The police want her to stay close by, in case they have to talk to her some more," I tell her. "But soon they'll figure out the truth: Abbie absolutely did not hurt your mother. The police are just being very thorough because it's a very serious situation."

"Did they want to talk to you, too? You were there that night. So was I."

I hesitate. We told Jude I was on a business trip while I was locked up. She would have been none the wiser about the entire situation if the police hadn't crashed my wedding.

"They did talk to me," I say, leaning on as much truth as I can without spilling my guts. "But I didn't stay long." Which is not entirely inaccurate.

"But what if...what if Abbie did hurt Mommy?" Jude asks worriedly.

"She didn't," I say firmly. "I don't think anyone hurt your mother. I think she took too much of her medicine and it made her very sick. That's all it was. The police will realize this soon, too, and then Abbie will be able to come home. I think it is a very unfortunate situation."

Jude nods. She doesn't look at me anymore, just picks at the skin around her thumbnail. I see a tear trickle down her face, but she wipes it away. "When can I see Mommy again? And when is Abbie coming home? This isn't fair."

My chest hurts. "I know, love. We'll visit your mother again soon." *Even though she's a lying whore*, I think to myself bitterly. "Once she's feeling like herself again, and the doctors say she's able to have visitors, we'll go see her. You have my word. And Abbie will be home just as soon as she can. It's a lot of waiting, I know, but I'm here now. We can wait it out together."

Jude sighs, her entire demeanor dragging down into the same cesspool I feel myself sinking into. We both can't be depressed about this. I have to be strong for my daughter.

"Why don't we go riding?" I say. When in doubt, always rely on horses with Jude. Still, she doesn't perk up, only shrugs her shoulders, her eyes trained on the marble countertop. "Maybe some fresh air will help clear our heads."

"I want Abbie." Jude sniffs. "I want Abbie to come riding with us."

I encase her hand in mine. "I do, too. But we can go without her, just this once."

"Maybe we can go stay with her in New York," Jude suggests.

"I wish we could. But it's best to stay here right now. There's a lot going on with her and the police, still—she's got quite a lot on her plate at the moment. But try not to worry. We have a whole team of lawyers working with the police to help figure this out." I squeeze her hand again. "We'll get through this, Jude. For now, let's get our riding gear on, and I'll have Cassie get the horses ready. I think we could both use some time in the saddle."

Jude nods her head and slides off the stool without saying another word. I hate this for her. I hate this for me. I hate this for Abbie. It's a miserable turn for all of us.

After a quick call to Cassie to ready the horses, I head to my room to change, silently cursing Natasha the whole time. As I'm pulling up my jodhpurs, I get a call from the PI handling my case. I slip into my bathroom, shut the door, and answer it.

"This is quite the goddamn case," Daniel says by way of greeting. "I'm still working on clearing Miss Montgomery, but I wanted to check in because I've discovered something else that needs your immediate attention."

I scrub my hand over my face and take a deep, steadying breath. I can't let myself spiral right now. "I'm listening."

"There's some money missing from one of your accounts."

"Okay... How much is 'some'?"

There's a pause. "Uh. A significant amount."

"*Daniel.*"

He sighs. "Two million dollars. She stole two million dollars from you."

"What did you just say?" I must have heard him wrong.

"One of your business accounts is short two million dollars, Mr. Ratliff. It was wire transferred to an offshore account in Miss Montgomery's name."

"That's impossible."

"You're welcome to check yourself. In fact, please do. Because believe me, I'd love nothing more than to find out I'm wrong about this."

And just like that, the floor drops out from under my feet, my vision going red. Abbie stole from me? She came into my house and integrated into my family and *stole* from me?

But this can't be right. She wouldn't do this. "There's been some kind of misunderstanding. We signed a prenup, on her insistence. Abbie isn't interested in my money."

"I'm sure she was happy to sign whatever the fuck she felt like, because she already had the money in her pocket. You didn't notice two million dollars go missing?"

His tone grates my nerves almost more than the information he's given. "It's a mistake."

"You've got blinders on, my man. Thinking with your dick. I've got all the paperwork to prove it. I'll send it right over."

Fury pumps through me. "Accuse her one more time and see what happens. You're wrong."

"Whatever you say, boss. I'm sending over the information, and you're welcome to do with it what you will. I'll call you when I know more."

He hangs up and I stand there, half dressed, unsure what to do. Abbie would never steal from me. I know her too well—that's not who she is.

But Natasha...

Natasha is just desperate enough to try to pull something like this off.

Chapter Twenty-Two

Abbie

THE APARTMENT IS cavernous without anyone in it. Lavish, yes, but bleak. Graham offered to keep a skeleton crew of staff here for me, but I declined. It would feel too weird, having all these people wait on me when I don't have one of the Ratliffs with me.

Because I'm not a Ratliff yet, no matter what Graham and I promised each other under the sheets. Legally, I'm still a Montgomery—and legally, I'm still suspected of attempted murder. Neither of those things scream "wife of Graham Ratliff." Graham is the kind of man who needs a partner who is poised, confident, someone who the public adores. Someone like...Natasha.

Except without all the crazy.

The longer I sit in this apartment, the more certain I become that I can never live up to that level of person. Yes, I grew up wealthy and my parents still have a large house, but nothing in my life ever compared to the life Graham and Jude have. Who am I, even? The nanny. The help. The daughter of the best friend who never lived up to the same potential. I'm nobody.

I don't deserve Graham or Jude. All my presence has done is cause drama. Big drama. Follow-you-around-with-cameras drama. Jude, especially, doesn't deserve this. And now she's going to know way more about this scandal than we ever wanted her to know, because the police broke up my wedding in front of God and every-body. I shamed the entire family. I am shit.

Though I'm starting to regret turning down the company, even if it would've only been a housekeeper or two. I'm curled up on the couch under a blanket, wearing sweatpants and a T-shirt I found in Graham's room, with every TV in the whole place turned on just for ambient noise. I've got Turner Classic Movies on in the guest room, the Disney Plus app playing cartoons in Jude's room, and reality TV (cooking competitions) in the living room. But no news channels, no radio, and no current events. I don't want to hear anything about Natasha or Graham or myself from the media. Because whatever it is, it's not going to be good. At least I've had a few Face-Time chats with Amanda, checking in and giving me pep talks. That's about the only thing that's keeping me sane.

The doorbell rings and I race across the apartment for it, relieved that the Thai I ordered on my food delivery app has finally arrived. I've barely eaten since I got here, but this morning I woke up with a craving for pad see ew and green curry. When I open the door, the delivery guy has his phone held up in one hand and the bag of food in the other.

I pull up short. "Um—"

"I knew it was you!" he exclaims. I hear the camera on his phone snapping away as he takes photos.

Holding a hand in front of my face, I grab the food and then back into the apartment, slamming the door in his face. My adrenaline is pumping, anger flaring through me at the audacity of this guy. I will never get used to this kind of notoriety. I feel violated and gross.

I drop the bag on the coffee table and then sink back onto the couch, my stomach twisted in knots. Maybe this is exactly what I deserve. This entire mess. After all, I took the nanny job to get closer to Graham, partly at my dad's insistence and partly because I just plain wanted Graham. Either way, my intentions weren't good—I went to the Ratliff estate to infiltrate a family and a home for personal gain. Financial and otherwise.

But God, my dad gave me no choice. We were so broke. He was months overdue on the mortgage, hundreds of thousands of dollars in debt, and had already sold off most of his stocks and investments just trying to stay afloat. He'd laid on the guilt, talking about how expensive my upbringing had been, how spoiled I was compared to him at my age. I didn't want him and my mom to lose the house. Mom especially. She loves that house. She's poured her love and care into every refinished plank of hardwood, every designer light fixture, every antique figurine and Pantone-approved accent wall and dupioni silk curtain panel. Where would they even go?

I could see my entire future, and theirs, slipping down the drain if I didn't cave in to my father's plan. So off I went.

Maybe it doesn't matter that as I got to know Jude and Graham all over again, I genuinely fell in love with both of them. Maybe there's no way to make up for my original reasons for coming. Maybe, even if Graham and Jude could forgive me, I can't forgive myself.

I'm still brooding, listlessly picking at my rapidly congealing pad see ew, when my phone rings. It's Amanda, on FaceTime. Yes! I scramble to mute the TV and then pick up.

"Hey, you." I try to sound upbeat, as if I haven't been wallowing in self-pity for the last several hours. "How's it going? How's Jude today?"

"We're okay, but um...I was actually hoping you could talk to her for a minute?" Amanda says. "She's not feeling the best. She really misses you."

In the background, I hear sniffling. My heart aches. "Jude, sweetie, is that you?"

Amanda turns and looks off screen. She quietly encourages Jude to take the phone, and after a minute, she finally does. Part of Jude's face comes into view, just the top of her head, but even from this angle I can tell she's a mess.

"Oh, Jude." The words tumble out of my mouth like a sigh. "I'm so sorry I'm not there."

Jude sniffs in response, her breathing jagged, still too emotionally distraught to speak.

"You know I would do anything to be back home, right? But I can't. Not yet."

There's a long silence and I decide to not fill it up. Jude is probably terrified, and hearing me say it's going to be okay is a waste of breath when it doesn't feel like it ever will be.

"I just want you to know that it's okay to be upset right now," I tell her. "It's okay to be mad or scared or confused, or whatever else. Because this is really hard. It really sucks."

"But I want to see you. And I want to see my mom. Daddy said she's still sick, even though she's awake. He said she...she thinks you tried to hurt her. But I know you didn't. She's just confused," Jude chokes out between sobs, still not looking into the camera.

"Oh, sweetie." This weighs so heavy on me, I can feel it in my chest. "I know this is a lot to put on you, and you've been so strong. But it's going to be okay. The police are going to figure it all out soon, and your dad's lawyers are going to help them, and your mom's going to get better and you're going to see her soon, too. Okay? And in the meantime, I'm living my best life down here in New York. I'm getting lots of ideas for fun things we can do the next time we're all here together."

"Okay." Jude wipes her nose and finally centers the camera so I can see her whole face. "I miss you so much."

"I miss you, too. So, so much." Sadness punches me in the gut as soon as I say the words. All I feel is overpowering grief. I can only imagine how Jude feels. "But I'll be back before you know it. The police just made a mistake about me, because your mom...like you said, she's confused, and now it has to get fixed."

Please God, let this get fixed. And soon. Please, let me get back to my people.

"I love you, Jude. More than all the stars in the sky.

We're all going to be together again soon, and you can call me any time. In fact, I'm so bored all by myself here that you'd be doing me a huge favor. So can you please do that for me? Call me a lot."

Jude nods, looking a little better. "Okay. Whenever I want?"

"Of course. And I need you to be good for Amanda, too."

But Jude isn't listening anymore. She's shouting over her shoulder, "Dad! Abbie said I can call her whenever I want to!"

Immediately, my heart races. I miss Graham so much it hurts. We were together just yesterday, but it already feels like it's been an eternity since I saw him or felt his touch.

"Is that Abbie, love?" His deep, lilting voice sinks straight to my core. He takes the phone from Jude and says, "Give us a few minutes, please, will you?"

"Sure thing," Amanda's voice says in the background. "We'll be in the living room."

"Bye, Abbie!" Jude says. Graham turns the phone to face her so she can wave to me. "I love you and I miss you and I'll be good for Amanda. And I'll call you all the time, okay?"

"Promise?" I say.

"Promise!"

I see Jude walk away and then the phone jostles and I'm suddenly face to face with Graham. Calm settles over me for the first time since he left New York.

"God, I miss you." He takes a breath. "It's not right, being so far from you."

"I hate this," is all I can say. I'm trying so hard not to crack, not to cry.

"I know, love. But I spoke with the private investigator this morning and I wanted to keep you updated on what he's found so far. It appears...that Natasha has been very busy."

Fear pumps my heart harder. The PI was supposed to be working in conjunction with the lawyers to clear my name. What the hell has Natasha been up to? "What do you mean, *busy*? Like, busy beyond accusing me of murder?"

Graham looks over his shoulder before continuing and then lowers his voice. "It looks like she stole some money from my account. Siphoned off two million dollars."

My jaw drops. I don't know what horror I expected, but it wasn't that. "Are you serious? But how—why would she think she could get away with that? Wouldn't she know she'd get caught? Was she expecting you to just let her keep it?"

"I don't know." His face sours. "We're still trying to put it all together. Compile evidence, get it all ready to go to the police. Since God knows they can't do any solid detective work themselves."

I nod. "Okay. So what do we do in the meantime?"

"Keep our heads down and wait. I know that's not what you want to hear, but believe me, I'm doing everything I can to figure out this mess. Bowen's firm and the PI are digging into the banking fraud as we speak, and we're putting together the best plan of attack to clear your name as soon as possible. I promise, I'm going to fix this."

I desperately want to believe Graham, but I don't know if I can. Because as far as I can tell, whether Graham and his team of lawyers can "fix" this or not, my life has already completely imploded.

All thanks to Natasha Ratliff.

Chapter Twenty-Three

Abbie

WHEN I WAS LITTLE, I had recurring nightmares in black and white. My dreams were usually in color, but the nightmares...it was almost like they needed one more layer of fright to truly terrify my five-year-old self.

The actual details were always fuzzy when I woke up. The only thing I could be sure of was that I'd been running from something horrible. Something hell-bent on catching me. I'm not sure what that says about my childhood psyche, but the bad dreams started to taper off right around the time I started high school. As if my daytime social anxiety was so omnipresent that I no longer had the headspace for nightmares anymore.

They've come roaring back this week, though. Plaguing me with shadowy visions.

I've fallen from buildings, from cliffs, from snowy mountain tops. I've drowned. Burned. Crashed a car. I've lost my voice, lost my ability to use a telephone. I've seen Graham and Jude turn their backs on me. Walked through the paper-strewn halls of my old high school, with everyone pointing at me and shoving tabloids in my face. I've been lost in a house that's a maze, unable to find my way out. Some of these dreams sound ridiculous after the fact, but they all leave me tossing and turning, waking with an intense heaviness in the pit of my stomach.

"What are you doing before bed? Watching horror movies?" Amanda asks during our morning FaceTime. Jude is at her lessons, so we can talk candidly.

I mumble out something that kind of sounds like the truth, because I'm embarrassed to admit it. It doesn't work on Amanda, though, who merely gives me *the look* and rolls her eyes. There are definitely perks to having a friend who knows me so well, but right now doesn't really apply, not when I'm trying to lie to myself.

"If you seriously just said you've been staying up late reading *all the news articles* about your case, then I have to say, it is blatantly obvious why you're having night terrors." Amanda frowns at me, sternness coloring her voice.

"I know I shouldn't, but I can't stop," I moan. "Everyone is calling me a homewrecker and a murderess. Can you believe that shit? They were divorced! Because *she* cheated on *him*! And it was an overdose! But no. Somehow Natasha's the media darling again and I'm the villain."

"I'm sorry, babe. It's just how the press works. They'll move on soon enough, just you wait, and then everyone will forget your name," she soothes.

"I hope you're right." I drop onto the couch, sighing in frustration. "I'm just so freaked out that the longer it takes to clear my name, the more likely it is that Graham is going to start doubting my innocence."

"He would never. He's been on the phone with his lawyers all day every day, trying to get your name cleared. Don't forget he was also arrested for attempted murder— he knows it's total bullshit. And he also knows Natasha better than anyone. He's not going to abandon you."

"Yeah." I chew on my thumbnail, watching the TV switch over from a Swiffer commercial to an ad for a news channel. My picture briefly flashes on screen in a montage of other recent news stories, and my stomach immediately clenches. "Jesus. This is the worst thing that's ever happened to me."

"It is pretty shitty," she concedes.

"Pretty shitty?" I scoff. "Amanda, I was arrested on my *wedding day*. For fucking *murder*."

"*Attempted* murder. Besides, all the cool kids get arrested for attempted murder these days. You, Graham, that football player from Nebraska. Look at it this way, you two now have something to really bond over. Who else knows what it feels like to have your ex frame you for murder besides you two?"

I know she's trying to add some levity to the situation to make me feel better, but it's not working. It's still too soon. I'm still in the thick of this, for fuck's sake.

"Maybe you should get out of the apartment for a little while," Amanda suggests, interrupting my sulking. "Some fresh air might do you good. Plus, a break from screens."

"I can't. I tried to walk to the Starbucks on the corner yesterday and I got pointed at on the way there and then stopped by two people before I even set foot inside the door."

"People *stopped* you?"

"Yup." My voice is clipped as the memories wash over me. "Apparently they felt it was their duty to tell me I was trash and that they hoped I'd go to jail and stay there. It was so humiliating and awful. So yeah. Not gonna be leaving the building anymore, unless it's absolutely necessary. Although I guess it doesn't even matter, since I found a shitty note slipped under the door this morning. Which, it had to be someone who lives here."

"Assholes," Amanda commiserates. "What'd it say?"

I'm just about to tell her when I hear a key in the lock. It's either Natasha or Graham. Please let it be Graham.

"Gah, I need to go. It's the door. I'll call you back."

"Go, go!" Amanda yells and we hang up.

"Abbie?" Graham calls out, closing the door behind him. His voice is so gentle, so concerned, that I can't help feeling comforted before I've even seen his face.

I get off the couch and pad over to him in my stolen loungewear, smiling guiltily as he gives me a once-over. "I, um, borrowed a few things out of your dresser."

"I'm glad. Those sweats look much sexier on you," he says.

He pulls me in for a kiss, and I immediately wish I wasn't standing here with a greasy ponytail and no makeup and a men's large T-shirt and sweatpants combo.

"Give me ten minutes. I need to jump in the shower real quick," I tell him.

But I don't even need ten whole minutes to get ready,

because all I have in the guest room en suite is a toothbrush, some tinted moisturizer I left here last time, and a tube of Jude's pink lemonade flavored lip balm. It'll have to do.

As soon as I go back to the living room, wrapped in the thick cotton guest room bathrobe with my hair still damp, Graham pulls me into a tight embrace. I lean into him hard, letting his heat radiate through me, drinking in the touch and scent and feel of him.

"It's been too many days since I've seen you," he murmurs against my ear. "I'm so sorry. I've been so busy with the PI and the lawyers and trying to get all of this figured out—"

"I know. Don't be sorry," I say, squeezing him harder.

Graham slides the robe off my shoulder and leaves a trail of hot kisses there, gently guiding me backwards down the hallway to his bedroom, fumbling for his belt as we go.

"I hate being away from you, love." His voice drops into something throaty and the warmth between my legs begins to radiate upward. "It's destroying me."

"Me, too." The words tumble out as he places more kisses around my neck and throat.

"We're going to get you home again soon," he promises. He kicks the door shut behind him and then unties my robe, pulling it open. "And then I'll never let you go."

He drops my robe to the floor and I stand before him naked, shivering as beads of water from my hair roll down my chest, causing goosebumps to rise all over my body. His eyes take me in slowly, until, with a hiss of lust, he lifts me in his arms. I wrap my legs around his waist, feeling his cock raging in his pants as he carries me over to the bed. After he throws me onto the mattress, he climbs over me, his greedy mouth finding my nipples.

"Fuck," I groan as he sucks on me, digging my hands into his hair.

Graham dips a hand between my legs and fingers me open, his thumb stroking long ellipticals from my clit to my opening. I'm already wet and hungry for him. He's still fully dressed, but I can't wait one more second. Wrapping my hand around his, I hold him steady and start grinding against his thumb. Still tugging my nipples with his teeth, Graham adjusts his fingers so there are two of them inside me, his thumb moving up to cover my clit.

I cry out as I fuck his fingers, harder and harder, needing this orgasm to wash me clean. When I beg for more he adds a third finger, and I roll us both over on the bed so that I'm on top of him, dragging my pussy back and forth over his plunging fingers, rocking so hard that my breasts sway back and forth over his open mouth, his tongue darting out to lave them.

Seconds later I'm coming, so fast I barely have a chance to feel it, the shockwaves hitting me hard but dissipating quickly. It's not enough, not by far. I need more.

Moving onto my knees beside him, I start tugging at the buttons of his shirt. I'm frantic, still keyed up, still breathing hard. One of his buttons goes flying across the room, and he lets out a quiet laugh, gently taking my hand in his.

"You can slow down, love," he says. "I'm not going anywhere."

His voice is so soothing, so full of love, that I can't even handle it. My eyes fill with tears and I curl up next to him and start to cry, my fingers twining in his shirt. Graham pulls me into his arms and repositions us back against the headboard, rocking me slowly as I weep. The whole time, he strokes my back, telling me it's going to be okay. That we are going to be okay.

By the time I get myself back under control, my whole face is a wet, soggy mess.

"I think I need another shower," I tell him.

"Alone? Or would you like some company?"

"I'd love some company. I just need a minute first."

After I get a little alone time, Graham joins me under the hot spray of the dual showerheads, and we take turns slowly soaping each other down. This is nothing like the fast, frantic shower I had earlier. There's no rush, no panic. I inhale the steam deeply, my stress and anxiety almost seeming to wash right off, right down the drain, along with the grapefruit-scented bubbles and the soothing warm water.

Soon we're kissing again, squeezing each other's slick, naked bodies, whispering endless I love yous. I have his cock in my hand and I'm stroking him firmly, ready to drop to my knees and take him in my mouth, when he lifts my chin and gazes into my eyes.

"I've been wanting to try something," he says. "If you're ready."

His voice reverberates down my spine, and his other hand slips down the curve of my ass, his finger sliding up between my cheeks ever so slowly before it comes to a stop over my asshole. He gives it a light press, and I shiver at the contact.

"*Oh*," I say, my voice trembling a little.

"You can say no, love. I'd never pressure you."

"No. I mean, yes. I'm ready. I want to," I say honestly. "I'm a little scared, but I trust you."

"And I trust you."

He kisses me, and it's soft, lingering. His finger stays pressed against my hole the entire time, pulsing lightly, turning my insides to liquid flame. When I start to moan, he pulls away.

"Turn around. Spread your legs. Hold on to the towel bar."

My heart is pounding in my throat. I swallow hard and do as he says.

I'm aching now, desperate for his touch. I widen my stance and back my ass toward him, lifting it as high as I can. I have no idea what to expect, adrenaline and anticipation coursing through me along with the fear and the lust. It's a heady combination.

Graham comes up behind me, reaching around to finger my clit. Then he slides his dick into my pussy in one smooth, easy motion, pumping once, twice, and then a third slow, *oh-so-slow* thrust before pulling out again. I moan his name, and that's when I feel the tip of his cock slide between my ass cheeks, hot and slick with our juices.

This is it. My God.

I close my eyes and try to relax, try to not clench up and make this any more painful than necessary. But

Graham doesn't make any sudden moves. He lines himself up with the pert hole he's only toyed with before and gently strokes my ass cheek with the hand that isn't wedged between my legs. The hot water sprays down on us, and my knees start trembling.

"I love you. I will never hurt you intentionally. But this...likely will hurt," he says, whispering in my ear from behind me. "So if it's too much, say the word and I'll stop."

"What's the word?" I ask.

"Anything that's not the word *yes*. I don't want to hurt you. I will stop at any point if you're uncomfortable, if you're in pain, if you've changed your mind. Is that understood?"

I nod, and he kisses the back of my neck. "Yes."

He presses into me, hard and sure, the tip of his cock slowly splitting me open, and it steals my breath away, leaving me tightening involuntarily.

"Are you all right?" he asks.

"Yes," I tell him, gasping for air.

Graham pushes in a little further, then stops again when I hiss with pain. "More?"

"Yes."

He works my clit as he thrusts deeper inside, so slowly, so carefully. With each micro movement forward, he takes a pause and waits for me to relax again: thrust and hold. Another gentle thrust and hold. Together, we move like this until he shifts slowly, easily, into something with a little more friction. It opens something within me that yearns for him in new ways. The pain eases. Graham continues to rub my sweet, aching nub as he softly fucks my ass.

"Abbie. Oh, Abbie," he moans. "Abbie, Abbie, Abbie. Give yourself to me."

He's rock hard inside me, and his voice, desperately invoking my name, only ratchets up my lust another notch.

"Yes," I whimper. "Yes."

Our connection is so intense that tears fill my eyes. I'm shocked to realize that it's starting to feel good, tingling bursts of pleasure shooting straight to my clit, which Graham tugs between his thumb and forefinger with each thrust.

"I love you," I gasp. "That's a yes."

"Abbie. I love you, too."

I start lifting up on my toes to meet his thrusts, backing against him, so both of us are contributing to the push and pull, so I'm the one dictating the rhythm.

"Yes, Graham, yes," I moan. "You feel good. You feel so good. Yes."

He stiffens and draws back a little, holding himself still, his breaths coming fast and shallow, and then he lets out a primal growl. I can feel the exact moment he starts to spill into me. Knowing he's coming pushes me right over the edge, and I cling to the towel bar as tight as I can, eyes squeezed shut, feeling a hard, deep orgasm rip through me. It's explosive, as if my entire body is contracting and releasing in waves of sheer euphoria, leaving me crying out and grinding my clit against Graham's hand as he moans through the final throes of his own climax.

———

When we get back to the bedroom, still toweling off, I see the clock on the nightstand and suddenly remember — "Fuck. I have to meet with Bow. I completely forgot we're meeting up this afternoon."

I drop the towel and scramble for the pile of Graham's clothes that I've stockpiled. Jeans I can cuff at the ankle and wear slouchy, a dress shirt I can tie in a knot over my midriff. It'll do.

Graham reclines on the bed, beautifully naked, and tucks a hand behind his head. "Would you like me to come with you?"

I mull it over as I roll the shirtsleeves up over my elbows.

"No. It'll just give the paparazzi more photo ops. They'll be all over us if we go anywhere together right now, and I don't want the tabloids to have any more to talk about."

"We'll let them cool down, then. Maybe I'll just stay like this until you return."

My heart flutters as I lean over to give him a kiss goodbye. "I'll be looking forward to it."

Chapter Twenty-Four

Graham

DESPITE TEASING Abbie about waiting in bed for her, I'm not able to lay around for long before I start to feel restless.

I get dressed and order groceries from the bougie organic market at Columbus and 106th that offers one-hour delivery, then straighten up the minimal mess that Abbie left in the living room. After I put her Thai leftovers in the fridge, I pull out baking sheets and pans and utensils and spices, gathering everything I need to prepare a home-cooked meal for her.

She can reject my offer of keeping a domestic staff here in the apartment all she wants, but she won't be able to say no to this dinner. Seared scallops, thin-sliced flank steak, a mean kale Caesar, and roasted asparagus. There aren't many gourmet meals I'm confident I can prepare perfectly every single time—blame my British heritage or my motherless upbringing, if you must—but this is one of them. It's fresh and simple yet elevated, exactly the type of cuisine Abbie likes best.

An appetizer of toasted, sliced baguette with burrata, honey, and figs will be the first thing I offer her when she gets back from her legal meeting. After everything she's been through lately, she deserves to be pampered a little.

I'm still banging around in the kitchen when I hear the doorbell.

"Just a moment," I yell.

My grocery order is here a lot faster than I expected, which is appreciated, so I dash back to the bedroom for my wallet so I can tip the delivery person.

But they must be in a hurry, because the bell rings out again, and I hear loud, rapid knocking on the door as I make my way back down the hall.

"Yes, yes, I'm coming," I call out.

I throw the door open, already apologizing. "Sorry, I just had to grab my—"

"About goddamn time you opened the—"

Except it's not my delivery person standing there. It's Ford Montgomery. Freshly tanned, in a finely cut suit, looking peeved.

We stare at each other, and it's immediately obvious that neither of us was the person the other expected to see. I hesitate, my words freezing in my mouth as my mind runs a million miles an hour.

Ford and I haven't spoken since he showed up at the police station to help me out, which was before I proposed to Abbie...so I have no idea what—or how much —he even knows about my current relationship with her. I've seen him destroy people for less than fucking his daughter. The fact that she is so much more to me is beside the point; Abbie is Ford's child and he isn't the type to give much consideration to gray areas.

But it's possible he doesn't know anything at all yet—he's been off on some tropical vacation with his wife, and if he hasn't been following the American tabloid headlines, he may have no clue what's been going on. Should I tell him about the engagement, the aborted wedding ceremony, Abbie's arrest, and the subsequent attempted murder charges?

I'm torn. He deserves to know the truth about everything, but it doesn't feel right to tell him without Abbie here. On top of that, I'm not sure where I stand with him at the moment. The way he's looking at me is downright inscrutable.

Finally, he barks out a laugh, breaking the tension. "Well, look who it is."

"Ford. I didn't know you were back from the Bahamas." I smile uncertainly, trying to feel him out.

He returns my smile, but his gaze shifts over my shoulder, into the apartment. "I'm looking for my daughter. Is she here?"

"Not at the moment, I'm afraid. Do you want to come by later?" I ask. "I'm sure she'd love to see you."

"Don't bullshit me, old friend." Ford smirks. "You can drop the act. I know she's wanted for murder—did you think I wouldn't find out? I spoke with Esmeralda yesterday to get an update, and hot damn did this go ass up. Not to mention what the press is saying."

My stomach drops. Does this mean he's seen all the despicable tabloid headlines, too? And that awful photo of Abbie in her wedding dress, her hands in cuffs?

209

I clear my throat. "It was all a misunderstanding. There's no truth to it, obviously. The police let her go."

Ford grunts noncommittally. "Well? Aren't you going to let me in?" he says.

I don't like his tone. I can't tell if he's merely furious that his daughter got arrested, and possibly blames me, or if he knows about the wedding and he came here to confront Abbie about it. Maybe it's both. Or maybe it's something else entirely.

Regardless, I take a step back and open the door wide.

"Been a while since I've seen the place. Looks good," he comments as he saunters in and glances around, eyeing the living room with interest. He's giving off the energy of a ticking time bomb, which I've seen in him plenty of times—but now, it has me on edge.

He pours himself a tumbler of whiskey from the bar cart without asking and then drops into an armchair. "This place is immaculate. Natasha always did have good taste, though."

"Money can buy many things, including interior design," I say, bristling. This man knows more about my fallout with my ex than anyone, and here he sits, flattering the devil. "Look, Abbie is at a meeting and I'm not sure how long she'll be. Why don't you come back this evening?"

"What, no time to chat with your oldest friend?" he asks. "I'm practically your god damn father-in-law now, aren't I?"

Ah. Finally, he's shown his hand. He's pissed about

the engagement he didn't hear about and the wedding he didn't get invited to. Fine. I can handle this.

I square my shoulders. "You're upset about us getting married. I can understand that—"

"*Upset?* You left Abbie for the sharks when the tabloids ran that salacious story about you two. I'm the one who had to convince you not to kick her out of your house so you wouldn't damage her reputation and yours, remember? But then you decided that wasn't enough to cover your ass, so you moved your ex-wife back into your house with my daughter along for the ride—which was a brilliant plan, wasn't it? Until Natasha OD'd, at which point you did a full one-eighty and decided Abbie was suddenly wife material? What in the actual fuck? Upset doesn't begin to cover it, Graham. No wonder the press is eating you two alive."

The way he's boiling down our relationship to all the paltry bits, glazing over the intricacies of the drama, lights a fuse within me. "I apologize that there was a need for discretion, but it's not the way it looks. Abbie and I...we fell in love." I try to keep the venom out of my voice. This is his daughter, after all. I can get defensive all I want, but how can I compete with the fierceness of a father's love? "Things have just been a bit complicated between us."

"You *fell in love?*" Ford lets out a derisive laugh. "She had a crush, a silly infatuation. But you, old man, should know better."

I take a breath. "Why exactly did you come here to see Abbie? Was it for the sole purpose of trying to break up our relationship? Because it's not going to happen—"

"*Relationship?* That's what you call sneaking around

with my teenage daughter all summer and then trying to have a secret wedding behind my back? I can only imagine the lies she told you to convince you not to invite me and my wife. She must've painted herself quite the little victim—"

"She did nothing of the kind." I draw myself up to my full height. "And it wasn't a secret wedding. As I said, there was a need for discretion, given the circumstances—"

"So you're saying my invitation got lost in the mail?" Ford eyes me over the edge of his whiskey glass as he drinks deeply, and then adds, "Funny, though, I'm not sure how you got lost asking my permission for my daughter's hand."

Guilt squeezes at me, but I shove it away. "She's a grown woman, Ford. She can make her own decisions. And the truth is, she did call to tell you, but then decided she didn't want to ruin your vacation. I respected her choice. I wasn't trying to disrespect you in the process."

"Bullshit. You know what ruins a vacation? Finding out your daughter's been arrested for attempted murder. On her secret wedding day."

"*As I said*, the police let her go. My legal team is working on her defense around the clock. We're all working as hard as we can to prove her innocence. I'm handling it."

"I doubt that. If you recall, *I* was the one who saved *your* ass when you were accused. Now my daughter is in the hot seat, and I'm supposed to believe you're 'handling it'? And then what? You think you're going to get her off the hook and you two will just ride off into the sunset together? Wake up, Graham. Your life is a shitshow, and you're not going to drag my daughter down with you."

He slams his empty glass down and gets up. My body goes tense as I brace for a physical altercation, but Ford just walks over to the window. He takes in the view, heaves a sigh, and turns back around to face me.

His voice is softer, calmer, downright lawyerly as he says, "Look, buddy, man to man, this is what I'm saying: You need to call off the engagement. Give her a chance to marry someone who can provide for her properly without dragging her name even deeper through the mud. Don't be selfish. Don't ruin her. She still has a chance to do well for herself. Thank God the police intercepted the wedding before you two could make it official."

All I can do is shake my head. "She will be my wife. But I swear to you on all that is holy, I will take care of her. I will *always* take care of her. She won't be ruined. That is a promise."

"You need. To end it," Ford repeats.

My fists clench at my sides. "We will be married, with or without your approval. I love her and she loves me, and we've committed to each other. There's nothing more to discuss."

He coughs out a laugh and shakes his head. "You know, I almost feel sorry for you."

"I don't need your pity."

"Oh, but you do, old friend. More than you know." His expression is gleeful and mean.

"Do you know why I sent Abbie to you to begin with? No, you don't. Because your head's too far up your own ass to even consider that someone could put one over on you."

My blood runs cold. "Explain. Now."

Ford walks back over to the bar to refill his glass, swirling the drink before taking a healthy swallow.

"This is the thing, Graham. Abbie *set you up*. She came to work for you so she could seduce you and rob you blind, by hook or by crook. Granted, the blackmail plot did backfire, thanks to your stable boy blowing the lid off the story first, but then she pivoted to the whole marriage thing, so overall I'd say she did pretty well for herself. Even if you haven't made things legal just yet."

A high-pitched ringing erupts in my ears. "You're lying. I understand you may not be comfortable with our relationship, but trying to tear us apart is—"

"There's nothing to tear apart," he interrupts. "My little actress played her role spectacularly. She seduced you. She got the ring. Hell, she apparently even tried to kill your wife to make sure there weren't any loose ends. Frankly, I'm impressed she went so far. Well. Sort of impressed. Can't exactly support attempted murder, but her dedication to her task has been quite remarkable. Not that I expected her to cut me out at the last minute like she did. But that's women for you, eh? Ruthless to the last."

Ford drains his second drink, then sets the glass down with a vile smack of his lips. Meanwhile, I'm standing here speechless and horrified, ice in my gut, my pulse jackhammering.

"It's not true," I protest. "Abbie doesn't want my money. She signed a prenup. In fact, it was *her* idea—"

"A prenup, eh? That little bitch," he says quietly. Then he shakes his head at me. "Don't you get it? She did that just to trick you all the better! You think she isn't planning to suck you dry once she has that ring on her finger? In more ways than one, old man, and not the way you want, believe me." He chuckles to himself, and my stomach turns. "There's no love between you two. There never was. She was just doing her job."

His words have the sinister ring of truth. I sink into a chair, my legs no longer capable of supporting me. "But...why?"

"Because I told her to." Ford stalks toward me, victory etched on his face. "I was in the lurch, Graham. Hit a bad spot, needed the help. Bank was getting ready to take my house, I had creditors breathing down my neck, debts piling up left and right. You knew this.

"You, the man with more money than God. You, the man with more bank accounts than toes. You knew, and you could have helped, but you didn't, did you? No, you greedy fuck, you hoarded your treasures like a dragon. Well, guess what? I'm the dragon slayer. I set you up. I did what I had to do to help my family. Though I guess you and I both got screwed in the end, didn't we? And now I'm just trying to put things to right. So. Break it off. Cut your losses. Move on."

The weight of his words hits me like an anvil. This doesn't feel real. Abbie would never do this to me. And yet. The stories, the tabloids, the way she dressed when she got to my estate, the way she clung to my family like we were her last resort...it all makes sense now.

Because we were her last resort.

"Get out," I say through gritted teeth. "Get the hell out of my house!"

He shrugs. "Give my best to Abbie. Tell her daddy dearest is waiting on a phone call."

Ford saunters away, and a moment later the door slams, echoing through the empty apartment. All I can do is sit here, frozen in shock, my entire world shattered.

For the second time in my life, I've fallen for an actress. A manipulator. A liar.

If I missed that...what else is Abbie capable of?

Chapter Twenty-Five

Abbie

I STEP out of the subway station and into the late summer heat, making my way down the packed, humid, noisy streets toward the apartment building. A thick file folder is clutched to my chest. Inside are legal documents I need to study, notes I took during my meeting with Bowen, every defense I have at my disposal to keep me safe from Natasha.

I have no idea if it will be enough.

My life is one big minefield right now—one wrong step could result in complete annihilation. But God, I can't go to jail. The idea of it is incomprehensible. I didn't do anything to that woman, didn't do anything but fall in love with the man she once loved—and never stopped using. If she thinks I'm going down without a fight, she is very sorely mistaken.

Natasha Ratliff may be used to getting her way, but she can't have everything. Not this time. She's not going to take away my new family, my new life. Everything I've worked for.

The meeting with Bow did a lot to lift my spirits. She fully believes in my innocence, and also believes Natasha is full of shit. It sounded to me like they never really liked each other, though Bowen didn't explicitly say so. Either way, she believes we have a solid defense. The lack of concrete evidence combined with medical statistics regarding coma patients and their mental states after regaining consciousness make for a very strong case. And honestly, having an objective party believe me so unquestioningly makes me feel like things will actually be okay.

Graham and I will get through this, together, and then we'll take one hell of a honeymoon to help us forget it ever happened.

As soon as the ritzy apartment building comes into view, I pick up my pace and hurry through the lobby, nodding to the kindly doorman who ushers me inside.

All I can think about now is the fact that I've got Graham upstairs waiting for me, waiting to rip off all my clothes and fuck all this stress and anxiety away. My center instantly goes hot as I picture him laying me down across the bed, pushing my thighs apart, licking his lips as he lowers himself between my legs...

I'm so distracted, I full-on collide with someone stepping out of the elevator.

"Sorry!" I jump back, praying I'm not about to be recognized by any of my haters who live here. But when I lift my eyes, my stomach drops. "*Dad?* What are you doing here?"

He eyes me coldly. "Paying an old friend a visit. Where have you been?"

Clearly, he's pissed off. But what about? Did Graham

just tell him about our engagement? Or, no—it's far too late for that. Surely Dad has seen all the tabloids and news stories by now. He must know that my wedding was interrupted by police, that I was arrested, that Natasha's first order of business upon waking from her coma was to point the finger at me.

I swallow hard. The shit has most assuredly hit the fan. Now all I can hope to do is some damage control.

"I had a meeting with my attorney. Do you want to come up and talk?" I ask.

His face remains sour, even as the corners of his mouth turn up in a smile. "Oh, no, I'm quite done talking. You see, I just had the loveliest chat with your hus—oops, boyfriend. Sorry, no, that's not right either. Your *ex*-boyfriend."

My stomach curdles. "What is that supposed to mean?"

"A secret wedding, Abigail? Truly? What are you, five?" he says with a sneer, ignoring my question. "Not that it isn't *incredibly* romantic, of course—" This he says with dripping sarcasm. "But did you really think you could hide a *marriage*? Sneak the ceremony in your house, where no one knows, so no one can smell your filth? Now the *whole world* has seen those photos of you. The bride in handcuffs."

His cruel words hit me like a slap in the face. My eyes dart around the lobby as I panic about who else is within earshot of the vitriol spewing from my father. The last thing I need is for gossip about this encounter to get sold to the tabloids.

Dad continues, on a roll now, getting louder as he

picks up steam. It's almost as if he's putting on a performance, the same way he does in court. As if he's enjoying himself.

"Did you really think you could get away with stabbing me in the back? Or were you simply too 'in love' to remember where your loyalties lie? You know, I've never taken you for a frivolous girl, but I'm now forced to consider that you may be a stupid one. Especially if there's any credence to the allegations about you trying to kill Natasha Ratliff."

My mouth opens and closes, but I can't speak for a moment. There's a lump in my throat and my chest is constricted. I feel like the wind has been knocked out of me.

"Can we talk about this upstairs?" I finally choke out.

"No. I have no desire to grant you the courtesy, you ungrateful little wretch."

"But—"

"We had an agreement," he hisses, leaning in so close I can see the bloodshot whites of his eyes. "You knew the plan. But you abandoned it. Which I realized the second I found out I hadn't been invited to your little wedding."

I blink at him, aghast. This is all about his goddamn *plan*? "Wait, but—the last time we talked, you gave me your blessing. You said—"

"I was being fatherly. I never thought you'd still go through with it, only to cut your old man out the second his back was turned. Graham told me all about your little prenup, too."

Fury distorts his features, his expression ugly. Suddenly, everything clicks: my dad was so pissed off when he found out that I'd tried to secretly marry Graham—and presumably keep all the Ratliff money for myself—that he decided to turn around and tell my husband-to-be about our original plan to extort him. Just to fucking ruin everything for me. Sheerly out of spite.

It takes my breath away. My adrenaline surges, my sight going dark around the edges.

I might be capable of murder after all.

He shakes his head, smirking again. "You should know better than anyone, princess, that Ford Montgomery does not get cut out of his own deals. So now you have to pay. Though I have to say, the murder attempt was a nice touch. I didn't think you had it in you to do something so diabolical, but you know what they say: the apple never falls far from the tree."

I square my jaw and throw back my shoulders. "*I am nothing like you.*"

"More's the pity."

Dad adjusts his cuffs, then sticks his hands in his pockets and starts to walk away. I'm watching his back, rage pumping in my blood, when he turns back around and says, "My condolences on the broken engagement, by the way."

Everything slows around me, and my ears start to ring. "What the *fuck* did you do?"

"Did you forget, in all your scheming, that Graham and I are friends? When I see someone trying to take advantage of a friend, I warn him."

Terrors trips down my spine. The word barely leaves my lips. "No."

He shrugs. "It was the right thing to do. Though I know you do struggle to separate right from wrong."

My father is a fucking sociopath. He doesn't look upset by this at all. He just ruined everything, *everything good in my life*, because I didn't play by his rules. Because I fell in love. Everything is shattering all around me because I fell in love.

"Why?" I manage, torn between tears and screaming.

He leans in close and whispers, "Never mess with the bull, Abbie. You'll always get the horns."

"I'm your daughter!"

"You're a liability," he spits back. "No daughter of mine would betray me like you have."

"I didn't betray you!" My voice cracks. There's a maintenance worker in the lobby who's paying way too much attention to watering the plants nearby, and I try to lower my volume. "You told me I was absolved of my guilt. You told me I didn't have to worry about it anymore!"

"And then you tried to cut us out. Got yourself a man in the bag, so fuck your family, eh? Well, now we both don't get what we want."

My chest rises and falls rapidly with my shallow breathing. I'm a mouse caught in a cat's paws. "Get out of here, or I'll call security. I have to go fix whatever it is you just did."

He smiles. "Good luck with that, princess."

And then he saunters away casually, like we'd just talked about the weather.

I pound the elevator button frantically, dizzy with panic. When the doors slide open with a ding, I rush into the elevator car, even though I'm terrified to find out what's waiting for me upstairs. All I can think now is that I have to get to Graham. I have to tell him the truth—the whole truth. I have to fix this.

But it might already be too late.

Chapter Twenty Six

Abbie

By the time I step off on the 25th floor, I can't stop shaking. I'm convinced that Graham is going to be gone already, unwilling to talk to me ever again after the poison my father spewed.

How do I recover from this?

I'd like to believe that Graham would have taken my father's words as bullshit. He has to know I love him. He was going to marry me. Officially make me part of his family. We were going to build a life together, hand in hand. Surely he would give me the benefit of the doubt.

But that's not how my luck has gone lately. So I'm bracing for the worst.

I'm not expecting him to be waiting in the apartment, arms wide open, ready to comfort me as I try to explain the lies my father just told him—because in all fairness, they aren't lies. Not really. I know exactly why I was sent to the Ratliff estate, exactly what my role was. And I know exactly how my father operates. The ugly truth has been unveiled, and now Graham is going to spurn me.

This is the end of us. The end of everything. I can feel it in my gut.

My legs tremble as I walk down the hallway, eyes focused on the apartment door. Taking a deep breath, I remind myself that I've been in worse situations this summer. I've been accused of far worse. And I've come back, every time. I have always come back.

I can come back from this, too. Graham loves me. For better and for worse. He said so.

But as I stand outside the door, keys in my hand, I know in my heart that I'm lying to myself.

When I walk into the living room, I see Graham standing next to the floor-to-ceiling windows, staring out at Central Park with his back to me.

Just seeing him relieves the angst in my heart. But then it sends me into another frenzy, because what if I'm about to lose him? What if he's about to walk out of my life forever?

I know he must have heard me come in, but he hasn't said anything yet.

"Hi," I say. I stand there awkwardly, ten feet away, unsure what else to do or say. I don't know what my next move is until I see his face.

He doesn't respond, just continues to stare out the window. I take a step closer.

"I had a good meeting with Bow," I go on, desperately hoping for normalcy. "She says we have a strong case. They can't prove anything, all they have is Natasha's word against mine. She says those kinds of allegations are easy enough to get thrown out."

Still, nothing.

"I, um...saw my dad downstairs." My voice wavers, but I keep pushing. There's no point trying to play innocent. "I didn't know he was back in town. He said you two talked."

Graham slowly turns around. On his face is the cold, cruel expression he used to wear so often—a look I never wanted to see directed at me again. His eyes, though... they're even worse. They're full of anger. I freeze in place. We are trapped in a silence that feels as heavy and loaded as a gun. I'm too terrified to move, much less speak. So I stand there, waiting.

"Do you take me for a fool?" Graham finally breaks the silence, his voice just as cold as the rest of him.

"Of course not." I swallow hard.

"Don't insult me with more lies. I know everything."

I'm afraid to pour fuel on the fire, but I have to say these words. "I love you, Graham. I love you with everything I have. That's the truth."

"STOP. LYING!" His voice fills the apartment like terrifying thunder. "I brought you into my home. I entrusted my child into your care. Fed you, sheltered you, paid you generously. And somewhere along the way, I fell for you. I was foolish enough to give you my heart. To get down on one knee. My God. To think I almost made the biggest mistake of my life."

I shake my head, tears blurring my vision. "Please, just let me explain—"

"I don't want to hear a single thing you have to say," he grinds out, as if each word is causing him pain. "I've heard enough already."

Grief stabs me in the heart with a long, hot knife. "It's not like you think. I swear to you, Graham, it's not."

"Are you going to deny that you came to work for me for the sole purpose of extorting me? Go ahead and try." He sneers again.

The tears roll down my face, but I brush them away. I know the only way out of this is the truth, as badly as I don't want to tell it. "No. It's true—my dad did send me to you with ulterior motives. I tried to tell you..." I trail off weakly.

But despite my protests, I know I'm guilty. I did try to seduce him. And I succeeded. There were plenty of opportunities for me to come clean, but I never did. I tried to bury it. Brush it under the rug in the hopes that Graham would never find out. What the hell was I thinking?

"You tried to tell me that you were after my money?" Graham snorts. "NO. All you told me was that you were a little girl with a crush. Now, you're a little girl with a fat bank account. I hope that two million dollars fucks you as well as I did."

"I was *marrying* you. I signed a prenup! I never wanted the money, I wanted *you*. Why would I go behind your back and steal from you?"

He remains unmoved. "Turns out, I don't know why you do anything."

"I didn't rob you, Graham." My hands are clenched, my nails digging into my palms painfully. I have to fight for my marriage, but it feels like a losing battle. "Yes, I initially agreed to try to seduce you to get access to your money, whether through blackmail or marriage. I was sent under terrible pretenses, and I had an ulterior motive. That was my dad's big plan.

"But it *failed.* Because I fell in love with you, Graham. So I *didn't do it.* I walked away. And now my dad is furious because I abandoned his piece of shit master plan, but I don't care what he thinks anymore. *All I care about is you.*"

"You know, I didn't believe his story at first. But then all the pieces started falling into place. And I knew there was no point in denying it. I couldn't lie to myself."

I'm full-on sobbing now. "I never meant to take advantage. I know this looks so bad, but I'm telling you, Graham, I love you. You and Jude mean everything to me."

"Don't you dare bring my daughter into this," he growls.

"You have to understand." My voice cracks. "He's my dad. He told me he was going to lose the house, that he and my mom would be homeless. I had no idea what I was getting into. I just knew I'd get to spend the summer at your house, and I've always loved you—"

"Stop. I won't hear another lie out of your filthy mouth."

I sink to my knees, all the strength gone out of my legs. "I just want to be with you. I want to be your wife. I want us to be together forever," I murmur softly.

Graham casts a disgusted look down at me. "You're good. You're very good. Shame you couldn't show Natasha a thing or two."

This hurts almost more than anything else. "You know I didn't do anything to Natasha."

"Do I?"

"Graham. After everything we've been through, can't you see my devotion to you? I love you. You have to see that. You have to know that. Please." I climb up off the floor and go to him, grabbing his arm.

He coolly shrugs out of my grasp and takes a step back.

"What I know is this: You came into my home under false pretenses to steal from me, you hustled your way into my life and gained access to my accounts, and then two million dollars went missing."

I shake my head, shocked. "What are you talking about? I thought you said Natasha was the one who—"

"Yes, she was quite the handy scapegoat, was she not? Unconscious in the hospital, all the better to take the fall for your actions."

"I didn't do it!" I dig the heels of my hands into my eyes and take a deep breath, but it does nothing to calm the frantic pounding in my chest. "And I never wanted to betray you, Graham. You're too precious to me. You have to understand. You have to understand."

"And *you* have to understand you've been found out. Rooted out like the vermin you are." Graham's tone is so repulsed that it sickens me. How can he not believe me after all that we've been through? "You have forty-eight hours to find somewhere else to live and someone else to represent you. I'll no longer be bankrolling your legal team or your lifestyle."

"Graham, please."

"And if you try to contact Jude," he goes on, "you'll hear from my attorneys."

"Don't do this," I beg, tears flowing down my face.

"The ring," he says, gazing pointedly at my finger. "I need it back. It's a family heirloom, and one that doesn't belong on the hand of a lying whore."

His words hit me like a kick in the stomach. I feel sick. "Please don't do this."

"Take it off. Now."

Sobbing, I twist the ring off my finger and hold it out to him. My hands are trembling.

He wrenches it from my grasp and tucks it in his pocket, giving me one last hard look. "Goodbye, Abbie."

"No." I shake my head and reach for him, but he turns his back on me and storms to the door. "Graham, no. Don't walk away. It can't end like this."

He pauses with his hand on the knob, and I hope for one tiny moment that he will change his mind. That he will remember what we have. How much we mean to each other.

"I can't believe I ever thought I loved you," he says, so softly I almost can't hear him.

And then he's out the door, slamming it so hard the walls rattle.

Chapter Twenty-Seven

Abbie

Days pass, and the world feels like it stops spinning. I'm only keeping track of the passage of time thanks to my phone, but in my head the past few weeks feel more like months. Life slows to an excruciating pace, every second reminding me of what I lost and how precious it was. I lost everything, all because of my father. I lost my partner, I lost Jude, I lost my home.

I lost my entire future.

I'm in agony. Graham won't pick up when I call, and I know better than to defy him and try reaching out to Jude through Mary or Esmeralda—not that I'm sure they'd answer my calls, either. All I have to hold on to are the photos I took all summer long, literally thousands of them, that are saved on my phone. I pore over them constantly, tears stinging my eyes, wishing I could go back to those sweet, perfect moments. Wishing this nightmare wasn't my new reality.

Until the fall semester at Cornell starts, I'm staying with Amanda at her parents' house in Stamford. After

Graham left me at the apartment in Manhattan, he'd called Amanda to dismiss her from her temporary nanny position and asked her to pack up all my things from the estate. He then had Ronaldo drive her home from Hudson Valley, after which she got in her car and came down to New York City to pick me up. It was one of the longest days of my life.

Since then, my BFF has tried her best to cheer me up, but I haven't been in the mood to do much of anything except hide under a blanket and cry. Trying to talk to her about my feelings just makes me feel worse. She's brought me countless cups of tea, braided my hair, forced me to eat toast and soup since I can't stomach real food right now, tried to distract me with social media and CNN and my favorite movies. Which I appreciate. But it's not doing much.

I usually love being at Amanda's parents' place—they've always treated me like their second daughter—but at the moment, leeching off them just makes me feel more pathetic. I'm not even ten miles from my own parents, but I don't want to go back home. It would require me to call my dad and ask for help, which there is no way in hell I'd do. Not after his betrayal.

This afternoon, Amanda invited me to hang out with her and her girlfriend, but I couldn't bear the thought of watching them be happy and flirty together when my own heart has taken such a beating. Amanda said she understood. Now I'm sitting in her bedroom by myself, mindlessly scrolling on Instagram, trying (and failing) to keep my brain in sleep mode.

I know I'm guilty of so much, but I didn't hurt

Natasha, I didn't steal that money from Graham, and I didn't betray my loves. But Graham doesn't believe me. It was so easy for him to take my father at his word, to cast me out, to turn his back on me for good. It's like he never loved me at all. If he did, he would have been fully invested in our partnership. He would have committed to us doing the work together to mend the trust that was broken. So we could move forward, and build a life together. The fact that he didn't just proves that his love wasn't real.

Another crying jag takes me, and I sob so hard into Amanda's spare pillow that I make myself sick. In the bathroom afterward, I splash my face with cold water and rinse out my mouth, studying my puffy, red face in the mirror. I'm a fucking mess.

When Graham rejects my call for the hundredth time, my entire body shudders, but I find that I literally have no more tears left in me to cry. I'm a hollowed-out shell. A black hole. Nothing. I'm nothing without him. Maybe I never was.

And then...something inside me snaps. The old Abbie would be horrified to see me acting like this. The old Abbie had self-respect. I can't let myself keep sitting here, wallowing and desperate, pleading with God and the universe for Graham to just pick up the phone and say he'll take me back. What's done is done. There's no turning back time. We're over.

It's time I get my shit together and take control of my life.

Starting with the attempted murder charges.

I *know* I'm innocent, but I can't move on from all of

this until the charges are officially dropped. Which means I need to visit Natasha Ratliff.

After a quick shower, I put on the most modest outfit I can find in my suitcase. Then I work on my face, skipping the Teenage Fantasy and raiding Amanda's makeup for something more muted, settling on a pale pink. I keep everything natural and light, so I look my age. Young and sheltered and largely ignorant to the ways of the world.

Amanda's mom is happy to drive me to the Amtrak station, and on the way there I buy my ticket on my phone and just barely make it onto the next train to Manhattan.

One fifty-four-minute train, a brief number six subway ride, and a half-mile walk later, I step through the doors of Mount Sinai hospital. The place is a swirl of activity, so it's easy to make my way up to Natasha's floor without being noticed. The closer I get to her room, though, the more my heart begins to thud. What if this doesn't work? What if they find me in her room and have me arrested again? I don't have Bowen to save me anymore. I don't have anyone.

But this is my last chance to clear my name. My only chance.

So I lift my chin, stroll past the nurses' station like I'm in a hurry, and confidently open the door to Natasha's room like I belong there. My stomach is in knots the whole time, but the act clearly works, because no one stops me.

Inside the room, I see Natasha propped up on a pile of pillows, tapping away at her phone as the television blares. She has her hair and makeup done—maybe not as immaculately as usual, but pretty close—but under the fluorescent lighting, in her thin hospital gown, she somehow looks smaller, less dangerous. Still, I know better than to trust appearances. I won't let my guard down. Not for a second.

Natasha turns to look at me, surely expecting a doctor or a nurse. The double take she does is almost Oscar-worthy.

"What the hell are *you* doing here?" she hisses, scrambling for the nurse call button.

"Wait." I hold out a hand. "Please. I just want to talk."

"Get out," she says, her thumb hovering over the button. "You have three seconds to leave or else I'm pushing this. Though I'm sure the police would love to have you back in cuffs."

"*I'm done,*" I blurt, the words rushing out of me in a tumble. "With all of it. You can have your life back. Graham and Jude, the estate, everything. I don't want it anymore."

Natasha doesn't lower her hand, but she doesn't push the button, either. "I'm listening."

"I came here to apologize. I just want to put this behind me and try to move on." I shake my head and swallow hard.

Her smile is smug. "Well. I knew you'd eventually come to your senses. I didn't expect it to be so soon, but I suppose an attempted murder charge really helps one to reconsider one's priorities, doesn't it?"

"I don't know how everything got so out of control. How I got in this deep. I guess, ever since I first met you, I was just...so in awe of you." I look down at my feet. "I mean, you had it all. You were talented and glamorous and beautiful and rich. And you had the perfect life and the perfect husband. And that's what I wanted. I wanted to *be* Natasha Ratliff. To be perfect, too."

"A childish fantasy. Not that I blame you for trying. You come from nothing. Of course you were hungry for more." Natasha nods solemnly, but I can feel her glee radiating off her.

"It just kills me that this is how it all turned out." I sink into a plastic chair and sigh heavily, the weight of the last few months bearing down on me. "After dealing with the tabloids and the paparazzi, my reputation going down the drain, the legal troubles...God, it was all for nothing in the end. It's just not worth it—I can't live like this. I'm not strong enough. You won."

"Don't beat yourself up, Abbie. It takes grace to admit defeat. And I respect that you made the effort to tell me face to face." She sounds absolutely delighted. "To be honest, I'm glad you realized you were in over your head. Before it was too late."

"I just want it to be over. I want to go home. But my dad won't even talk to me now." I look up, blinking back tears. "Is there any way—no. I shouldn't even ask."

"Do go on," she coaxes, eating it up.

I hesitate, and then continue. "It's just that...if you recant your statement, and I'm not a suspect anymore... maybe my parents will forgive me. Maybe I'll be able to go back home."

"Oh, you poor thing," Natasha tuts. "You know, I was just like you once. Ambitious. Idealistic. A dreamer, even

—but hungry for what I wanted. Willing to do whatever it took to achieve my goals, and fuck anybody who tried to get in my way. Do you know what my secret was? I figured out how to turn everything into an opportunity."

"What do you mean?" I ask, gazing at her with adulation as I scoot my chair closer. "I thought that's what I did."

"You certainly tried. But you lack experience! You're too trustful, too naïve. You had no contingency plan in place." Natasha is all but gloating. "You *always* need a contingency plan. You have to be able to launch yourself off of setbacks. To pivot. Move on to Plan B, or C, or X."

"I'm...not sure I understand," I murmur.

"No, of course you don't. You're still so young, so green. You're not ruthless enough." She shakes her head. "But take me, for example. Do you think I meant to OD, or end up in a coma? Of course not. *And yet.* I was able to work it to my advantage. I took control of the narrative. Blaming you was the perfect way to stop the wedding. So you see, it's just like I said. You have to learn to seize every opportunity. That's the difference between you and me."

For the first time in what feels like forever, a zing of hope pumps through my veins.

"That's not what's different between us, Natasha." I pull my phone out of my skirt pocket and hold it up, showing her that it's recording. "I see opportunities, too. I'm just not a liar."

Shock and rage bloom on her face as she realizes that I have her entire confession in the palm of my hand. "*No.*"

237

As she starts cursing up a storm, I bolt for the door. Thank God she's hooked up to all those machines and monitors and can't jump out of the bed to throttle me, because I'm sure she wants to.

"What have you done, you little *cunt*?" she screams at my back.

I pause in the doorway, glancing over my shoulder at her one last time before I go.

"I'm taking control of the narrative," I tell her.

And then I float out the door.

Chapter Twenty Eight

Graham

THE HOUSE DOESN'T FEEL right today. It feels empty, sterile, fragmented. I can't shake the feeling that something is amiss as I walk down the hall to the kitchen to get another espresso.

I'm not sentimental enough to entertain the possibility that it's the absence of Abbie, because she's been gone for almost two weeks now, and all for the better. Her presence in my life was beyond disruptive. Hell, it continues to be. I've spent far too many hours dwelling on the ways she's interfered and how she's turned this house upside down, and I'm still getting my business matters back on track and my work caught up. The only thing Abbie didn't ruin was my relationship with Jude.

I stop in the middle of the hallway. *Jude*. That's what's not right. I should be hearing her infectious laugh and relentless stream of words bouncing off the walls, but all is silent. She's been morose ever since I told her that Abbie would no longer be her other mother.

And when I finally, grudgingly took Jude to the

239

hospital to see her real mother, Natasha had barely paid attention to Jude at all. We were there for less than half an hour before Natasha got annoyed with all of Jude's questions about why Natasha had accused Abbie, and Natasha insisted that she needed her afternoon nap. Jude was crushed.

After sending Jude to the waiting room down the hall, I told my ex-wife what a miserable human being I think she is. She tried to convince me that she really did believe Abbie drugged her, tried to tell me that there was still hope for me and her to rekindle our marriage, but I wasn't having any of it. It took all my willpower not to throttle her in that hospital bed.

Before I walked out, I left Natasha with an ultimatum—I said that Jude wouldn't return until she made the effort to call her and invite her to visit. I also said I wouldn't subject our daughter to her narcissism and manipulations any longer, and that Jude and I would both be waiting for her to decide she was ready to act like a decent mother again.

Jude has been calling her mother every day, but Natasha has yet to invite her back to the hospital for a visit. And Jude hasn't asked to go again. Yet.

It's blatantly obvious, now that I think about it.

The house is missing my daughter's joy.

My brow furrows as anger steals over me anew. Abbie has no idea how much she stole outside of that two million dollars. I storm back to my office, grab a decanter of whiskey, and pour two fingers into a tumbler. I'm about to walk it to my desk when I pause, reconsider, and pour another finger.

"Mr. Ratliff?" Esmeralda calls through the door, rapping gently. "Would you like the paper now? You weren't at breakfast, so—"

"No," I call back. I stare out the window, watching the sun hike higher in the sky, wondering, not for the first time, how I could have been so damn foolish. "I'm tired of the news."

Esmeralda pops her head into my office anyway. "Business section?"

I sigh and take a drink of whiskey. It's early for it, but my soul needs soothing and this is the only way I know how. My father was a drunk, my father's father was a drunk, and I'm quite certain the affliction has long nourished the roots of the Ratliff family tree.

"Leave it, then," I finally concede. "I'll look it over later."

"Is there anything else we can do?" she asks as she pulls apart the paper and sets the applicable section down on my desk.

"Act as though nothing has changed." I look up to meet her eyes and immediately regret it. The pity on her face churns my stomach. "Frankly, I'm concerned about Jude."

"She was very attached. Her last nanny was very good with her," Esmeralda muses, careful not to say Abbie's name. I shoot her a frown. "What? She was. Do you remember how Jude used to be? She changed so much this summer. It's just too bad about...it all."

I cock an eyebrow at her, but don't argue, because Esmeralda is, as usual, correct.

"How can I help her? I appreciate you and Mary

241

taking turns caring for her, more than you know, but soon enough I'll have to get her back to Manhattan to start third grade, and I'll be back at the Midtown office. She'll be so lonely. I'm afraid she'll never bounce back. Especially with everything going on with her mother..."

"Spend as much time with her as you can," Esmeralda councils. "She needs extra love right now. I'll see if I can get Cassie to take her on a trail ride today. Perhaps you could join."

"I have a full day. Meetings until bedtime."

Her mouth flattens into a straight line. "How many meetings did you give up for Abbie?"

"Don't say her name." I wince and take another drink. "That name is banned from this house, you know that."

She snorts. "You're acting Jude's age. Never mind, that's an insult to your daughter."

"With all due respect, go away. Please."

Esmeralda places a gentle hand on my shoulder for a fraction of a second and then whisks out of my office, closing the door softly behind her. I shove the newspaper off to the side and don't bother looking at it again.

The remainder of the morning is a blur of video conferences, phone calls, and emails. I'm starting to regret skipping breakfast, the headache I've been ignoring suddenly moving into my sinuses, when my cell rings with a call from Bowen. I consider ignoring it, calling her back later, but why not make my day a little bit worse? After all, I'm sure it can't be good news. It never is.

"Whatever it is, just spit it out," I say instead of hello.

"Are you sitting down?" she says.

My gut clenches. "That bad? Go on, then. I'm listening." This whole goddamn case is giving me ulcers. Fucking Natasha.

"Your favorite person has recanted her statement."

I freeze at my desk, not computing. Obviously, she means Natasha, but there's no way that demon would recant her statements. She's in too deep. That's not her way.

"Graham, you there?"

"I'm going to need you to explain that a little better, Bow."

"Natasha recanted her statement to the police. She admitted it was an accidental overdose, self-administered. The DA dropped all charges against you and Miss Montgomery."

My jaw drops. "What? Natasha would never do that."

Bow clears her throat. "Haven't you...seen the news today?"

"Obviously not."

"Her camp is selling it to the public as her being confused after waking from her coma—safe to say I know exactly where they got *that* idea from. She's spinning her overdose as the result of stress and strain caused by the rumors surrounding your affair. Or some shit like that. Anyway, the press is eating it up. She's going to come out of this smelling like a rose. And with the sympathy of her fans, unfortunately."

"Sympathy for the devil, eh?"

"Indeed," she sighs. "But congratulations on your freedom. You can rest easy. At least, for now. God only knows what that bitch might be saving in her back pocket for next time."

I stand and start pacing around my office. "You're not wrong. Natasha never backs down from a fight. Is she back at Central Park West now?"

"She's supposed to be checking into one of those celebrity rehab centers once she gets released from the hospital. Knowing her, she'll turn it into a reality TV show."

"I would not be surprised."

"Also, there's one more piece of business we need to discuss," Bow says. "You still need to remove Ford Montgomery's Power of Attorney. Now that the case is over, there's no need. Especially since PoAs can get messy."

"Shit. I completely forgot about that. Can you take care of it?"

"Already working on it." Bow starts typing, so fast it sounds like machinegun fire through the phone. "I'll have it handled and the paperwork sent your way this afternoon."

We hang up and I start shutting down my laptop to go trail riding with my daughter. I can finally breathe. I'm free from that godforsaken succubus.

I suppose that makes two vanquished succubi now, doesn't it?

God, the Montgomerys are a real piece of work. As if Abbie's betrayal wasn't fucking devastating enough, her father—my oldest friend, the man who was supposed to be my closest confidant—has turned into my enemy as well. How does shit like this happen? I trusted him.

Trusted him so much I gave him power of attorney.

And then I pause, hands hovering over my laptop.

Ford's power of attorney.

My brain starts clicking, and the pieces start coming together. I'd forgotten, amid the stress of the case, that Ford had power of attorney when Bowen was unavailable. Ford had access to all of my accounts, my business, my entire estate, my entire fucking life when I was arrested.

Ford, who showed up at the Manhattan apartment not two weeks ago to destroy my life, fresh from his trip to the Bahamas and wearing a brand new suit...even though he was so broke, he'd sent his daughter to work for me over the summer just so she could seduce me and extort me for my money. *Ford*, who had access to both my bank account numbers and all of Abbie's identifying information. *Ford*, who has a long history of fucking over anyone and everyone when he's up against a wall. That motherfucker. That *motherfucker*.

Everything suddenly becomes crystal clear.

I was so quick to blame this all on Abbie, the nineteen-year-old girl who would do anything to help her family. Abbie, who abandoned her dad's despicable extortion plot for love. Abbie, who brought my family together. Abbie, who was relentlessly attacked by the public, by Natasha, by everyone, and who still stood by my side until the very end.

Who was being used here? It's so obvious now, I can't believe I didn't see it before.

I can only pray it's not too late to make amends.

Chapter Twenty-Nine

Abbie

IF THERE's one good thing that has come out of any of this, it's that my mother finally reached out to me.

I spent the whole summer thinking she was on my dad's side—not that she had any idea about the real reason he sent me to work for Graham, of course, but that she was equally disappointed by my behavior, embarrassed by my highly publicized affair and disgusted by all the trashy headlines, maybe even believed I was capable of attempted murder.

Or else that she just didn't care at all.

But when the news hit all the major media outlets this morning about Natasha recanting her statements, the first person who called me was my mom.

"My poor baby," she kept saying, her Georgia accent thickening as it did when she got worked up. "I can't imagine what you've been through. That horrible, horrible woman."

I was cautious at first, convinced her sympathy was just a ploy orchestrated by my father. A way for him to manipulate me again, take me emotionally hostage. To get me to do something else for him. But at one point Mom's voice dropped low and I could tell by the echo that she'd locked herself in the bathroom. That's when she'd started spilling her secrets.

"I've missed you so much," she told me, her voice catching. "I've been dying to call you all summer; I had such a hard time with you being away at college this year, but your father..."

"What?" I prodded, after she trailed off.

"Well, it's just that...he told me I had to give you space. He said you're an adult now, and I'd be smothering you, that you felt too guilty to tell me so yourself. So I did, I gave you space. Let you live your life, like he said. But now I wish I hadn't."

The shock of this latest betrayal hits me like an ice-cold wave. "Mom, Dad lied. I never said that. I never wanted that," I swore. "I missed you, too. I guess I thought, ever since I moved out for college, you wanted *your* own space. And then when I never heard from you this summer, I just figured...you had to be ashamed of me."

She started crying, and I had to wipe my own tears away as she went on apologizing.

"No, baby. Even when the gossip rags were saying all those things about you, I knew they couldn't be true. Not my Abbie. I shouldn't have listened to your father. God bless it, I should have just called. I should have called *every day*, I should have driven up to see you. I just thought you'd feel put out. And then when we weren't invited to the wedding, it just seemed to corroborate everything your dad had been telling me all along."

"No," I told her. "It was Dad I didn't want at the wedding. I was afraid of what he'd say."

My heart just about cracked in half as we talked for over an hour, catching each other up on our lives. I told her about the fall classes I'm excited to take at Cornell, and she dreamed up a spring break trip to Tahiti for us to go on. The strange thing, though, was how little she mentioned my dad. How, when I asked about their trip to the Bahamas, all she said was that it had been "fine." How her voice got all clipped and cold whenever he came up.

"Won't you come home for dinner tonight?" she asked before getting off the phone. "I'll make all your favorites. Shrimp and grits and fried green tomatoes—I can make a hummingbird cake for dessert, too, or peach cobbler and ice cream. Or what about—"

"Wait, Mom," I'd interrupted. "I don't know about all that. Didn't Dad tell you that we're not talking? He and I...had a falling out a few weeks ago. I don't think he'd want me there."

A "falling out" was putting it mildly. My father had cost me my marriage, my new family, my life. My hopes, my dreams. My relationships with both Graham and Jude. What he had done, intentionally and spitefully, was unforgivable. I didn't ever want to see him again.

There was a pause on the line. Finally, Mom said, "Whatever happened is between you two, but please don't punish me for what he did. I don't want him keeping my child from me. Not anymore, and not ever again. Please come, Abbie. I haven't seen your face in so long, and you'll be back at school soon—"

I'd tried to resist, tried to suggest meeting at a restaurant, but she was adamant that we shouldn't let him be the final say on who would or would not be welcome in our family home. And she wanted so badly to cook for me. So in the end, she won. I couldn't say no to my mom.

Which is how I ended up here now, knocking on the door of my parents' house, my heart in my throat.

Amanda offered to come with me tonight for moral support, to act as a buffer between me and my dad, but I couldn't ask her to sit through the awkward silences and ugliness that I'm sure I'll have to face. Because honestly, I'm not expecting this dinner to result in some kind of magical reconciliation. Or to be anything other than a complete shitshow. Which is why, when my BFF dropped me off, I told her to be on standby in case I need a ride home early.

The door swings open, and before I can say hello, my mother is stepping onto the porch to wrap me in her arms. I blink back tears as she rocks me back and forth, the familiar scent of her gardenia perfume enveloping me.

"Dinner's just about ready. I hope you're hungry, baby girl. I was so nervous I got started cooking too early, and now, well. It's already time to pull the cheddar biscuits out of the oven."

"Smells great," I tell her, though I feel uneasy as I step into the house.

Everything is exactly the same, of course. But I still feel like I don't belong.

I let Mom lead me into the dining room, where Dad is sitting at the table with his glasses on, reading something on his tablet. When I say hello, he barely spares me a glance and only grunts in response. The tension in the room is so thick, I practically have to wade in it to get to the place setting my mom laid out for me. But instead of the two of them positioned at opposite heads of the table, per usual, it's me and Mom sitting side by side, across from Dad. Interesting.

Mom brings out all the dishes as Dad continues to ignore me, and after our drinks are poured—sweet tea for me and Mom, more whiskey for Dad—Mom bows her head to say grace.

Dad and I stare each other down as she does, neither of us ever having been particularly religious. When she finishes, I reach for the biscuits, but Dad snatches them up first.

"We need to discuss our plan of action going forward," he says, loading up his plate and handing each dish to Mom afterward, completely skipping over me.

"Whatever it is, I'm not getting involved," I say flatly.

"I wasn't talking to you," he snaps. "You've already proven yourself a failure."

"Ford," Mom warns.

"It's the truth. She's ruined our family name. She spent her entire summer fucking off, and she's got nothing to show for her time away but a criminal record and a nasty reputation."

"Her name was cleared," Mom says, her voice icy. "Eat your greens."

Wow. I have never in my life heard my mother speak

to my father like this. Sure, I've heard them fight, but those fights usually consist of my dad yelling and accusing, and my mom crying and trying to explain herself. But this outright sassiness? It makes me proud.

She must really be pissed at him for keeping me and her apart all summer. It doesn't escape me how hard it must be for her to go against the way she was raised in the South, either—her parents groomed her from birth to be sweet, demure, soft-spoken, obedient. To smooth away conflict, not partake in it. To be the perfect trophy wife.

Maybe her priorities have changed.

Dad just snorts and turns his cruel gaze back to me. "You might not have tried to kill Natasha, but everyone knows you're the little homewrecker who broke up her marriage."

"They were already divorced," I protest.

"They were in the midst of reconciling," Dad insists.

I frown. "That was just for show. It was damage control. A PR stunt. You know this."

"That's not the point." He spreads an obscene amount of butter across his biscuit and I can only hope he chokes on it. "It's all about public perception, Abbie—and the perception is, you're a whore."

Mom's fork hits her plate with a clatter so loud, it makes me jump.

"Don't you *dare* call my daughter that name." Her voice is steely. The claws are out. "If you can't be civil, you can leave the table."

Dad cocks a brow at her and stuffs a forkful of shrimp and grits in his mouth. He seems annoyed at her, but not shocked. I wonder just how long they've been fighting like this.

The irony is, my dad is sitting here calling me a whore, but he's the one who sent me to seduce Graham in the first place. Which, technically I succeeded at, albeit temporarily. I'm dying to say as much out loud, to spill to my mom that *he* put me up to it, but I don't want to poke the bear. I just want to make it out of this dinner in one piece, and not upset my mom any more than she already is.

As we eat in chilly silence, Mom's amazing comfort food tasting like ash in my mouth, I feel her give my hand a quick squeeze of solidarity under the table. It's the kind of squeeze that says, "We're going to get through this." Thank God school is starting soon, and I won't have to deal with this shit outside of semester breaks and big holidays. Unless the people at Cornell end up being as bad as my father.

Maybe I should change my name. Or drop out. There's no way everyone won't know who I am and what I was accused of...those rumors are going to follow me around campus until I graduate. Can I even handle three more years of gossip and shit talk? Will Amanda be able to protect me from it? Will anyone even care about the truth? What if this follows me after I get my degree? For the rest of my life, even?

Fuck. Maybe my dad is right. Maybe public perception is the only thing that matters.

Suddenly, the doorbell rings, interrupting my brooding. I wonder if Amanda's intuition led her back here to rescue me.

Mom all but jumps out of her seat. "I'll get it."

"Sit your ass down," Dad says through a mouthful of grits.

"I *said* I'll get it," Mom shoots back, storming out of the room.

A moment later she reappears, her cheeks flushed. In the hallway, following after her, is—*holy fucking hell*.

It's Graham.

His eyes lock on mine, and I almost spit my iced tea.

"Am I interrupting something?" he asks coolly.

Dad whips around in his chair, his whole body going stiff when he sees the imposing figure standing behind him. My heart is still racing at the sound of Graham's voice—that familiar voice, lilting and fierce and powerful. But why is he here? We're done. He's over me. He hates me, he all but said as much before he walked out of the apartment in New York.

I drop my gaze and notice the fear that flickers across Dad's face, there one second and gone the next, and I'm suddenly even more interested in why Graham Ratliff is here in my family's home in Darien, when he should be tucked away in his Hudson Valley estate.

"Graham! What are you doing here?" Dad frowns, rising from his chair.

"I came to set things right," Graham says, his face like stone.

Set what things right? My heart starts to pound. Dad and Mom share a quick look, his of panic, hers of confusion.

"Look," Dad says, "if there's some order of business to discuss, we can set up a call this week. But you can't just barge into my house in the middle of a family dinner and act like—"

"Oh, but I can," Graham interrupts, surveying the table and my parents, his eyes barely skimming over me. He leans casually against the sideboard. "You see, I have a very interesting bit of news to share. As you all may or may not be aware of, two million dollars recently disappeared from my bank account, only to reappear shortly thereafter in an offshore account. One with Abbie's name on it. But it wasn't Abbie who stole the money, was it?"

"What?" I blurt. My whole body goes hot, my stomach twisting as his words sink in. *My* name? Jesus. No wonder he was so convinced I stole from him. The crime literally has my name all over it. But how is this possible? I didn't do it. I'd never—

And then I look across the table at my father.

"Graham. Come on, man. This isn't...this is—" Dad stutters, his face going pale.

Graham waves away the words my dad is tripping over. "There's no sense in trying to talk your way out of it, old man. I have all the evidence I need that you transferred the funds while you had power of attorney. Clearly, your plan to use Abbie to get my money wasn't moving fast enough for you, so you took matters into your own hands. "

"Plan to...use Abbie?" Mom says haltingly, her hand going over her heart. Then her eyes narrow. "Ford, what is he talking about? What was the *plan*?"

It's exactly as I suspected—my mother had no clue what was going on. Of course she didn't. She never would have stood by and let my father manipulate me the way he did. I can't believe I ever doubted her.

"You really didn't know?" Graham turns to Mom, anger radiating off him. "Your husband sent your daughter to my house this summer to seduce and extort me. Because he's broke. I guess he figured pimping out his child was the only solution."

Mom gasps, a look of horror on her face.

"Bullshit," Dad spits. "You have no proof. This is nothing but speculation and theatre."

Graham reaches inside his jacket, withdraws a stack of folded papers, and throws them onto the dining table. "There's your proof. And plenty of it."

Dad pushes back from the table and stands, pulling a fist back, but before he can swing, Graham decks him square in the jaw. Dad staggers into a glass cabinet, hard enough to break some of the dishes inside. Mom watches, a hand over her mouth, her back against the wall.

Graham turns to me. "Abbie. I am so sorry. I should have never doubted you. And if you'll give me another chance, I will spend my life making it up to you. Can you forgive me?"

He holds out his hand, but I'm frozen, still processing everything that just happened.

"I...I don't know," I say truthfully. "It's not that simple. I don't even know if...we can work."

"We can. We can work," he says softly.

I shake my head. "No. It's not that simple. Do you have any idea what you put me through? I'm not going to be in a relationship with someone who doesn't trust me. With someone who can just throw me out like trash

255

without a look back. I thought we were going to have a life together, and you took it all away—you didn't try to see if we could figure it out as a team, you didn't give me the benefit of the doubt, you just...walked away." I've been getting louder and louder as my words run together, my anger flaming in my chest. I'm practically shouting now, and even my parents look shocked. "Do you have any idea how it feels to have every single man in your life treat you like a toy? Something to play with and use and then discard when you decide you're done with it? I've had it with powerful men abusing me."

My chin starts to wobble, and I blink back the sting of tears. I'm furious. Indignant.

"I'm not your fucking toy," I say, stepping back from him.

Suddenly, I feel a warm arm around my shoulders. It's my mother. Standing at my side.

Graham closes the gap between us, dropping to his knees, gazing up at me with pure love. "No, you're not. You're not a toy at all. And you're right, I fucked up, I threw you away, threw us away, and I will never stop regretting it. But Abbie, I swear by all that is sacred, *I love you*. I love you and I trust you, with my heart and my soul, and my daughter loves you, too. You are our family. Come home with me. Please. Give me another chance. I need you. We need you."

I look him in the eye, and what I see there helps me decide.

When he holds out his hand this time, I take it.

Chapter Thirty

Abbie

WHEN WE PULL up to the estate, Graham insists he's going to carry me over the threshold.

I let him.

After he deposits my bags inside, he comes back out to scoop me up in his strong grip, and I sigh happily as I twine my arms around his neck.

"Welcome home," he whispers as we enter the foyer, and I shiver at the brush of his lips against my ear.

"I'm never leaving," I say. "Well. At least not until I have to go back to Cornell."

"I'll be right behind you," he says.

He kisses me as he sets me down, and my heart feels like it's taking flight. Between picking up my things from Amanda's house and then driving up from Connecticut, it's gotten very late—on top of which, I'm exhausted from the emotional roller coaster of the day—but the second my feet touch the cool marble floor again, it's like I'm reinvigorated. I bet I could run a marathon right now. The way Graham runs his hands up the backs of my thighs, however, gives me other ideas. Ideas that have nothing to do with running.

"I think I need to be welcomed home properly now," I inform him slyly, trailing my finger slowly down his bicep.

"Oh, I agree. And you'll need a proper apology from me as well." His words are light, but his tone is pure sex.

Heat spreads through me like wildfire. "I might have some ideas about that."

"I can't wait to hear them."

With a low growl, he picks me up again, his palms cupping my ass. I wrap my legs around his waist and hold on tight, kissing his neck greedily as we head up the stairs. The whole house is quiet and dark, with everyone asleep, and I feel almost like I've stepped into a dream.

We enter the bedroom, Graham kicking the door shut behind us, and I feel all my stress melt away as the softness of his lips against mine reignites the passion in my heart. When he sets me on the bed, our clothes come off in a frenzy of impatient tugging and unbuttoning and kissing and laughing, and then he finally lays me out reverently before him.

Then he goes to his dresser drawer and takes something out, bringing it over to me with a crease between his brows.

"My love," he murmurs, dropping to one knee beside the bed. "This is yours. For always."

I see what he's holding out to me—my engagement ring. And a solid gold band to go with it- the wedding band he never had a chance to give me on our wedding day. I nod, blinking back tears, and he slides the rings onto my finger. My heart skips a beat as I look down at them, gleaming in the light. They're a perfect fit. They feel right.

Graham stands and climbs over me on the bed, his body deliciously warm against mine, and kisses my forehead, my cheeks, my chin. Goosebumps race over my skin as he moves lower, over my neck, my collarbone, my chest. Each kiss sets me on fire.

"My love. My divinity."

His tongue circles my areolas, and then he's gently sucking and pulling on my nipples, stealing my breath as my back arches and my fingers dig into his scalp. He alternates between my breasts until I'm moaning and twisting beneath him. Then he kisses lower, my belly, my hip bones, until he's between my legs, placing soft kisses on my inner thighs. It's driving me crazy, the sweet press of his lips, his tongue, his hair tickling the most sensitive skin on my body.

"My everything," he groans.

And then his tongue finally, blessedly, touches my clit and the world alights into a million colors.

The flat of his tongue laps me open, tracing a line up my slit, ending with another soft nibble on my clit. He repeats the cycle several more times, leaving me breathless and twisted, only to press my hips back down with a firm hand and continue with renewed vigor. When he slips a finger inside me, plunging deep, the world cracks wide open. I can't stop saying his name.

It's fucking beautiful.

"Do this forever," I moan. "Forever."

"I'll never stop," Graham solemnly vows, voice

muffled as his tongue performs tricks that I barely remember from before.

When I come, I swear I see the ends of the universe. He licks me slowly, thoughtfully, like a man savoring his last meal, and I laugh as I come down from the heights he just took me to. Frissons of pleasure run from my head to my toes, warm satisfaction washing over me, but I want more. So much more.

"Come here," I instruct him. He looks up at me from between my legs, curiosity and hunger radiating from him. "I want to suck you."

He moves slowly back up, the feel of his skin on mine driving me insane so soon after my orgasm. I lick my lips as he kneels on either side of my head, my mouth ready and open when he positions his cock over my open mouth. Grasping the top of the headboard, he thrusts forward at the same time I suck him into my mouth. From this angle, he hits the back of my throat easily, bringing tears to my eyes. I bob my head, making him groan with the hard suction of my cheeks, relishing the feel of him, the power I have over him again.

"Naughty girl," Graham murmurs, breathing hard. His hips grind fast, jolting like he can't control himself, his cock drilling deeper into my mouth. "I've missed my naughty girl."

I respond by gently stroking the soft skin below his balls with my thumb, circling gently, then dipping even lower to press against his hole. He growls and throws his head back, panting slightly. *Ooh.* He likes that. Maybe as much as I do. I toy with him a little more, sucking and probing and stroking, enjoying the sounds pouring out of his mouth.

"Careful," he warns. "I'm not coming in your mouth."

"Hmm?" I ask, a questioning moan I can barely manage around his length.

He thrusts faster, clinging to the headboard, jackhammering against my tongue. I can taste the tang of precum, feel him growing even harder. I look up to lock eyes with him and see a wicked grin cross his face, but after one more thrust, he pulls out of my mouth with a regretful grunt. I reach for him, but he shakes his head, denying me.

My lips are swollen and half numb, my jaw aching, the taste of him lingering.

"Get back here," I demand.

But he doesn't. Instead, Graham lays on top of me, a full body press, the two of us so close I can feel his heart beating against mine. He kisses from my ear to my lips, then over to the other ear. Cupping my face in his hands, he lines his cock up against my opening.

"I need to feel you come on me." It's not a request, it's an order. God, I missed being bossed around. "I need to feel this pussy contract on my cock."

"Then make me come again." I hold his gaze, so deep and intense.

"Every day of your life, my love," he promises.

He plunges into me, filling me completely, and it feels so good and so right that I immediately orgasm again. I cling to him as our bodies climax in sync, his moans mingling with mine as I cry out with the force of the contractions. The sweet pleasure of it is endless, taking me higher than a mountaintop, rolling through me in wave after shattering wave.

We make love for hours. As far as apologies go, this is my favorite one ever.

"As long as you do this for every apology, you can screw up as much as you want," I tell him, brushing a damp lock of hair out of his eyes.

"I hope I never hurt you like that ever again," he says.

I was teasing, but he's so sincere. Graham turns toward me and twines his fingers with mine. He searches my gaze, brushes a thumb over my lips. He looks at me like I am precious.

"Abbie, I love you more than the moon loves the stars. I should have trusted you. I suppose it was just...easier to believe the worst. To believe that another person had betrayed me. That what we had was too good to be true, because...I never deserved it to begin with."

His confession shocks me to my core. I've never seen Graham so vulnerable. And what he's saying breaks my heart. "Why would you think that? You deserve all the happiness in the world. You're a good, strong, decent man. You deserve to love and be loved for all that you are."

He shakes his head. "I never thought that. Not deep down. But you, Abbie—you make me want to believe it's true. I want to believe in our happy ending."

"Believe it," I tell him tenderly. "I love you, Graham Ratliff. And I'm not going anywhere."

I climb on top of him, tracing the line of his jaw as I kiss him long and slow. When I finally break away, we're both out of breath.

"I vow to trust you, always, from this moment onward," he says.

"Forever?"

"Forever," he whispers, pulling my lips back to his, and his kiss tastes like an everlasting promise.

I work my way down his body until I'm sitting gently on his cock, leaning back on my palms to give him a better angle, letting him fill me completely. I missed this feeling so much, being so stretched and so satisfied. He fingers my clit and we rock together, slow and steady, losing ourselves in the pleasure, until we both come together in a toe-curling rush of bliss. I love the sound of him groaning my name, the feel of his fingers digging into my hips as he thrusts himself into oblivion, the white-hot fire of his seed spilling into me. I love knowing I have that power.

We collapse together afterward, breathless and sated, limbs entwined. This is what forever feels like, I realize. This comfort, this pleasure, this delicious euphoria. And I'm the luckiest woman in the world to have it.

"He used you," Graham murmurs quietly, his fingertips stroking up and down my back. "He used his own daughter. To steal from his oldest friend."

"My dad's a shit," I agree. "But so was I."

"No. Abbie, listen to me. He victimized you. You were manipulated and controlled. It wasn't your fault, and you're not to blame. Not ever. But now...now you are free."

I sigh into him. "I am. But what you said before—about how you didn't think you deserved what we had—I think I felt the same. I didn't think I deserved this happiness, either. Or, I don't know. Maybe I thought, after what I did to you, it was only fair to have it taken away."

"You took my happiness with you, my love. And someone else's. But now you're home, and you know what? This family is going to be even stronger."

I nod, tears filling my eyes. "I never wanted to hurt Jude. I'm so sorry she had to go through all of this."

"She hasn't been the same without you. That girl really loves you. And she's going to be absolutely over the moon when she realizes you're back."

"I can't wait to see her tomorrow," I whisper.

Graham tips my chin up and gently places a kiss on my lips. "I've got a better idea. Get a robe on. We're going to make pancakes with Jude."

I laugh as he climbs out of bed and pulls his robe on, then goes into the closet to take out a spare for me. "You're serious? Graham, it's midnight!"

"It is. Which is why she will be so incredibly excited to be woken up by her favorite person to get into some late-night culinary mischief."

He throws the robe at me and smiles as he watches me put it on. Then we tiptoe down the hallway to Jude's room, where we burst in to invite her to the happiest family reunion of her life.

Epilogue

Graham

FIVE YEARS LATER

"I'm going to be late!" Jude calls over her shoulder, pushing through the crowds to the stables.

"Wait up!" Abbie laughs. "We don't want to lose you!"

"It's the stables! You know where to find me!"

Abbie shoots me a look and we both roll our eyes and smile. "Teenagers," she says.

I pick up little Posey and lift her onto my shoulders. She squeals with delight as she settles into one of her most favorite places in the world. I would carry this girl to London and back if it meant hearing that joyful squeal every time.

"Careful," Abbie warns.

She's got baby Max wrapped around her chest, with a protective arm tucked around him. She's stunning in mom mode. I knew she would be a good mother when I saw how engaged she was with Jude, all those years ago, but watching her care for our smallest cargo from their first breaths, their first furious little screams, has been an entirely novel experience.

And still, even with two new babes to care for, Abbie and Jude are still thick as thieves, gossiping by the pool, going on trail rides, enjoying weekend shopping trips with Gigi—Jude's nickname for Abbie's mom—the only grandmother that my daughter has ever known. After divorcing Ford, who is still serving jail time, Abbie's mom moved into the estate house with us. She's been running a successful interior design firm from there ever since. She and Esmeralda get along like a house on fire, and I couldn't be happier with the arrangement.

Jude doesn't seem to give her grandmother half as much teenage attitude as she gives me and Natasha. And although I'd love to see my daughter grow out of that sassiness at some point, I also love knowing that Jude and her Gigi care for each other so much. It's gone a long way toward filling the gap that Natasha left when she moved to the UK—and even though my ex-wife has done her best to be a mom to Jude on her monthly visits from London (per our modified custody agreement), Natasha still struggles to put Jude first. When she does show up for Jude, though, she really makes the moments count, for which I am grateful. And Jude manages her mother's caprices well. I hope in no small part because Abbie and I have worked so hard to ensure that all our children are surrounded by so much love.

Our family, as blended and unconventional as it may be, truly is a thing of beauty.

I pause outside the stables, allowing Abbie and Max to go first, and take a minute to just drink it all in. Jude has been training for this event for months, our entire world devoted to nothing but horses for so long that it's hard to remember what other hobbies we ever had. And now, we're here to cheer her on for the championship of the season.

It will be nice to relax after this. For a little while, anyway.

I feel like the luckiest man alive.

"Go, Daddy, go!" Posey wiggles her adorably roly-poly four-year-old body on my shoulders. "Gotta find Juju!"

Translation: *Hurry up, Dad. We have to find Jude.*

"Let's go get her then, love." Holding her legs tight, I bounce her gently as I make my way through the barn, homing in on the cascade of giggles up ahead, where Abbie and Max stand outside of Desi's stall.

Jude and Cassie are in there already, brushing Desi and talking strategy. Cassie gives me a stern look as we approach.

"We need to focus, and you all are distracting," she says mock-scoldingly, arms crossed over her chest.

"I told you," Jude says, but a smile is still tugging at her lips.

"What, we can't come to wish you luck?" Abbie says, leaning over the gate to kiss the top of Jude's head. "Knock 'em dead, kid. You're going to do amazing."

"Remember, my little warrior: you shall vanquish them." I shoot her a wink. That's the pep talk I've been giving her for weeks, every time her nerves have started to catch up with her.

Jude laughs and shoos us away. "Out! I have to get ready. Cassie needs to do my hair."

"Fine, fine. We know when we're not wanted, right, Poe?" I glance up at my favorite toddler. She blows a raspberry and giggles.

"We'll see you at the winner's circle. Now get," Cassie commands.

So we obey. We wave goodbye and find our way to our seats, Posey begging for everything under the sun on the way there. She wants a funnel cake, she wants pink lemonade, she wants *frozen* lemonade, she wants a little flag to wave. Please and please and pretty please.

"There you go, love. There's your flag. Wave it around, then," I mutter, shaking my head and sharing a look with Abbie. "We've spoiled her rotten, haven't we?"

Abbie grins. "Look how happy it's making her, though. And plus it helps it feels like a party in here instead of just...watching horses prance around."

"You know as well as I do that's the whole bloody point."

She laughs at me, rubbing her hand in circles over the back of a sleeping Max. He's been an exceptionally good baby, which was a nice change after his colicky sister. Year four, though? Year four has been amazing. I remember Jude at this age. She was a joy and a wonder as well.

"Daddy?" Posey chirps. "Can we get a snack, pwease? *Pwease?*"

She clasps her hands together and I feel my resolve weakening. Here we go again.

I glance over at Abbie, who is shaking her head. "Only *one thing*, Graham. And she doesn't need a bunch of sugar, or else we'll never get her to sit still until it's Jude's turn."

"I'll try to find something healthy. Ish."

Abbie sighs, but her beautiful smile still shines through. "I'll go find our seats, you two grab the food. See you in a few."

The second she turns her back, I make a beeline for the concession stands, Posey crowing with delight from my shoulders. We get funnel cake with raspberry jam, we get mini corn dogs, we get white cheddar popcorn. I even get her a balloon, because the way she says, "Pwease?" melts my heart.

"You're absurd." Abbie laughs when we finally reach our box seats, surveying the mess I'm carrying in my arms. "Absolutely absurd."

"I'll have you know these are vegetarian corn dogs and the popcorn is local and organic," I tell her and give her a quick kiss.

"Ew." Posey covers her eyes.

We settle in and watch the other riders, pointing out different techniques to Poe. She's just starting her lessons now, with a pony that we let Jude choose at auction, but I can already tell that my youngest daughter is going to be good. How can she not be? Her older sister is a champion rider, and Cassie is the best instructor in the state.

Finally, it's Jude's turn. We all stand and cheer as she's announced, and then quiet back down to watch her

269

work her magic. She and Desi have an unbreakable bond, and Desi does everything Jude asks. Together they tear up that field, acing tricks with poise and grace. By the end, she gets a standing ovation from the whole crowd. I can't keep the smile off my face.

"That's my sissy!" Posey yells excitedly to everyone she can. "That's my sissy!"

When they award Jude the first-place ribbon, my heart swells with pride. She's worked so hard for so long, and the payoff is sweet as honey. I notice one of the boy riders going up to Jude to congratulate her afterward, and judging by his body language, I get the impression he fancies her. Looks like Miss Jude and I will be having a talk later. She's far and away too good for him. Too good for any boy, if I have anything to say about it. Though I have a feeling that Abbie will want to put in her own two cents. May cooler heads prevail.

Back in the stables, we find Jude brushing down Desi, beaming brightly, hair sticking to her forehead from wearing her helmet in the summer heat.

She's brilliant, my little girl, and growing up far too fast for my liking.

"Abbie! Dad!" she calls when she sees us. She pops out of the stall and tackles us in a sweaty group hug, grinning widely. "Did you see how well Desi did?"

"We saw how well you *both* did," Abbie says. "You were amazing."

"Phenomenal!" I clap her on the back.

Posey clings to her older sister's leg, squeezing tightly. "You won! You won!"

"This calls for a family photo," Cassie proclaims, coming up behind us. "Everyone squeeze in with Desi!"

My whole beautiful family comes together, arms wrapped around each other, for a quick photo. When Cassie shows it to me, my heart feels full to bursting. Posey's grin is so wide you can't see her eyes, radiating infectious joy. Jude looks proud and accomplished, like the self-possessed young woman she is. Even Max looks bright-eyed and alert, an impressive feat for Mr. Naptime himself, his duckling-fine hair sticking up like a mini mohawk that has me laughing.

And standing there in the middle, surrounded by our children, are me and Abbie, arms around each other, looking every bit like life couldn't get any better.

I don't suppose it could.

If you loved Graham and Abbie's story, you will love The Billionaire's Intern by Lia Hunt!

THE BILLIONAIRE'S INTERN is a classic virgin-meets-billionaire romance - if your idea of classic is scorching hot angst with a plot twist that'll leave you begging for more...

No one's ever called me friendly.

You don't get to where I am by being approachable.

I'm used to seas of people parting for me. Especially in the lobby of the building I own, filled with people who work for me.

Guess no one told the new marketing intern.

She spills her coffee all over me and then offers to replace my custom couture with Kathy Ireland.

Emery is a sweet little blinky-eyed Kansas girl. A kitten in the middle of our shark tank. It's just common decency to protect her. Take her to lunch and get to know her. Wonder why she looks at me like she wants me to eat her alive, but pulls back every time I'm ready to bite.

Okay, so that last one isn't decent at all. In fact, every fantasy I have about her is downright filthy.

Discovering I'm her first?

Well, it gives me even more wicked thoughts about the big... *city* I can show her.

I've been burned before. Fool me once, right? I built a billion-dollar company by planning for every possibility. Making sure nothing gets past me again.

But I sure didn't see this one coming.

Paige Press

Paige Press isn't just Laurelin Paige anymore...

Laurelin Paige has expanded her publishing company to bring readers even more hot romances.

Sign up for our newsletter to get the latest news about our releases and receive a free book from one of our amazing authors:

Laurelin Paige
Stella Gray
CD Reiss
Jenna Scott
Raven Jayne
JD Hawkins
Poppy Dunne
Lia Hunt
Sadie Black

Also by Sadie Black

HIS NANNY TRILOGY

The Billionaire and His Nanny

The Billionaire and His Scandal

The Billionaire and His Forever

About the Author

Sadie Black lives in her head as an ex-member of the British royal family, a current fashion icon, and couldn't be more annoyed that she has to pay taxes on a job called "governess."

Printed in Great Britain
by Amazon

10331461R00164